1

MAGGIE

There's a blood moon the night murder finds its way to the tiny Maine town of Coyote Cove. A rosy glow outlines the lifeless face as I roll up in my Jeep, lights off. A few of the early fall leaves shake loose from the trees, dancing across the narrow gravel road.

As I stare at the body, it briefly crosses my mind that it could just be a drunk. Wouldn't be the first time I'd come across a man passed out while patrolling the lonely dirt roads that twist their way through the wilderness of logging country. Even as the thought enters my head, though, I know this time is different.

I'd had dinner at Em's, a kitschy little diner out by the highway that draws tourists like bees to honey. Or blowflies to a dead corpse. The food is decent enough, but the real attraction is the life-like moose statue out front that promises a great Kodak moment. That, and it's one of only three places to eat in town.

I was on my usual stool at the counter, working on a burger, when a group of tourists bumbled in. Still excited from the thrill of spying a moose on the twilight tour, which they'd paid way too much for, their enthusiastic voices carried so that they shared the recap of their adventure with half the diner. I didn't pay them much attention until they started discussing what else they'd seen out on those logging roads.

It's a scene I can picture all too well.

Rough-looking men, greasy hair catching in the wind, rifles slung over the shoulders of filthy t-shirts, leaning against the bed of a shabby pickup, snarling dogs caged in back. Spitting tobacco on the ground through sneering lips as they watched the tour van drive by with cold, hard eyes. Mouthing obscene gestures at the sightseers, then laughing at the sight they'd given them to see.

Over the counter, my eyes met Peggy's, her drawn-on eyebrows arched so high they almost met the platinum bouffant balanced on her head. No doubt we were thinking the same thing. Poachers.

So I'd left my meal and hit the road, decided to do a little trolling to see if I couldn't keep the black bear population from losing any members that night. Not really my job as the police chief of a two-cop town, but I like bears, and I don't like people breaking the law under my jurisdiction, so I figured, why not? And now this.

Inching my Jeep forward, I aim my spotlight and turn it on, knowing I'm blowing my cover, but I suspect I have more important things to worry about than poachers right now. I take in the color of the skin, the half-open eyes, the slightly parted lips, the protruding tongue—the glistening patches of drying blood on his dark flannel shirt. Even from this distance I recognize stab wounds when I see them. But what I don't recognize is the victim. Means the ruined flannel shirt must be LL Bean instead of Wrangler.

I shut my eyes, trying to block the swirl of memories that come at me, from the life I thought I'd left in the past. Breathing deeply, my right hand finds the radio in the center console, my

THE
GIRL
WHO
LIED

BOOKS BY SHANNON HOLLINGER

SHANNON HOLLINGER

THE
GIRL
WHO
LIED

bookouture

Published by Bookouture in 2023

An imprint of Storyfire Ltd.
Carmelite House
50 Victoria Embankment
London EC4Y 0DZ

www.bookouture.com

ISBN: 978-1-80314-886-1
eBook ISBN: 978-1-80314-885-4

To my husband, Ben. There's no one else I'd rather get lost with.

fingers curling around it. My lieutenant is probably just about to call it a night. There are a number of reserve officers at my disposal, but, to be honest, I don't think any of them will be much help at an actual crime scene. Coyote Cove doesn't see much besides domestic disputes, drunk-and-disorderlies, and the occasional tourist kids with sticky fingers.

A low rumble sounds from the sky in the distance and I realize the situation is taking a turn for the worst. I straighten in my seat, opening my eyes. There's no escaping reality—it will find you wherever you try to hide. This incident is proof of that.

Switching channels on the radio, I message my lieutenant. My skin shrinks two sizes as I wait for him to answer. I go over protocol, everything that will need to be done in my mind. I'm about to radio again when a crackle of static bursts from the black box in my hand.

"Hey, Chief. What can I do you for?"

Lieutenant Murphy's husky voice carries over the radio, the slightly cartoonish way he accentuates *chief*, the way most of the men in this Podunk town do, not lost in translation. Even after four years most of them still have a hard time accepting that their police chief is a woman. Too bad for them.

"Hey, Murphy, I've got a bit of a problem. I need you to call the guys down at state, have them send a major crimes unit up here. Tell them we'll need a medical examiner and a van, too."

The radio is silent after my transmission. I imagine Murphy sitting in a chair, tipping it up on the hind legs like he often does, scratching at his head while trying to interpret the meaning of my words.

"You said state, doc, and van? For what?"

"Murphy." I've never had any patience, no use pretending now. "I've got a homicide victim out here on one of the logging roads out by Craig's Pond. Just south of marker two-thirteen, west of Mount Buffalo."

"Huh. Really?"

"Yes, really."

Murder has found me, followed me to my safe haven. I can't identify the dominant feeling I'm experiencing—fear, sorrow, anger—they're all in there somewhere, but right now instinct is taking over. Memories from a lifetime ago spill over the dam in my head, flooding my brain. It may have been a different life, but it was my life. I still remember what to do. I run a quick inventory on the Jeep's contents.

"Send a couple of guys over here with buckets and shovels. Lots of buckets. And a pickup with a covered bed to transport them in."

"What for?"

"Murphy, we've got a murder on our hands and a storm coming in. We need to secure as much evidence as we can before it gets washed away. I need a way to transport the body, too. See if the hospital can get an ambulance out here. If not, try the funeral homes, see if they'll help us out."

"Shouldn't you wait for the staties to get there?"

Staties are something I'm still getting used to. In Maine, the state police handle all major crimes. Normally, I hate the idea of someone trying to step in and run things in my jurisdiction, but this is one investigation they're welcome to. Unfortunately, the nearest outpost is in Skowhegan. That's over a hundred miles away. No way the staties will make it here before the storm breaks. And if I let all the evidence get destroyed, they'll be here even longer.

"I'll take any shit they want to sling for this, but I need you to get me some backup out here ASAP. Can you do that for me?" I think about Murphy's two squinty-eyed kids and his angry wife. About his double-wide trailer hidden in the woods and the few small crimes that happen every year. "This is our chance, Murph. This is probably the most action we'll ever see, and I need you in on it with me."

I hope this does the trick, even though it's half lie. This isn't my chance. I've played that hand of cards already, ran out here to the high woods of Maine to lick my wounds and hide. When Murphy radios again, there's a change in his voice.

"Roger that, Chief. You can count on it. I'll round up a crew and meet you out there ASAP. You be careful. Over and out."

Closing my eyes, I lean my head back against the headrest, the radio clutched to my chest. This cannot be happening. But it is.

A crack of thunder jars me into action. Strapping the radio onto my belt, I nudge my hand against my sidearm, checking for the reassuring weight of its presence. Opening the door, I judge the distance between myself and the body. It's a good fifteen feet away. I adjust the spotlight before heading to the back of the Jeep.

Popping the hatch, I don a pair of disposable nitrile gloves, shoving some spares into my jacket pocket. I smash a box of plastic bags into the other pocket. Rustling through a stack of miscellaneous junk, now known as supplies, I discover a tarp still new in its plastic wrapper, which I shove under my belt against the small of my back. I squeeze a roll of twine over my left wrist, then fumble my cell phone out from my back pocket, replacing it with a pair of scissors, and close the hatch.

It's always made me feel silly, having a smartphone way out here where the technology is wasted. It's the last vestige I cling to from my former life. Between the mountains and the woods, it rarely gets even a 3G signal, but tonight it will serve a different purpose. Bringing up the camera app I clear my mind, recall my training, and begin to shoot my way into the crime scene.

The wind lashes against me, yanking strands of hair from my ponytail, pelting me with waves of stinging sand. I take my driver's license out of my wallet and lay it beside a series of tire marks on the road in front of the Jeep. Using light and shadows, I shoot different angles to highlight the tread patterns.

I don't hold out much luck for shoe prints, but I search anyways, snapping a shot of every dimple in the sand even remotely suspicious. Reaching the body, I quickly circle, photographing the surrounding area around it before I focus on the victim. I aim without truly looking, going through the list of shots in my mind. Hands, face, wounds, clothing, body, all photographed close-up, mid-range, and distant.

I shoot from every angle, every side, before exchanging the phone for the scissors. I bag his hands, wrapping the twine around his wrists to keep trace evidence from being lost or contaminated.

I smell the rain and know I'm running out of time, wishing that I'd hear the approaching engine of assistance. I grab a stick and use it to draw an outline of the body. The wind immediately begins to erase my work, so I do it again, forcing the stick to dig deeper.

Then, taking the tarp out of its wrapper, I brace myself, hating what I'm about to do next. I break protocol and wrap the corpse like burrito filling in a tortilla, grunting as I put my weight behind pushing the body over and over.

I'm trying to decide which would be worse, driving my Jeep over the victim and crime scene to keep it sheltered from the rain or giving the storm free access, when a bolt of lightning strikes a tree to my right. The night lights up like aliens have landed. For a moment I feel the electricity lancing through my body, my heart skipping a beat. It skips another as my eyes land on the teenage girl standing behind the SUV, her clothes disheveled and torn. Then the sky opens up and the flood begins.

2

HEATHER

It's like the bolt of lightning brings me to life. I can't remember anything before the cracking boom rumbles through my head—not what's happened, not where I came from, not even how I got here. It's like it flicked the switch, turning my lights on, and before there was simply nothing but waiting alone in the dark with nothing to do.

My eyes are focused on a woman. Police Chief Riley. I have no idea how long I've been standing there, watching her. I'm staring at her and she's staring at me, and by the look on her face something is wrong about this.

The rain pounds us with fat, heavy drops, the kind that actually hurt when they hit you. Her hair is plastered to her cheeks, wrapping wetly around her neck like it's choking her. As I watch, she hugs herself like she's cold. I don't feel my wet hair. I don't feel cold. I feel nothing. I am numb.

Another crash echoes through the sky. Chief Riley jumps, her arms dropping to her sides. She walks in my direction, her movements odd and jerky under the strobe-light effect of the stormy sky. I see her mouth moving. I strain to hear her words.

"Are you all right?"

I don't know, am I? I realize how strange it is that I don't know the answer to this simple yes or no question. She's only five feet away when a pair of lights break through the gloom and land on her, bobbing as the approaching vehicle bounces along the rutted road. She looks behind her at the car and then back to me.

A soggy clump of hair falls, blocking my vision, and I'm spurred to action for the first time. I move to push the hair out of my eyes but freeze, catching sight of my hand. It takes me a minute to realize that I'm the one screaming.

Somewhere behind the racket of my ear-piercing shrieks I hear the chief talking to the newcomer. I can't understand the words, but recognize the authority of the tone. A moment later, a jacket is laid gently over my shoulders. The rain is letting up a little but still I cry, the screams turning to body-racking sobs. Soothing words are whispered in my ear, calming strokes pet my back, but it makes no difference. I can't react.

Then my wrist is in her hand. Despite the rain her palm is hot, searing my flesh. Like that, my crying stops, just as suddenly as it began. I can't let her touch me. I have to get out of here.

I push her, spin, struggling to get away, lifting one sodden shoe and then the other, trying to run, wanting to escape, but my body doesn't cooperate. Pain flares through me and I fall to my knees, gasping air like a fish. As I catch my breath, sounds begin to form into words again.

"Heather, it's Chief Riley. It's Maggie. I need you to tell me what happened."

But I can't do that.

My head hangs limply as I stare at the toes of her boots. I hear her knees crack as she squats in front of me. I feel her soft hands gently take hold of my wrists.

"Honey." Her voice is soothing, her tone understanding. "You're out wandering in the middle of nowhere. Your clothes are torn. And something bad happened out here tonight. If someone hurt you, if you know what happened, I need you to tell me about it so we can protect you."

I raise my eyes to hers. Even in the dark and through the rain I can see the sincerity in her startling blue gaze. I wonder for a moment what it would be like to have eyes such a striking shade of blue. Would looking in the mirror be like losing yourself in the aqua waters of the Caribbean? Would the world look any different, any less hopeless from behind those eyes? Would life be any better, easier with eyes that color instead of the drab brown of my own?

I know she wants to help me, but I can't let her. It's too late for that. I'm beyond help.

My eyes flick over her head to where some of the men from town are loading something rolled up in a dark green tarp into Mr. Hensley's black hearse. I watch Lieutenant Murphy, Chet from the gas station, and David and Frank, the brothers who run the hardware store, finish heaving their burden into the back. Mr. Hensley shuts the door.

In a small town like the one I'm from everyone knows each other. These men know who I am, maybe even more than I know myself. By morning everyone will be wondering what I was doing way out here on the logging roads, in the middle of the woods, by myself. Too bad I can't answer their questions.

Chief Riley gives my wrists a little lift, a gentle reminder to bring me back to the present.

"Heather?"

I look at my hands, wet with rain but nothing else, and make a decision. I may be beyond help, but it might not be too late to save myself from worse.

"Heather?"

"I'm sorry, Chief Riley." I'm amazed by how normal my voice sounds, how easy the words come out. "It's been a really bad night." I give her an apologetic smile. "I didn't mean to worry you. I was just scared."

She regards me with... suspicion, relief, concern? I notice the rain has stopped.

"Nothing happened to me, I just... I feel so silly. I went for a walk. I wasn't paying attention, and I guess I lost track of time because it got dark. I didn't notice until I came up on a couple of coyotes on the trail. I don't know why I panicked. It's just, the nasty things always make me so nervous. I started running and lost the path and couldn't find the way back. Then I saw your lights and I was so relieved, but when I got here, I saw..." I gesture at the hearse and shrug apologetically. "I guess I just kinda freaked out."

She's still giving me that look, like she's trying to worm her way under my skin to see what's going on with me for herself. I tug my wrists free from her grasp. "I feel real bad for scaring you," I add.

Those blue eyes are drilling through my skull. After what seems like an hour, she speaks. "I'm just glad that you're okay, that nothing bad happened."

I smile and nod. "I feel so silly," I say again.

"Well," she groans as she stands. She offers me her hand, but I pretend to need to push myself off the ground with both fists as I rise. "I'll be tied up here for a while but I'm sure we can find you a ride home."

"Thanks, Chief, that would be awesome."

She gives me a tight smile and a nod. I get the feeling that she doesn't entirely believe my story. Luckily, she has more important things to focus on than me.

While we walk over to the others, I smile at the nervous glances, relieved when Mr. Hensley agrees to give me a lift home. I'm halfway into the passenger seat, already counting my lucky stars, when Chief Riley's voice strikes fear into my heart.

"Heather?"

I freeze. I have to dig deep, use all my willpower to make myself look up and meet her gaze. I know instantly that this is a mistake, that she sees something in my face that confirms whatever suspicions she may have.

"Yes?"

"I'd appreciate it if you didn't mention anything about this —" she gestures toward the back of the hearse "—to anyone. I don't want to cause any unnecessary panic."

"Uh-huh, sure." We stare each other down for a moment. Then I slip my other leg inside the hearse and buckle my seatbelt. "No problem." I pull the door shut, ending our staring contest. And starting the war.

3

MAGGIE

I spend the next two hours helping my motley team shovel the top three inches of heavy, wet sand from around the crime scene into buckets. My soggy clothes are full of grit, and I briefly remember beach days and soggy bathing suits. Blue skies and sunshine. The smell of salt, the sound of the surf, water lapping at my toes, waves breaking against my body. Surely that was someone else's life.

I cordon the area off, stringing yellow crime scene tape from the nearby trees, making an odd, octagonal enclosure. I promise everyone a beer next week, my treat, and send them on their way. We'll be meeting back here at first light.

I watch the taillights of the last vehicle fade and then I walk over to where I first saw Heather. Using my Maglite, I find the impressions of her shoes, still visible in the damp soil. I snap a few pictures on my phone, briefly following her trail into the tree line.

Her steps are short and light, zigzagging through the trees. She was walking. Or more like meandering, with no purpose or direction. It makes no sense.

I know she's hiding something. It's more than just a hunch,

a detective's gut feeling, or women's intuition. I know it as surely as I know that this case is going to be a headache.

I lose her tracks among the thick layer of pine needles that blanket the forest floor. I consider going a little farther, seeing if I can't pick her trail back up, but it's late and I have an early morning. I need to get home. I snake my way back through the woods to my Jeep. Starting the engine, I throw the car into gear and start the slow journey across the pitted dirt roads back to the highway.

The entire drive I repeat the scene in my mind. The crack of thunder, flash of lightning, Heather's face as she stood there on the edge of the shadows. Fast forward, slow motion, no matter how I play it the memory is the same—Heather started screaming not when she saw the body behind me, but when she had looked at her hands. Hands that, from a distance, looked like they were stained red.

I remind myself that I had murder on the brain when I saw her. That the world was shaded in ruddy tones from tonight's blood moon. That there are at least half a dozen logical explanations for what I thought I saw that don't make a teenage girl a murder suspect.

Pulling into my driveway, I take a moment, struggling to put the job on the back burner. Compartmentalizing is key when you're a cop. Once you get in the habit of carrying a case through the front door with you, you never stop. I have never once let a case into my cozy little cabin in the woods. Of course, I brought enough baggage with me from before to fill a dozen cabins, but that's another story.

My dogs, Tempest and Sullivan, are at the door by the time I let myself inside. They jump up to greet me, pulling at me with their front paws as they stretch their backs and demand attention. Sharp teeth graze my hands as I pet them, gentle reminders that I'm their property and shouldn't leave them.

The terriers scamper ahead, one white butt and one black

leading the way as I head for the kitchen. The air is fragrant with spices, making my stomach growl and my mouth water. I feel bad, the memory of the greasy burger I started on at the diner making me cringe. I had no idea he was going to cook dinner.

Steve is my neighbor. And more. I'm never exactly sure what to call him. Our relationship is hard to define. He's sitting on a stool at the counter reading the *Wall Street Journal*. He glances at me over the top of his reading glasses.

"Hard day?"

I give him a look that says *don't ask*, but realize too late that I really want to talk about it. Welcome to today's episode of the issues of being a woman.

"There's a plate in the oven for you."

I've never met a man like Steve before. I pause as I'm crossing behind him, make the decision, and kiss him on the top of his head before washing my hands. I know I should shower and change, but I just don't have the energy right now.

Grabbing a hot pad, I retrieve the plate from the oven. I sit on the stool beside him, my uniform dried stiff like a filthy rag. A napkin with silverware awaits my arrival.

Steve moved to Coyote Cove the year after I did. He came up for a weekend with his girlfriend and fell in love with the sleepy little town, nestled in a little hollow of Moosehead Lake, deciding that he never wanted to leave. Shortly thereafter he left the high-powered job and the high-maintenance girlfriend in the city to move to the North Country. Or so he'd have me believe. There's more to the story, but I'll allow him his secrets as long as he allows me mine.

He bought one of the luxury cabins on the west side of the road mostly reserved for second homes and vacation rentals. I live on the east side of the road. Whereas his cabin is on the lake with a spectacular view of the mountains in the distance, my cabin is simply off the road with a nice view of the woods.

Besides the view, the only difference is a few hundred thousand in value and a hefty chunk of monthly mortgage payment. It's a difference I can live with.

Steve sells annuities over the phone now. He seems to enjoy it. Just like me he never really talks about the career he left behind. Mainly he regales me with tales of the dog's daily hijinks. He's taken to bringing them over to his place during the day while I'm at work.

The man is stealing my dogs. I once heard him call my Parson Russell "daddy's exquisite little princess" when he thought I couldn't hear him. What was worse is that I could tell that she liked it.

I watch Steve out of the corners of my eyes as I chew. He gives the paper a noisy jerk, folds it up, and lays it down on the counter. Removing his glasses, he sets them on top. They've left a small red crease on the bridge of his nose. As he turns, the handful of silver hairs that pepper his head catch the light and wink at me. He laces his fingers together, leaning an elbow on the counter.

"Well? I know you want to talk about it."

Steve gets me. I like to think that I get him. I guess my main insecurity about our relationship is that I wonder if it stems from a lack of options. We're the only two people in this tiny little town who are single, educated, and in the same age range. I question whether he would still pick me if there were other options available.

"I'm not even sure where to begin." I sigh, suddenly exhausted. Laying the fork down, I give the plate a small push away.

"The dogs defended the lake from a flock of geese today," he says as he stands.

"Did they really?"

"Yep. They're heroes." He spins the seat of my stool so that I'm facing him.

"Are they now? Have they received medals?"

"Uh-huh." Looping his arms around my back he pulls me off the stool. "And a key to the city."

He holds me tight against him, my body drawing the strength it needs from his. Pulling back a little, he looks at me in that way he has that makes me feel that it's okay to be me. We kiss. His lips linger on mine and then he takes me by the hands and leads me to the shower. As I follow, I wonder how I got to be so lucky, because I definitely don't deserve it.

4

MURPHY

Even though he makes the scene by first light, Chief Riley is already there. He watches her tromp around the edge of the woods with the same mixed feelings she always stirs in him. He doesn't really care if she'd been a detective in a city before coming here. The fact of the matter remains the same. His boss is a woman. It's a slight that's impossible to forget, especially with his father always adding it to the top of the list of ways Murphy has disappointed and shamed him in life.

Maggie is in her late thirties, tall and fit. Her auburn hair has red highlights that flare like fire when they catch the light, and her eyes are so blue he does a double take every time he looks away from them. A couple of the guys down at the Loose Moose Tavern call her gorgeous, and he can't disagree. She could almost pass for a model, except that her nose is a little too sharp, her smile a little too goofy, and the skin around her jaw is starting to sag a bit. She shouldn't be the Chief of Police. She should get out of the way of men like him and be a housewife.

Every time he thinks this way a streak of shame burns through him. His mother had been a strong woman. His father had done his best to beat it out of her until the day she got strong enough to leave, and Murphy hasn't seen her since. He knows one of the reasons Chief Riley makes him uncomfortable is because she's salt in the wound that his mother made.

Murphy climbs down from the cab of his truck. "Morning, Chief."

She looks up and waves. He walks away from the crime scene, over to where she's crouched down among a couple of weeds in the dirt. Watches her scoop up a sample of soil in a small plastic container. There's another container with a couple of small plant leaves in it by her boot.

"Find anything?"

"Probably not."

"But you think our victim came from this direction?"

"No. There were no prints around the body last night, not enough blood at the scene. He was dumped. I took some photos of the tire tracks on the road, but with all the traffic out here I don't really have much hope that they'll pan out."

"Huh." Murphy scratches his head. It's been a long time since he left the academy, and he's never had cause to use most of what he learned, but, last night, it started coming back to him. And none of it would explain why she's taking samples from an area that's not related to the crime scene.

He wants to ask what she's doing but is afraid he'll sound stupid. He looks hard at the area around her, trying to figure it out on his own. Deep impressions of footprints from the night before are starting to crumble as the sand dries. The prints are small, narrow. Female, but not made by the heavy boots the chief wears. They must belong to Heather McGillis.

He wonders what the hell Heather had been doing out there the night before, crying and carrying on the way she had. He'd told his wife about it after he'd gotten home, and she'd promised to call and find out. Like a quarter of the town, Heather was somehow related to his wife.

Maybe the chief thinks Heather has something to do with

the murdered man. The thought makes him feel slightly concerned. His wife would be damn pissed if he had anything to do with busting one of her kinfolks.

Alma had been a sweet little wisp of a country girl when he'd knocked her up and married her eight years ago. With each kid she'd doubled her size and with every year she grew angrier and more spiteful. All the more reason why he needs the job more than Chief Riley.

Engines sound in the distance, disturbing the morning silence. He turns, watching as a trio of vehicles emerge from a cloud of dust and park along the side of the road behind his truck, the faded Coyote Cove Police Department emblem on the tan door looking particularly shabby this morning.

Two plainclothes emerge from a black Nissan sedan, squinting around at the scrubby dunes and woods like it's their first time in logging country. A pair of officers exit a marked Ford Crown Vic Interloper, their dusty blue state police uniforms the same shade as their car. The doors to a white van marked "Evidence Response Team" remain closed.

He looks the newcomers over with narrowed eyes, dawdling behind as Chief Riley strides over to the detectives, offering a hand. He squats, pretending to be looking at something of interest, buying more time.

"What're we looking at here?"

Murphy glances at the speaker. The detective is short, stringy, probably late fifties, with dark, leathery skin. His pants, Murphy notes, are the same yellowish-brown his kid's vomit had been when he had the flu. The partner is taller, his face beefy and red even though his body appears fit.

"Body dump," Chief Riley replies.

"So... where's the body?"

"We've got him tarped and bagged in a cooler at the local funeral home."

Puke pants shakes his head as if he's sure he's heard wrong.

Murphy stands, choosing this as the moment to approach. He hovers behind the chief's shoulder, waiting.

"You what?"

Her voice is confident, unapologetic as she replies. "We moved him. Had a hell of a storm come through here last night. I bagged his hands and got him wrapped in a tarp before it broke. We skimmed the top three inches of soil into buckets," she gestured to a twenty by twenty-foot depression in the sand.

"It's soaked, but it'll be fine to sift once it dries. I sent one of my reserves over to the nearest photo lab to pick up the pictures I took. Got a bunch of tread marks, but we get a lot of traffic out on these roads, so doubt they'll be of much help. Haven't found a weapon yet, though. Figured my lieutenant and I would do a search after I briefed you."

The detective grunts, his mouth pulled in a deep frown.

"Chief Riley, by the way. This is Lieutenant Murphy." She half turns so there's nothing between Murphy and the detectives anymore.

"Lou Campden." Puke pants introduces himself, then gestures to the man to his right. "My partner, Hal Robbins."

Murphy gives both their hands a shake. Had he been chief and found the body, Murphy would have left it where it was and watched it overnight from his car, taking shots at any coyote that got close enough to try and scavenge. He wonders how the detectives would have responded to that.

"I'll get my guys to do a grid search of the area for a weapon, see if they can't find anything else of interest, if Lieutenant Murphy here would be kind enough to give our ME and analyst an escort to the funeral home where the body's at?" Detective Campden asks.

Murphy nods.

"You have an office where we can set up shop?"

"Our building isn't very big, but you're more than welcome to use it." Chief Riley smiles, but her brows furrow, and

Murphy notices the slight change in the tone of her voice. He realizes that she doesn't want to deal with the bigwigs from state any more than he does.

Strangely, it makes him feel protective of her. She's done her job, and she preserved what they need to do theirs, responding to the crime in a way that lets the staties know that they aren't dealing with some backwoods dimwits. Now it's time for them to take the stiff and the evidence and go. Too bad they don't seem to be taking the hint.

5

MAGGIE

I glance into my rearview, checking to make sure that the detectives have pulled off the dirt logging road onto the highway behind me. My thumbs drum on the steering wheel while I drive into town, the trip taking longer than it ever has before. I want to text Steve, tell him that the state police want to stick around, set up headquarters for their investigation here, on my turf, but I don't. He wouldn't understand why that would upset me. Mainly because I haven't told him.

Emotions that have faded like paint over time are threatening to surface. I thought moving to the other side of the country was far enough to escape. But maybe it's impossible to dodge your past. Maybe it hangs like an albatross around your neck until you face your fears and deal with it, get over it, move on. Maybe that's the purpose of life. I sure as hell hope not.

I pull into the lot and park next to Sue's car. The rusty green Pinto has seen better decades. Glancing at the building, I pray that she received my voicemail—no craft projects, friends, or grandchildren in the office today—please make it look like the clerk for a two-cop office has some work to do.

I slam my door shut as loudly as I can to give her warning.

Detective Robbins shoots a questioning look in my direction. I pretend not to notice and lead the way up the wooden ramp to the door.

When we walk in Sue's typing away so quickly that I know the keys she's hitting equal gibberish. She looks up over the rim of her glasses, her eyes flitting over me and landing hard on Detective Campden.

"Good morning, Chief." She stands, smoothing the front of her skirt. I wonder if she went out and bought it special or if it's just been living in the back of her closet since the 1970s, because I've never seen her in anything other than flannel pajama pants. Even in winter when the snow is four feet deep, she just layers them on. "And you must be from the state police." She holds her hand out, fingers down, like she expects them to kiss the back of it.

"Well, hello there."

Detective Campden daintily takes her fingers in his own and I think she may just get her wish. It occurs to me that a love connection might make the detectives delay their stay, so I do my best to speed things along.

"Morning, Sue. We've got a full day ahead so hold my calls, please, unless there's something urgent."

Detective Campden ignores my efforts. "Sue." He repeats her name with such reverence that I can't help but roll my eyes. During the course of their orbit they meet Detective Robbins's also-rolling eyes.

"Truly my pleasure, Sue."

I cough into my fist. Robbins checks his watch.

"And you are?" Sue asks.

Not your soul mate, Sue, now move along, I think, my impatience growing.

"Detective Campden."

"And this is Detective Robbins," I say. "We'll see you later,

Sue." I usher lover boy out of the room and into my office with a hand on his back.

"Delightful lady," he says after I've shut the door.

I blink hard to stifle another eye roll. "Yes. Anyways, Detective Campden, please feel free to use my office and whatever other resources I have at my disposal during your stay." *Except for Sue*, I add silently, gesturing for him to take my chair behind the desk.

Detective Robbins seats himself on the stool against the wall that held my office plant until last week, when I finally accepted the truth and tossed its brittle, dead skeleton into the trash. He busies himself with penning notes onto a preliminary report sheet that he's brought with him on a clipboard.

"I don't want to impose." Campden is looking wistfully at the door.

"Not at all." *Down boy.*

With a sigh he settles into the chair, knees popping. "Nice," he comments as he shimmies himself comfortable. "So, I'd like to start with getting a feel for Coyote Cove, the kinda comings and goings that take place here. You said he wasn't a local, so we'll need a list of all the places nearby for out of towners to stay—motels, hotels, B&Bs, rooms for let, vacation rentals, etc."

I nod.

"I'd also like to do a canvas, see if anyone saw anything out of the ordinary. You said those back roads get a lot of traffic? Not just the loggers?"

"Lots of locals ride out there, ATVs and snowmobiles, depending on the season. People aren't supposed to hunt out there, but they do. And it's a popular route for the moose tours."

It's his turn to nod. He seems distracted.

"Detective, there is one thing I haven't mentioned yet. A local girl who wandered onto the scene while I was out there last night. Seemed pretty distraught."

"Uh-huh. Yeah. Definitely want to hear more about that, but first—the restroom?"

"Back out in the lobby. Sue'll show you."

I catch Robbins's eyes circling toward heaven. Campden springs out of the chair and bounds out the door like a lamb through fresh April grass.

"He ain't what he used to be." Robbins grins at me. It's the first time I've heard him speak. His voice is nice, smooth. There's something soothing about it. I wonder if Campden lets him do the talking when they speak to victims.

"He'll be back and ready to focus once he's made plans to see her tonight."

"That so?"

"Wasn't always this way. Think he's hitting the age where he's afraid he's gonna die alone. Happens to single men at sixteen and sixty."

I have no response.

"This is a real small town, huh? Pretty rural." Detective Robbins stares at me over the report he's supposed to be filling out.

"Moose outnumber people three to one in Coyote Cove."

"Is that so?" He shakes his head, a look of bewilderment on his face. "What the hell are you doing here?"

"Excuse me?" I look behind me, sure that I've heard him wrong, or that he's talking to someone else.

"Someone with your skills..."

"I don't know what you mean."

"Don't give me that." His accusing eyes regard me from below raised eyebrows. "It ever occur to you that maybe first thing we do when we get a homicide in a small town is look at the history of the cop that found the body? You'd be surprised how often corruption rules in the country. Or maybe you wouldn't. Someone with a closed-case record like yours..."

"That was a different life."

"Bullshit. You and I both know that there are too many frauds on the job. Any idiot takes the exam enough times winds up calling himself detective. But then there are the ones like you, the ones with the knack, whether it's skill or luck or both, but we both know that it's too rare to just give up and walk away. It's not right to run and hide out here in the woods, *Detective*."

There's something about the way he says the word, maybe it's the emphasis he puts on it, but for some reason it strikes fear into my heart. "You don't know me. You don't have any idea what you're talking about."

"Don't I? You think I'm gonna spend the rest of my career working under *Mighty Mouse* out there? You think I like it? I don't. But he's the best there is at the Skowhegan Office. Third best in the state, and his close rate isn't even half of what yours was."

"Detective Robbins."

"No, I'm sorry, but I just can't understand it. You're as good at the job as you were and you leave it all behind because one case, *one case* ruins your perfect track record? So, you move out here to—"

"Detective Robbins." I say his name between clenched teeth, using the same tone I would use had he touched me inappropriately. Maybe it's that, or maybe it's something he sees in my face. Either way it shuts him up, and, for that, I'm thankful.

With a grunt he spins on the stool and goes back to filling out the report, but it's too late. I feel the long-forgotten beginnings of a panic attack creeping up on me. I pull at the collar of my uniform. Suddenly it's too tight, the buttons too constricting. I focus on my breathing, knowing I need to get some fresh air before I lose control.

"Everybody playing nice?" Campden struts back into the room. Guess Sue said yes.

I smile widely. "I've got a few things I need to check on. I'll be back later with some lunch." Before he can respond I rush out of the room, mumbling some random excuse to Sue on my way to the car. It isn't until I see her crossing the street that I remember what I forgot to make sure Campden knew about last night.

6

HEATHER

Sometimes I wonder if I was someone bad in my last life, like that evil Muppet in the movie or that Hitler guy we learned about in school, because I don't think I've done enough in this one to deserve what I get. Last night was the worst night ever. I don't know how I'm going to just go on living like it never happened. How do you survive when you're trapped inside the person you hate most in the world?

I wake up this morning to my little sister Penny crying in my face. She's standing in front of the couch where I slept wearing nothing but a dirty diaper and a layer of sticky toddler grime. She smacks my cheek and then howls even louder, like she was the one who'd been hit. I sit up, trying to escape, and am hit with the worst cramps I've ever had.

I turn the TV on and leave Penny screaming by the couch as I stumble to the bathroom. I pop one of Momma's OxyContin first thing, avoiding my face in the mirror. My hair has dried with an odd, egg-shaped lump on the right. I wash up and wet my hair, trying to get it to lay flat. It springs right back up. I search the drawers for a rubber band, settle for a banana clip, twisting my hair back.

My clothes from last night are balled up in the corner behind the door. Thinking of all the crime shows Momma watches on TV, I scoop them up and grab a box of matches and a bottle of lighter fluid from the kitchen, then I carry them out back. If only everything could be dealt with this easily.

The fire lights with a big whoosh, flames leaping up hungrily to eat my clothes. My face sweats from the heat. Maybe a bit from the pain and fear, too.

There's so much I've got to do, but I overslept, and I can't afford to be late to work again. My stomach grumbles, but I know better than to look for something to eat. Instead, I grab the baby and shove her into Momma's room, still wailing. Momma doesn't wake but her snoring lets me know she's alive.

I have no other choice, so I pedal my bike toward town. The pill's kicked in so I'm not hurting too bad, but I'm not steering very straight, either. I wish I had a different life. I could have been smart and a good student and gotten a scholarship to some college that would have gotten me out of this crappy little town.

But that was never really an option for me. I was never going to be one of those bright, shiny, successful people, even if I hadn't dropped out of school on my sixteenth birthday. Technically, it was five days before because I had some absent days saved up that I figured I might as well use, but I didn't sign the withdrawal papers until it was officially legal.

There aren't many job openings in Coyote Cove. Most places are worked by the people who own them, but I managed to get myself a job as a maid at the local motel. I had high hopes that some rich tourist would see me and want to take me with him. Problem is, no one with money would ever stay at the place I work.

I'll be eighteen in just over a year. If I haven't found my way out of here by then, I'm going to try getting a job at the Loose Moose as a bartender. Then I'll be able to save enough to get a car.

For now, though, I've got to keep cleaning the crusty rooms at the crappy Maggot Motel. It's technically Margot's, but trust me, there's only one Margot there and she's outnumbered by a ton of bugs, so what I call it is a better fit. On the plus side, I steal enough toilet paper and shampoo that it helps make the budget at home stretch a little farther.

Momma used to work construction. She was one of those sign holders who help direct traffic on the road when it's being worked on, until something fell off a truck one day and smashed her foot. She used to talk about how she'd live like royalty off that disability check once my brother Jimmy and I were out of the house.

The joke's on her because right after Jimmy moved to a logging camp, she popped Penny out. Didn't even know she was pregnant. That happens more than you'd think. You don't even have to be one of those fat ladies like on TV—Momma's not. She's thick, sturdy, country strong, but I wouldn't say fat.

I chain my bike to the rack outside the trading post and jog across the street to the motel. Ducking into the office, I grab the keys and get started. As I unlock the door to the storage room where we keep the cleaning cart, I remind myself that I've got to find a way to smuggle a jug of bleach home with me. On all those crime shows Momma watches, the people always use bleach.

7

MAGGIE

I watch Heather walk into the motel like it's any normal day. Maybe it is for her. Maybe she was telling the truth last night. And maybe I'm Papa Smurf.

I don't know much about Heather McGillis. I know she's a high-school dropout who lives with her mother, but the same could be said of half the people born in Coyote Cove. Ironically, the school ranks in the top ten for the state. It's not like a good education isn't an option. Still, the dropout rate is unusually high.

I've heard it's because students go stir-crazy attending the same building for their senior year as they went to for kindergarten. I guess I can understand that. The city council's been talking about holding different class ranges in different buildings, but there just aren't enough students or money to make it happen.

Heather lets herself into a motel room with a cleaning cart. I bite my lip, feeling the old familiar thrill I used to get when the stars lined up and the pieces of an investigation would start coming together. I imagine it's how hunters must feel when a trophy buck wanders into their sights.

Since he wasn't a local, and no one's reported him missing, the victim was probably staying at one of the rooms available in town. There aren't many. I get out of my car and cross the street, entering the office of Margot's Motel, and find Margot herself sitting behind the desk.

Margot Graves is a shrunken woman, dried like a piece of jerky. She holds a seat on almost every board and council in town. She chairs the food drive, the toy drive, and fosters any homeless pets that turn up until she finds them a good home. She's also the meanest little old lady I've ever met. At least half of the calls I respond to each year are either from or about Margot Graves. Luckily, I'm on her good side.

"Morning, Chief. Who's got a bee in their bonnet this time?"

"How're you doing Margot? Would it ruin your day if I said I'm not here to haul you in?"

She stares at me with her tiny, black, lashless eyes and it appears that she *is* disappointed. I stifle a smile. The last thing I want to do is piss her off before asking a favor, but I wouldn't want to upset her anyways. The truth is, I like Margot.

She and I are more alike than most people may think. For whatever reason, I lack the female bonding gene. I never really had any women I was close to besides an old colleague I hardly ever see. I was never one to hold hands with my girlfriends, give hugs, talk on the phone, recruit someone to go to the restroom with me—I never saw the point.

From an evolutionary standpoint, women engage in such bonding behavior to form social networks that will increase the odds of their offspring's survival. Before modern civilization, having other women to allomother a child enabled the mother to spend more time obtaining food, provided more eyes as safety resources, and helped teach younger females to care for young before they had their own.

I'm an evolutionary dud. Even as a child I knew I never

wanted kids, looking upon baby dolls with abject horror. It's this deficiency that Margot and I share and that provides the cement of our bond. We see that dud gene in each other and in turn recognize a kindred spirit.

"'Course, if you want to be difficult, I could always bring you downtown. I've got a couple of staties at the office today that you could beat up on."

She grins, the few teeth she has left worn down to nicotine-stained nubs, but I can still see how pretty she must have once been. Margot moved to Coyote Cove over forty years ago. She averages a husband for each decade. Rumor is there were a couple before she moved here, too.

"You know I love fresh meat, but those staties are too soft. I can't stand to see a man cry."

"Such a saint."

"I try. So, why are you here then? I'm guessing this isn't a social call, seeing as how neither of us is the type of woman for idle chat."

I wonder if I'm going to grow up to be just like Margot in another thirty or forty years. I suppose I could end up worse.

"Between you and me?" I look from side to side to make sure no one else is within earshot, even though I know there isn't. Margot leans forward. I've got her full attention. "There's been a murder."

Margot gasps. I know that I'm being overly dramatic. I also know that Margot wouldn't have it any other way. And yet, there seemed something ingenuine about her reaction. Almost like she was expecting what I told her.

"A local?"

I shake my head. She turns to the computer and pecks at the keys. A moment later a sheet of paper shoots out of the printer. Her spotted, gnarled hand trembles as she makes a few notes and then hands it to me. It's a guest roster. Beside each of the names she's written a description. Two fit the general look of the victim.

Taking a pen from the cup on her desk I make a star next to both possible names and hand the paper back to her. She pulls a file from the drawer, rummages through it, then makes a couple of photocopies that she hands to me. There's no need to look at the second sheet of paper. The first shows the driver's license of the victim. I nod, take a picture before I fold the paper and put it in my back pocket, while I study Margot's expression from the corner of my eye.

She wouldn't have made it this easy for me if she had anything to do with my victim, would she? Although, she's smart enough to know she'd look suspicious if she led me to believe the victim hadn't been staying here and I later found out that he was. And, sometimes, being helpful is the best subterfuge.

"The cleaning girl's got the keys." Margot stands on spindly legs. She springs across the room on them with the prowess of a panther. I follow close behind, knowing as I do that I should call the detectives and let them take care of it.

I shouldn't have anything to do with this case. No good can come of it. The last thing I need is to lose the tenuous hold on the tiny shrapnel of happiness that I've managed to get my fingers on in this far-flung corner of America.

I follow Margot down the concrete walk, suspecting that there's nothing to discover in the victim's room. Knowing that even if there is, it's already too late. My life here as I know it is over.

8

STEVE

I never had a dog growing up, and I never wanted one as an adult, but somehow these furry little beasts have seduced me and stolen my heart. Just like their owner. Now, I can't imagine life without either. I want to confess to Maggie and tell her the real reason that I'm over at her place so much. I want to be honest with her. The problem is that there are already too many secrets on both sides.

I don't work much anymore—just one of the secrets I'm keeping from Maggie. I make enough on residuals to make ends meet. I just don't have the drive in me to pick up the phone and make a sale.

I think I'm depressed. I've fallen in and out of it my entire life, not that Maggie would know—another secret. This time, though, I feel like there's something I can do about it. Like there's a light cord hanging at the end of the tunnel and all I've got to do is reach out and pull it.

I can love these tiny tyrants freely, without censorship or reservation, and they love me back unconditionally. It's something I've never experienced before and I seek it out now like a drug, always yearning for my next high. I spend most of my free time with them now.

I'm napping on the couch, a pup nestled under each arm, when they bounce up and start barking. There's nothing new about that, except that they're fussing at the door to the basement, which *is* odd. Anxiety claws at my chest as I take timid steps forward, forcing myself to investigate.

I hear the water gushing before I reach the door. The burst pipe is spraying like Niagara Falls. Running down the stairs, I search for the water main. This isn't something I'm good at. I'm from a family where the men paid other men to do the dirty work.

Maggie's the only one of us with a toolbox. She'd know what to do, but she's not here. And since I can't take another straw of incompetency upon my back, and I don't want to have to tell her that I stood by and watched her house get destroyed, I pretend that I'm someone else.

It doesn't take me long to find a valve that does the trick, a few quick twists quelling the leak to a trickle, leaving me quite proud of myself. I'm feeling manly. I feel like I should grunt or beat my chest like a gorilla, maybe give a cowboy yell, but the moment has passed and now it would just be weird.

Instead, I take a look around, assessing the damage. It looks like, at some point in time, someone was going to finish Maggie's basement. A single row of cement blocks runs along the floor marking the outline of how they were going to divide the room. For once they're something besides a pain-in-the-ass tripping hazard—now they're working to contain the water, flooding a couple of the boxes Maggie has stored down here.

To be perfectly honest, a little thrill zaps through me at having an excuse to snoop. I move the wet boxes onto the folding table Maggie uses for laundry and start unpacking the contents to dry. The first box is filled with a stack of framed items. I open the second and find a few photo albums with yellowed edges, and below those another box inside, light gray with a tie down lid. As I remove the cover, I discover that it's an evidence box.

I wonder if this is something she's supposed to have. And, if not, why she would keep it. I set it on the table and stare at it like there might be a body inside, which I know is ridiculous, but there's an odd force radiating from it telling me that this is a secret that I should let Maggie keep. At least until she's ready to tell me herself.

Turning my attention back to the items from the first box, I start separating things, using a towel to dry off any moisture until the table is covered with framed awards, commendations, and diplomas. I'm amazed at just how many Maggie has. I realize I'm trespassing, but I can't stop myself.

Maggie has a master's degree in both criminal justice and forensic science. She has certificates from FBI training programs in criminal profiling, tactical response, crime scene survey, and impression evidence—I'm not even sure I know what all of that is. There are acronymed awards, awards named after cops, awards for service, performance, and valor. I knew that Maggie had been a detective in Florida, but I had no idea she had been so successful. Why would she keep it a secret?

Thumbing through the photo albums, I find that they're filled with articles about Maggie and her cases. I learn that the woman I love worked homicides, busted a serial killer, shot and killed an armed assailant holding a child hostage. I read about Maggie's former life like it's an adventure novel until I get to the clips at the end of the second book. I glance at the evidence box, skimming the name and date.

Stumbling back a step, I swallow hard past the sudden lump tightening my throat. Rub my hands on the legs of my pants, but they still feel dirty. I know Maggie's secret.

I shouldn't, but it's too late. There's no going back. No forgetting that I now know what she ran from, why she's hiding up here in a dark little corner of the Maine woods when, with her qualifications, she could probably work for any police agency in the country.

What I've done is unequivocally wrong. I feel like I've stripped Maggie naked and left her exposed for the whole world to see. I've violated a trust she never gave me. I suspect that she'll know immediately the next time I look at her. I wish I could undo what I've done, unlearn her secret. But I can't.

Carefully, I repack the boxes and head back upstairs. The dogs jump up, welcoming my return. I ignore them, look up the number of a plumber and make the call. I need to erase this. It never happened. I understand now, and I love her more than ever, but that might not be enough.

9

MAGGIE

Margot and I find Heather cleaning the room next door to the victim's. When she sees me, the blank look on her face turns to horror. That expression tells me everything I need to know about Heather McGillis.

She thinks that I'm here to arrest her. The question is, why?

Margot is slick and doesn't directly ask her for the keys. She asks Heather how many rooms she has left to clean, what other chores she has left for the day. Then she tells Heather that she'll tend to the remaining rooms, asking her to weed the front garden bed instead. I can tell Heather's confused about how my presence plays into this change of task, but once given the opportunity to escape, she can't leave me and Margot alone in the room fast enough.

An interesting fact—reading expressions is hardwired into the female brain. Within the first three months of life a baby girl's eye contact and face-gazing skills will increase by over four hundred percent. During the same timeframe a baby boy's skills in these areas will not increase at all. It's intrinsic for girls to study emotional expressions—facial reactions are how they determine the success of their interactions with others.

Some of my female genes may be faulty, but this is a skill I dominate at. It was one of my best tools as a detective. Just now, Heather's expression told me she is scared, guilty, and ashamed. She is terrified that I know her secret. Whatever it is—and I will find out—it might not have anything to do with my dead guy.

Margot has finished replenishing the guest toiletries in the bathroom. She wheels the cart out of the room and over to the victim's. She hesitates, looking at me for approval.

I shake my head. "I better call the state detectives, let them have the first look. We'll need to fingerprint the door, knob, and frame before we enter."

Margot nods, looking relieved, and I suspect she doesn't want to see what may be on the other side of the door. This is her safe place, and she doesn't welcome murder in her refuge any more than I do in mine.

"Why don't you go on back to the front? I'll let you know if we need anything."

"Make sure they don't make a mess," she threatens.

I watch her skeletal frame slink back the way we'd come and disappear through the office door. I think how nice it must be to be able to just walk away from something like this. Sighing, I dig my cell out of my pocket and dial the office.

Sue picks up. I can hear Detective Campden talking in the background.

"Coyote Cove Police Department, how may I help you?"

"Hey, Sue, it's me. Can you do me a favor and send lover boy and his partner on down to Margot's. Room 14. You can tell them that I got an ID on the vic and I'm posted outside his room if they'd like to call their forensic tech and join me."

Sue must be holding the phone against her belly while she relays my message to Campden because I can hear her stomach gurgling, which is ironic, because my own is practically shout-ing, telling me to avoid the staties. As a rule, I always trust my gut—it's like a second brain. There are more neurons lining the human gut than the spinal cord. Physiologically, it's so your digestive system can work independently from your brain, but those neurons also react when you experience a flood of emotions, which results in the so-called "gut feeling".

Sue gets back on the phone. "They're on their way, Chief."

I already see Robbins and Campden hurrying down the wooden ramp down the street.

"Thanks, Sue."

"Hey, Chief?"

"Yeah?"

"You be careful, there being a murderer out there and all."

"You too."

"Don't you worry about me. I'm sitting here with a twelve gauge across my lap."

I can't help but smile because I know it's true.

"Hey, Sue?"

"Yeah?"

"I want to be just like you when I grow up."

"You could do worse. Now you play nice with those boys. And make sure that I get picked up on time for my free dinner."

"I'll do my best."

"You always do."

Sue leaves me with that. The line goes dead just as Campden and Robbins reach me. I imagine I can see Sue peeping at us through the blinds down the street.

"You know you shouldn't have been snooping into this on your own. You should have left it to us." That's how Campden greets me.

Robbins quickly averts his eyes from mine.

"I had no intentions to *snoop*, Detective. I was talking to the owner about an unrelated matter and figured I'd ask about her guests since I was here anyways. It was a random stroke of luck."

"Keys." He snaps his fingers and holds his hand out. I drop

them onto his outstretched palm like they're infected with Ebola.

"Here." I hand him the photocopy of the victim's driver's license. "In case you wanted to know who the victim is."

He snatches the paper and pockets it without giving it a glance. "You been in here yet?" he asks, his hand closing around the doorknob. I fight the urge to wince.

"No. I figured I'd wait until everything had been dusted for prints before I touched anything, this being a possible crime scene and all."

He drops his hand like he's just been burned. His eyes narrow, which, for some reason, accentuates the sharp angle of his ears from his head. "Thank you, *Officer*. Detective Robbins and I have a lot of *real* work to do now. You may leave. If I need anything else, I'll be in touch."

I give him my best eat-shit grin. "Well, as long as it doesn't intrude upon your dinner plans with Sue. I try to not interfere with my employee's personal lives. I prefer to run my business in a more professional manner than that."

I hear the name he calls me while I'm walking away. It just makes me smile wider. It must suck to be that incompetent, but I wouldn't know.

10

HEATHER

I watch Chief Riley and Margot from the reflection on the windshield of Margot's old Buick, relieved to be safely around the corner from the chief's accusing stare. They speak outside a closed door, then Margot leaves, heading toward me. I scramble onto my knees at the edge of the flower bed and grab a handful of green, ripping it out and setting it in a pile beside me.

Glancing over my shoulder, I see Margot vanish into the office. I return to my weeding, realizing that I tore half the leaves off a violet plug in my haste. Carefully, I pluck the tiny sprigs of grass and weeds out by their bases, not wanting to cause any more damage. I've done enough of that already.

But I can't figure out what's going on. I stretch until I can see Chief Riley in the windshield again. She's still just standing outside a closed motel room door. It makes no sense. It feels good to be off my feet though. My muscle spasms are starting to relax.

Two strangers clomp across the parking lot, their footsteps the heavy trod of city people. It's funny how you can sometimes tell where someone's from by the way they walk. City people slap their feet down like they have to stomp the ground under them into submission. Maybe cement needs to be walked on like that. Maybe it has something to do with the term concrete jungle. I don't know. What I do know is that country folk tend to walk softly, letting their foot conform to the ground underneath. You try walking with a rigid foot over uneven earth, and it just doesn't go right.

The strangers pass behind me and join Chief Riley. Suddenly, it hits me that maybe this all has something to do with the body from the night before. I feel sick as I realize that maybe I'm a suspect, and that's why Chief Riley keeps looking at me like she knows I've done something evil and wrong. I can't stomach the thought, but the more I think about it, the more I believe it's true.

I can't go to jail. I'm just a kid. I'm supposed to have my whole life in front of me. I deserve the chance to experience at least a few years that don't suck. Part of me is already planning my defense. But then I have a better idea.

11

MURPHY

Murphy had thought that accepting the crime scene technician's invitation to help process the victim was a good idea. He figured it was something the chief might do. It didn't hurt that the tech looks like she's right off a college cheerleading squad, a young brunette with bouncy hair and a bubbly personality that makes it seem like anything she does will be fun. Now that he finds himself standing over the green ‚tarped body, though, he's having second thoughts.

He hovers next to Chris Hensley, the funeral home director. The tech, Bridgette, and the medical examiner stand on the other side of the body cart. Murphy looks at the ME, expecting him to run the show.

Dr. Tony Marchetti is on the short side, round bodied, with a thin ring of hair clinging to his scalp, and a voice that's much too loud if you're in the same room as him. Murphy watches him make faces, twitching his nose like he has an itch. To Murphy's surprise, Bridgette takes the lead.

"We'll begin by unwrapping the victim. I'll photograph, then look for trace, lift any fibers, check his nails and hands, bag his clothes—the usual. Then we can transfer him to a bag for the

Doc here to take home. I'd also like to preserve the tarp, take it with me to check for transfer. I think the easiest way would be for me to work with him on the floor."

Murphy notices that she's looking at him expectantly. He plays her words back through his mind, trying to figure out what he missed.

"I've got something we can lay down first. Then Lieutenant Murphy and I will get him settled where you want him." Hensley crosses to a cabinet, withdraws a bagged roll of clear plastic. "Paint sheeting," he explains, opening the package. "I order it in bulk, has all kinds of uses."

Hensley hands an end to Murphy and backs away from him until the length is spread out. He unfurls a few feet from the roll. Murphy watches closely and follows suit.

"If we could just borrow a foot from you both, we'll have this done in a jiffy."

Bridgette pins a corner beneath her black work boot. Dr. Marchetti does the same as he pulls at his nose with one hand. Murphy matches Hensley foot for foot as they sidestep down the length of the embalming room. The plastic sheeting covers almost the entire floor.

"I'll have to remember this stuff," Bridgett says while waiting for Hensley and Murphy to skirt their way around the edges and return to the cart.

Hensley tosses Murphy a pair of disposable gloves and pulls a pair on himself. He waits for Murphy and then takes hold of an end of the rolled tarp.

"We'll take him to the middle, so Ms. Parsons has room to spread out the tarp and work."

Ms. Parsons? Murphy realizes Hensley is talking about Bridgette. Even her name screams cheerleader. Only, in a few minutes, she's going to be touching a dead guy. None of this sits well with Murphy.

He already feels a wave of heat creeping up his collar,

warming his head. Sweat begins to seep from the pores along his hairline as he and Hensley waddle the body into the middle of the plastic. The back of his neck is damp, his armpits wet as he retreats from the corpse, his back hitting against the wall.

Bridgette takes a series of pictures. The tarp crinkles loudly as she unrolls it. He stares at the clock on the wall, focusing on the second hand as it ticks its way around the timepiece in sixty tiny steps. Camera clicks fill the otherwise silent room.

Murphy's eyes flash to Bridgette for a second as she crouches over her toolbox. It seems like she's good at her job. He wonders how good.

He lets his eyes wander a little further, to where she's rolled one end of the tarp down against the dark-flannel-swathed arm and jeaned leg of the victim. He watches her hands as she presses clear plastic hinge lifters to the clothes, sealing the fibers trapped beneath to a shiny paper background. He looks at the dark splotches on the shirt, hard spots of dried blood.

Murphy half hears a comment she makes to the doctor about not having to break rigor to remove the clothes. His heartbeat slows. His body dries.

He observes Bridgette holding the victim's hand in her gloved fist, scraping the contents under the nails into a tiny manila envelope. The skin is pale and kind of waxy looking. It hardly looks real.

He slowly moves his eyes up the body until they land on the face. The bile hits the back of his teeth with the force of a water balloon, spraying out in front of him as he tries to flee the room, the image of the glassy eyes, half-opened and accusing, scarred into his brain like a tattoo.

12

MAGGIE

I leave the state detectives without a backward glance, walk down the street, and get into my Jeep. I'm not sure what to do, where to go, but I feel the need to accomplish something. I'll let the detectives fumble the homicide investigation for a while. At the moment, I'm more concerned with whatever secret Heather McGillis is hiding.

I know she'll be at the motel for a while longer, so I decide to stop by her house. Might as well talk to her mom and see if she knows anything. Maybe I'll get lucky, and she'll let me take a look around.

I head toward the logging road where I discovered a dead man only the night before. Heather doesn't live too far away from the crime scene. She could have easily walked there from her house last night. That part of her story I can believe.

Her reason for why she was out there roaming the woods by herself at night is a different matter. That I don't buy at all. I have a feeling, a tingling, second-brain-in-the-gut sensation that whether it happened to her or by her, something bad went down out in those woods last night—besides the corpse being dumped on the side of the road.

I park along the street in front of the tiny clapboard house that's aging poorly on a scrubby, mostly dirt lot. I move carefully across the cracked walk, weeds spreading like wildfire from between the breaks, and onto the sagging porch. Sidestepping, I find a board that doesn't feel like it's going to collapse beneath my feet before I knock.

I hear a child wailing and the TV blaring inside. The door used to be red, but is now a shade of faded purple and gray. The remaining paint is flaky, lining the door like the ruffled mushrooms that grow on trees. I knock again, louder. The TV mutes, but not the child.

I can feel the person approaching the other side of the door through the vibrations in the board under my feet. There's a creak while they look at me through the peephole, debating whether or not to ignore me. Finally, the door swings open, rusty hinges screeching in protest.

Heather McGillis's mother, Mary, faces me with a vacant look. Her eyes are glassy, empty. She's on something.

She steps back and waves me forward without a word. The inside of the house is no nicer than the outside. Framed pictures of cats hang on the walls, the glass fronts smeared with dirt and grease. Dust balls and fur line the edges where the floors meet the walls in thick clumps. The pattern of the linoleum floor is worn beyond recognition.

I follow Mary into the kitchen and sit where she beckons me to. She pours a mug of coffee and sets it before me without asking. I smile and nod thanks. I want nothing more than to drink it, but I'm afraid to consume anything from this house. She settles in the chair across from me and stares down at her hands.

The screaming child toddles in, stares at me with wide eyes from the doorway, then launches back into her tirade. A trail of snot hangs from her nose, a green slug oozing its way through the filthy grime on the baby's face. Her diaper hangs low, full. I realize how this is going to end, what I'm going to have to do. So does Mary.

"I know why you're here." Her voice is low, her words slightly slurred. She looks up, her bloodshot eyes meeting my own. "Thank God. I never meant for it to get this bad. Guess I should have called you myself, but I never would have thought that it would take this long for the neighbors to do it."

Her eyes go to the baby then back to me. "I just can't do it. Thought I could, but... Too old, too tired, too worn out. I just ain't got nothing left. She'll be better off with someone else."

I nod, encouraging her to keep talking.

"There ain't no need for fostering. I'll sign the papers, they can have her for keeps. Least I can do."

Mary stands and shuffles to the sink. She grabs a dirty hand towel, wets it, and returns to her seat at the table. She snaps her fingers and the baby waddles over in front of her. Mary roughly wipes at the dirt on her daughter's face, trying to clean her up. Her cries stop, as if she knows her pleas for help have finally been heard and now she can rest. "She don't got much to take with her."

"What about you, Mary? Do you have someone to take care of you?"

"Heather does what she can. It'll be better with the baby gone. Ain't neither of us the mothering type."

Neither am I, but I sure as hell could have done better than this, I want to scream. I want to shake her, smack her around a bit, and leave her soiled and naked wearing nothing but a diaper filled with her own filth. Instead, I pull out my cell phone and dial.

As soon as Sue answers I explain the situation. Coyote Cove is too small to have many of the programs most towns have, including Child Protective Services. I've only come across one other situation where it was needed in my four years here.

Sue's the closest thing we've got to a social worker. She's

also a state-approved temporary foster home. I hear her gathering her purse and keys through the line as she promises to be right over. I keep the phone to my ear even after the line goes dead, pretending to listen while I watch Mary's face from the corner of my eye.

Finally, I feign a goodbye and slip the phone back into my pocket. Then I turn to face Mary.

"Heather is still a minor." I state the fact.

Mary flinches as she realizes the implications. "Barely," she whispers.

"We'll be removing the baby from the house today. But I'm going to need to take a look around. I may need to speak with Heather."

Mary's knuckles turn white as she holds on to the edge of the table. I observe as what little composure she has starts to crumble. Her eyes dart around the room as if she can find the answer to her problems written somewhere on the grubby walls.

"You can't take my baby." Her voice shakes. I know she's talking about Heather, not the toddler. "I *need* her. We need each other. I'll... I'll die if you take her."

"Mary, I'm going to do everything I can to help you. And Heather. But I'll need full access to the house. Depending on what I find, well, the good news is that Heather is old enough to be emancipated. That may not even be necessary, but I've got to do my job and investigate."

Mary is nodding like a bobble head. "Yes, whatever you have to do. Please. Look anywhere. Just please don't take my baby."

I don't feel bad for manipulating the situation to get what I need, but I feel horrible that I have no intentions of removing Heather from this house. Worse still that I'm here behind her back to dig for whatever secrets she's hiding. But I have to follow my instincts, and now I have what I need—permission to do so. It takes every ounce of willpower I have to not jump up and start searching immediately.

Instead, we sit in awkward silence, Mary staring down at her hands on the table and me trying to not fill the air between us with my unspoken judgment. It's hard work. Finally, there's a knock at the door and we both breathe a sigh of relief. I know it's Sue—no doubt she redlined her speedometer the whole way here.

As Mary gets up to let her in, I meet the baby's bewildered eyes and try and let her know that things will be better now. I think she understands. Moments later, Sue appears in the kitchen doorway, takes one look at the baby, throws a look of disgust at Mary, and then scoops the child up into her arms.

"What's her name?"

"Penny."

"Where are the diapers? And the tub? I'm giving her a bath before I dress her for the car ride." Sue bounces the baby on her hip. I wonder if she's realized yet that this will put a damper on her dinner plans.

Mary leads her down another hall, head hung low. I follow. There's a door on either side. One is Mary's. She remains in the doorway, watching while Sue searches the pile of baby stuff on the floor for a clean diaper and clothes. I turn toward the other room, pipes groaning in the walls behind me as Sue turns the water on to bathe the baby. I open the door.

Heather's tiny bedroom looks like a typical teenager's. Posters on the wall, piles of clothes on every surface, magazine clippings taped to the mirror. I snoop, opening drawers, leafing through papers, peeking under the bed.

On the cardboard box Heather uses as a nightstand, I notice a folded paper that looks like it's been handled a lot. The edges are dirty, and the creases have almost worn through the page. Opening it, I read it, snap a few photos, and return it to where I found it.

In Heather's bathroom I find some smudges on the floor behind the door. I snap photos and use one of her Q-tips to take a sample, storing it in an evidence bag from my pocket to keep it from getting contaminated. Then I bag a soiled hand towel. I wander out of the room, through the house, and out the back door. The smoke smell hits me immediately.

I find the firepit encircled by rocks in the back corner of the lot, too close to the wood line. The ashes are dark. They look and smell fresh. I use a third bag to gather what I can and find small fragments of singed material in the cindered debris.

My mind is connecting dots that I don't want to see. I don't like where my thoughts are going. I need to take a step back and examine the evidence without jumping to conclusions, because I think Heather McGillis might be in big trouble.

13

MURPHY

"It happens to a lot of people." Murphy knows that Hensley is trying to make him feel better, but it's not working. He takes a sip of ginger ale and shifts on the stool so that he's facing the wall.

"A guy I worked with, Dan, he threw up *inside* the body the first time he watched a postmortem. No kidding." This from Bridgette, still collecting evidence from the corpse on the floor.

Murphy avoids looking at her. He wants to defend himself. He wants to tell them that he didn't throw up because he saw a dead body, that he threw up because of who the dead body was, but he knows that's the stupidest thing he can do right now. He wishes he could disappear.

He has some vacation time saved up. He wonders if it would be suspicious if he asked the chief if he could use it now. The case isn't actually theirs. Maybe he could mention something about now being the time, since there were other cops in town and the chief wouldn't be left on her own. All he really wants to do is lay low until this whole nightmare is over. Stick his head in the sand and pretend it never happened.

His pocket quacks. Murphy fumbles the phone out, sees

that it's his wife calling. He notices the amused looks as he rushes out of the room to take the call. Now he's the hillbilly cop who pukes at dead people *and* who has a redneck duck-call ringtone. Great.

"Yeah?"

"Where are you?" He can tell by Alma's voice that his wife is looking for a fight.

"At work."

"Where?"

"I'm at Hensley's Funeral Home right now."

"Hmm. I haven't been able to get a hold of Heather."

"She's probably at work."

"Yeah, well, her momma ain't answering the phone either. You know *she's* at the house."

"Maybe she's busy."

Alma snorts, an ugly sound that makes him cringe. "Not likely."

"I don't know what to tell you. What do you want me to do?"

"I want to you to find Heather and bring her over for dinner tonight."

"Alma, I don't know her. I don't want to do that."

"You do know her. She's family."

"Your family. Bet you don't even remember how y'all are related."

The silence on the line lets him know she's trying to remember. "That don't matter none," she snaps eventually. "Just do it." The line goes dead.

"Love you too, honey," Murphy says sarcastically to the empty air.

He considers taking off. He could just pick a place and start a new life. Like the chief did. It had worked for her. He thinks about his sons, wonders if they'd feel as betrayed about being abandoned as he did when his mom left.

"Everything all right?" Hensley asks, poking his head around the corner.

Murphy nods, pondering his sons' chin dimples. Neither he nor Alma has a chin dimple. Not like Bryan, his best friend does. He bets that when his boys grow up that their chin dimples look just like Bryan's. Just like it.

"We were getting ready to order some lunch. You want some?"

"Nah," Murphy says. "I've got to get going. Got some business to attend to. I'll catch up with you later."

Of all the unknowns running though his mind as he heads outside and climbs into his truck, the question that bothers him the most is how long he has until someone discovers the victim's identity—and his connection to the murdered man, found stabbed to death out on one of the back logging roads.

14

HEATHER

The cops are still in the motel room when Margot sends me home for the day. There's a ton I need to do, so the short shift was a lucky break. Leaving the woods, I push my bike through the sand and back onto the road. I could pedal again now, but I need more time to think before I have to listen to Penny cry all night. Besides, I'm off work early so it's not like Momma's expecting me home anytime soon.

A trio of deer graze on the other side of the street. They raise their heads, their dark eyes curious as they watch me. How would they react if they knew the truth about me? Would they run away? Would they knock me down and trample me under their sharp hooves? Or would they just listen? Just keep staring at me with innocence and acceptance? Maybe even be my friends?

Something inside me needs to say it, to speak what I've done out loud. To share my secret with someone else, so I'm no longer the only one to carry the burden. I know that it's ridiculous, but I decide to go for it. I am going to confess my sins to the deer.

Stopping directly across from them, I try to decide what to

say. They're deer, there's no use trying to sugarcoat it. I can just spit out the words, as horrible as they are.

"Last night I..."

Their ears twitch, their eyes flicking behind me. My words break off as I look over my shoulder and see the truck approaching. The deer shake their tails and then dart into the woods, disappearing to safer ground. I've lost my chance. I doubt I'll get another one.

I walk on, leaning heavily on the bike as I push it, like the weight on my shoulders has increased. I expect the driver to turn off on the crossroad, to return me to the deafening silence of my thoughts, but it doesn't. The engine grows louder, getting closer until it pulls up alongside me and slows. There's a whine as the window lowers. Keeping my head down, I refuse to look.

"Heather."

My eyes stare at the ground. "Yeah?"

"Get in."

This surprises me. I stop, not sure what to do.

"Alma wants to talk to you. She told me to bring you over for dinner tonight."

My eyes jump to Lieutenant Murphy's. His expression is blank. I feel my head shaking ever so slightly from side to side.

"You know how she is, she won't take no for an answer." He hangs an arm out of the window, bounces his hand softly against the door a few times. "You don't want me to get in trouble, do you?"

"I've gotta get home. Momma needs my help with the baby."

His eyes dart away from mine suddenly and I know something's wrong. I'm not ready to find out what. Maybe I should run while I still have the chance.

He must be able to hear my thoughts because the driver's door creaks open. His feet scuff loudly across the blacktop and then I no longer have my bike to lean on. I watch helplessly as he sets it into the back of his truck. He gestures to me with his head. "Come on, get in."

A part of me wants to bolt like the deer through the woods to someplace safe. But unlike them, I'm not very fast. I feel queasy as I slip my backpack off and put it on the passenger floor and get into the truck. It's going against what Momma would call my better judgment, but that was just her wishful thinking. I never really had any of that. That's pretty clear by now.

As the truck jolts down the road, I lean my forehead against the passenger window and stare into the woods, but the deer are long gone. We're all alone out here, which makes me worry because there's no one to see me in this truck as it takes a left and disappears around a curve. That's when I realize—we're going in the wrong direction.

15

STEVE

Maggie comes home unexpectedly early. I'm still chatting with the plumber in the driveway, thanking him for his help. I assisted him with his taxes last year, along with half the rest of the town. Led a free class at the library, took everyone step by step through the process. I figured it would end up saving me a lot of time and headache.

I'm the closest thing there is to an accountant in this tiny burg, and no one really has the money to pay for help even if there was one. It also helps make up for the somewhat antisocial personality I have the rest of the year. Maggie waves as the plumbing van drives past her and chugs away down the road.

"What's that about?"

"Pipe burst." I had been hoping that I could have the repair done and the basement clean and dry before she got back, that she'd never have to know about the leak. "All fixed now."

"Any damage?"

"A couple of boxes got wet. I put them on the laundry table."

She nods.

"You should probably take a look. See if anything needs to be dried off."

I know I'm acting weird. She knows I'm acting weird. She's going to take one look at the boxes and know that it's because I've been snooping.

Maggie gives me a long look. She breaks it by giving me a kiss.

"I'm going to take the dogs out to the logging roads for a bit." Her voice is nonchalant, but I can feel something behind her words. "We're going to play detective. Would you like to come?"

My mouth drops at the invitation.

"You don't have to," she says hurriedly, mistaking my reaction. "I understand if you don't want to go, really. We can talk when I get back."

"No. I want to go."

"Really?"

"Of course. I've always wanted to play detective."

"No, really." Her eyebrows arch halfway to her hairline.

"Maggie, I want to go."

"You probably shouldn't. What I'm looking for... whatever it is, it's going to be bad if I find it."

"Now you're trying to talk me out of going."

"No. Yes. It's complicated. It might be nothing, just a walk in the woods, in which case yes, I want you to go. But if my gut is right, you don't want to be there. I don't want you to have to experience... anything bad."

I take her hand in mine. "I'm going. And if it turns out that your gut is right, then I'm glad that you don't have to experience whatever the bad is alone."

"Yeah, you say that now." She squeezes my hand then slips from my grasp, heading into the house.

I follow, watching as the dogs greet her. Maybe I'm a sap, but I can't look at those pups without feeling my heart lift. Maybe that's what having a baby is like, if you like babies.

Maggie lifts her face to mine from her crouched position on the floor as she puts harnesses on the dogs. "You made sure everything in the boxes was dry, right? The evidence box?"

My mouth works like a fish out of water.

"It's okay. I mean, I've been wanting, trying to, well... You should know. And I'm bad with words. This kind of just, it's a good thing. Really."

I'm shocked. It feels amazing, to have the woman I love willing to let me in on the part of her life that was so painful that she dropped everything to move 1,500 miles and a new world away from it. My joy is short lived because I realize that if she shares her secrets with me, I'm going to have to share mine with her. I wonder if she can still love me after that.

16

MURPHY

Murphy wonders why Heather doesn't mention that they're driving in the wrong direction. She's never struck him as very smart, but surely she knows her way around the area where she's spent her entire life. He sneaks a peek at her when he thinks she isn't looking. Her eyes are open. She sees where they're going. She doesn't look scared, just defeated.

He drives them down a series of loops and turns, the truck bouncing roughly on the gravel logging roads. It seems like they've traveled miles, but he knows that they're still within running distance to Heather's house if she could find her way. Maybe that's why she doesn't look scared.

They're not too far from where the chief was last night when Heather showed up at the crime scene. He wonders if he should drive her to the exact spot but decides against it. Decides instead to pull off the road where he is, stopping the truck. Unclipping his seatbelt, he turns to face her, his knee raised on the seat, an arm across the back. Heather stares at his hand blankly.

"I need you to tell me what you were doing out here last night."

Heather doesn't answer, just continues to gaze at his hand like she didn't hear him.

"And then we need to figure out what you're going to tell everyone else it was you were doing and make some kind of trail to prove it."

At this she looks at him. Her lower lip quivers, her eyes red and watery. "Why would you help me?" she whispers.

"I won't even know if you need help unless you tell me. Do you need help, Heather?"

She nods at him, eyes wide.

"Then I need you tell me what happened. This isn't Lieutenant Murphy asking, just regular ole Dale. I promise."

"Why?"

"What's it matter? If you need help and someone offers it to you, you take it, right?"

Heather shrugs. Murphy knows he's not getting through to her.

"Dammit, girl. I don't have time for this. Someone died out here last night, and the chief? She's wondering why you just so happened to wander onto her crime scene. So you're going to tell me what you were doing whether you want to or not. You got me?"

"Yes." Her hands twist in her lap.

"So, what happened? Were you out here killing last night or was it something else?"

"I'm not sure." Tears stream down Heather's cheeks. Her body trembles, but her voice is strong.

Murphy recoils in his seat. "What do you mean, you're not sure? How can you not be sure of something like that? It's either a yes or a no. So, which is it?"

"I think..." Heather is sobbing now. If she notices the way Murphy is looking at her, she doesn't seem to care. Like she can't stop. Like it feels too good. Like she needs to get it all out. "I think maybe I was. But I didn't mean to. Honest."

17

MAGGIE

I sense a strange vibe coming from Steve as I drive out to the crime scene. A tension, like maybe he's having second thoughts about me. Or changed his mind altogether. I wish I knew. My hands wrap tighter on the steering wheel as I juggle questions about my own life with those of the case. The truth is, I don't think there's enough room inside me for both.

The crime scene tape is still up. I park on the opposite side of the road. Steve looks at me like he wants to say something, but then turns and gets out of the car instead. I hop out and open the back, grab my pack, and strap it on, then exchange seatbelt clips for leash clips on the dogs' harnesses. It never fails to amaze me that there are people who don't wear seatbelts, or, worse, don't make their kids wear them. Seems like a no brainer to me.

Steve is standing next to the SUV looking lost.

"It's not too late if you want to change your mind."

"No, not at all. I'm just not sure what to do. I don't want to mess anything up."

"Just treat it like any other walk with the dogs. Relax and keep your eyes open for things they shouldn't have."

I hand him a leash and lead the way into the woods, using the same general path I had followed last night. My hope is that the dogs will catch scent of Heather's trail and follow it. Of course, they're not tracking dogs so it's mostly just wishful thinking. Or maybe I really just don't want to be here, doing this, whatever it is, by myself.

I slow my pace so that Steve catches up and we can walk together. This means a circus act of flipping the leads over each other to keep the dogs from getting tangled, but it's a dance we're pretty good at. What I'm not good at is figuring out what's going on inside his head right now. Because the way he keeps casting glances at my face, not making eye contact? I feel like I'm in middle school waiting to find out if my crush is into me or not.

"Do you still like me?" I study the trees on my left, waiting for his answer from my right.

"What? Of course, why?"

"I don't know. I guess I thought that maybe you might have learned something about me that made you feel different."

"Well, yeah. I already knew you were the smartest person I know, I just didn't realize you were the smartest person anyone knows."

"I'm being serious."

"So am I." He brushes his shoulder against mine and smiles. "You've always been an intimidating woman, Maggie. I didn't know how much of an overachiever you were until today, but being a rock star doesn't make me love you any less."

I stop. The dog tugs on the end of the leash and almost pulls me over.

"You all right?" His brow furrows and something, maybe fear, casts a quick shadow over his face.

"Yeah." I start walking again. "You've just never said that before."

"Doesn't mean I haven't wanted to."

"So what's changed?" I'm praying that I haven't just received a sympathy vote.

"Nothing. Except now, what do I have to lose? If you rejected me before, then I'm a guy with a broken heart, but now I'm just a guy with a crush on a rock star. Huge difference. At least as far as my ego is concerned. Why? Don't you?"

"What? Love you?" I act like I'm thinking it over. Shrug as I draw out the word. "Maybe."

"Maybe?"

"Well, maybe I love you a little less because it took you so damn long to say it."

"What? You're the woman, you're supposed to say it first."

"Who made that rule?"

"Everyone knows."

"I didn't. I thought the woman was supposed to wait for the man to say it first, so she didn't scare him off."

"Well, maybe in the beginning, but..."

The dogs stop. We stop, too, falling silent as their noses stab at the air. My hand drifts to my gun. I undo the snap on my holster, hand Steve the leash I'm holding.

The look on his face is priceless. I'd pull out my phone and take a picture if I knew we weren't in any danger, but I have no idea what it is the dogs smell. Could be bear, coyote, moose, people, dead people... I creep as silently as possible. The trees are thinning ahead, leading to another stretch of road.

Looking back at Steve, I signal him to stay put for a moment and continue forward. A truck comes into view between tree trunks. As I get closer, I recognize it and wonder what the hell Murphy is doing out here.

"It's Murphy," I tell Steve in a loud whisper. "I'll be back in a sec."

Stepping out onto the road, I approach the vehicle. There's a series of movements behind the darkly tinted window, two faces peering out at me in surprise and then one ducking down out of sight. My hand instinctively falls to my weapon as I whisper a silent prayer that Steve stays with the dogs in the woods.

It's too late to retreat, so I'll have to play stupid instead. There's no telling how this is going to go down. Or why my police lieutenant is out here in the woods alone with my suspect, Heather McGillis.

18

MURPHY

Murphy considers himself lucky that he saw the chief as soon as she stepped from the woods to the road. He has Heather duck down, considers his options as he watches her slide off the seat and curl herself into a ball on the passenger floor. He debates whether to get out of the truck or not, decides with the height of the vehicle he'd be safe just rolling the window down to talk to Chief Riley, which he does.

She stops while she's still several yards from him. Shielding her eyes with her hand, she looks at the empty land around them, stretches of sand dunes bared by logging nestled among wooded thickets. There's no sense to the patchwork of barren land. Trees have seemingly been plucked at random.

"You looking for the weapon, too?" she asks.

Murphy sighs, relieved that she's given him an excuse to be out here, that he doesn't have to think of one of his own.

"Yeah. Just been driving around, looking for anything. Any luck in the woods?"

She shakes her head. "Nah. Saw some fresh coyote tracks, but that's it."

"Didn't that girl say something about being chased by

coyotes last night?" He can't resist. The opportunity to lay the groundwork for an alibi is too tempting.

"Yeah, something like that. Maybe we better put a warning out if they're getting that bold."

"Not a bad idea."

Maggie nods. "Yep. Well, I'm about ready to call it a night. Got a bit of hiking to do to get back to the car and, now that we're talking about it, I want to get it done before the coyotes come out."

"Another good idea. I've got to be on my way, too. Alma will have my hide if I'm late for dinner."

"Then I'll catch up with you later."

"Yep. Later."

Murphy has the truck started and in gear before Maggie can get back to the woods. He keeps an eye on her in the rearview as he travels down the road until she disappears from sight. She doesn't look back once. Gives him no reason to think she suspects him of anything. So why does he have a niggling feeling that the chief knows exactly what he was trying to hide from her? And what's he going to do about it if she does?

19

MAGGIE

I watch Murphy drive off before I return to Steve and the dogs, wondering if we should head back and move the Jeep. Do I really think Murphy might do something? Or am I just being suspicious?

By the time I'm back at Steve's side I've decided that we should keep searching. It takes much longer to get to the road the Jeep is parked on by vehicle than foot. Murphy would know that if I were headed out, I'd be long gone before he could drive there.

Steve's eyebrows are raised and he's giving me a questioning look. I crouch down and give the dogs a rub, buying time. I'm not sure how much I should let him know. Finally, I decide that I've kept far too many secrets for far too long. I'm going to tell him everything.

"That was Murphy. He was out here with Heather McGillis, the girl who just happened to stumble upon the crime scene last night and freak out, screaming bloody-murder style. Right next to a bloody murder, which she may or may not be a part of. I can't imagine she was, I think she was up to something else, which is why I brought us out here—to find proof. But still, she was with him, not even a quarter mile from the body dump, and they both just did their best to hide it from me."

Steve nods, wearing a thoughtful expression as he considers what I've said. "Then let's keep going."

"You sure?"

"Yes," he says. "We came out here with a job to do, so let's do it. I don't want you working with a lieutenant that you can't trust."

"And I don't want you trusting either of them if you happen to see them."

"You don't have to worry about that."

The dogs pull hard, eager to move again. We cross the road Murphy was parked on and enter another patch of woods. They throw their heads back, the whites of their eyes showing as they sniff the air without skipping stride. They're scenting something, and whatever it is has them weaving between trees, loping through the forest.

Steve and I follow behind them, jogging to keep up. Then the scent becomes stronger, hitting me like the back of a hand across the face. Steve wrinkles his nose. "Sick."

I put a hand on his arm, stopping him. Hand him the leash I'm holding. "Stay here."

"What is it? Something's dead, right?"

I hold his gaze with mine for a second. Watch the understanding dawn behind those warm, brown baby-seal eyes. He crouches down between the dogs to calm them.

"Someone?"

Nodding, I turn and let my nose lead me where I need to go. There's no use explaining the nuances that distinguish human decomp from other forms of rotting flesh. The slightly sweeter scent, the way your nervous system involuntarily alerts if you attune yourself to it, like some primal inborn knowledge that lives inside you clicks on to warn you. Danger —your kind dead. I've often wondered if other species can distinguish the scent of decay of their own from others, or if it's a human trait.

The dogs pant loudly behind me. The forest floor crunches under my boots as I continue forward, searching. I notice dark, stained leaves. Places where the brush has been cleared down to the soil among the tree roots. I take pictures of everything.

My nose tells me I'm in the right spot but I'm missing it somehow. Closing my eyes, I invoke those ancient senses that I believe exist on a cellular level, registering every air current that caresses me, every body hair that stirs within its wake.

My reward sounds like a lone fly, wings buzzing at ear level. Although it's been unusually warm the last couple of weeks, it's late in the season for flies. I target the path of the insect with my senses until I imagine that I can actually feel the vibration of its flight through the air. When I open my eyes, I see a bundle tucked into the crook formed where a large tree limb offshoots from the trunk.

After snapping a few shots, I prepare myself for what I'm about to do next. I take my pack off and remove a pair of nitrile gloves. They slip over my hands like they're volunteering for the duty they're going to perform. I remove an oversized plastic bag, the kind you store bedspreads in over the summer. I open it and settle it on the ground so that it's ready. My delivery will be quick and smooth.

Lifting my arms over my head, I close my fingers around the plastic-wrapped package, lift it down from the tree, and place it in the waiting container. I lift a corner of the grocery bag to confirm what I suspect. A corner of a tiny, scrunched baby face is all I need to see. I draw a deep breath, steadying my legs beneath me.

I collect a sampling of stained leaves and put them in my pack. I run crime scene tape in a ten-foot circumference around the tree I found the baby in. Finally, I kneel on the ground next to the open bag, silently apologizing to the tiny occupant as I close the seal. I hold the package awkwardly in the crook of my left arm. With my right I let crime scene tape spool off the roll, marking the way to the scene as we hike back through the woods to the Jeep.

Even the dogs are somber as they retrace our steps, leading Steve and me back to the car. I sneak a look at his face and see that his expression has turned from horror to anger, a look I've rarely seen him wear, and never with the intensity he has now. He catches me looking at him.

"What happens to people who do stuff like that? What kind of sentence do they get? Never mind. I don't want to know because it's not enough. That girl should be tied to a tree and left for the animals."

A part of me feels compelled to argue, to explain that as a man he'll never know fear the way a woman does. That he'll never experience how helpless and desperate teenage girls can feel, how hormones that yoyo to extremes on a daily basis can keep them from thinking clearly. But I don't explain. Because I do know, and I still can't think of any way I could muster up the slightest bit of compassion for Heather McGillis. The girl is a murderer, and I have everything I need to prove it.

20

HEATHER

I eye the man sitting beside me. He's always told me that I should call him Dale, but I can't even think of him by his first name without my face growing all red and hot. So even though Momma and his wife are some kind of distant cousins, and we're basically family, I've always thought of him as mister, like one of my teachers.

Right now, Mr. Murphy's knuckles are white on the steering wheel as he drives us farther from Chief Riley. His eyes keep checking his mirrors like he expects to see her in them any minute, catching up to us on a witch's broom, or maybe running after us like in *Terminator*.

But all that really matters to me is that, once again, I was interrupted trying to make my confession. I'm starting to think that the world wants me to keep it to myself. Maybe that's the best idea.

"We've got ten minutes before we're at the house and Alma's all up in your business, so you better spill the details quick so we can work out what we're going to tell her."

I shake my head, looking down at my hands. I feel his eyes on me.

"What? You think changing your mind is an option? That you can just tell me you think you might have killed someone last night and not say another word about it? You want to play that game, I'll take you down to the station and lock you up right now, let the staties have you."

"It doesn't matter. What I've done. No one's ever gonna know."

"Yeah, well, if there's any evidence of it in those woods back there you better think otherwise, fast."

"What do you mean?" I rub at a missing spot in the vinyl covering the door panel. The edge feels jagged, like a knife blade under my thumb. Kind of like my insides do.

"You realize that Chief Murphy wasn't really out there looking for a murder weapon, right? She was out there looking for whatever you were up to last night."

I flush with heat. Sweat bubbles just under my skin but doesn't break the surface. What he's saying can't be true. "What?"

"Do you know how stupid it would be for one person to go looking for a knife out there? And does the chief strike you as stupid? She was a full road over from the crime scene, in the direction you came from. So if you left something out there that could get you in trouble, you better come clean now. You've got eight minutes."

My heart pounds in my chest like it's trying to fight its way out. I wouldn't blame it. I wouldn't want to be stuck in me either. I'm probably all rotten and black inside.

"I had a baby out there last night. I wrapped it in plastic, and I left it in a tree. It was a boy." Now that I've said it, I feel like it might not have been such a horribly bad thing after all.

Mr. Murphy slams on the breaks, the truck lurching to a sudden halt. I fly forward, my face almost knocking against the dashboard. I look at him, wondering what just happened. Maybe we hit something and I just didn't feel it.

But when I see the look of disgust on his face I know I'm wrong. And that what I've done was bad. Real bad. But no one wanted the baby, not me or the father. No one was going to miss it.

"What's the plan?" I ask.

He cocks his head like he's not sure he heard me right. "Plan?" he echoes.

"Yeah. What are we gonna do? What are we gonna tell Alma and Chief Riley?"

"Chief Riley."

"You said you were going to help me."

"I don't think there is any helping you." He shakes his head sadly, like I've let him down or something. "I can't have anything to do with this."

Mr. Murphy jerks the car backward, making a rough three-point turn.

"Where are we going?"

"I'm taking you home."

"What about dinner? Alma?"

"You're not welcome in my house."

"What? Why? And what about Chief Riley? What if she's out there right now finding the baby?"

"I hope she does. And I hope she throws your ass in jail for the rest of your miserable life."

I'm stunned. I can't go to jail. He promised to help me. But it's obvious that's not going to happen now.

I'm desperate. "I'll tell her you knew."

Mr. Murphy stops the truck again, yanks the keys out of the ignition and gets out. He crosses around the front of the truck, jerks the passenger door open and grabs my arm, pulling me out of the cab. He lifts my bike out of the back of the truck and pushes it at me.

"You do what you've got to do, and I'll do what I've got to do. You tell the chief whatever the hell you want, see if I care.

'Cause right now, it's looking like if anyone's going down for anything around here it's going to be you. Small town like this— it'll be a witch hunt."

As he gets in the truck and drives off, leaving me in a cloud of exhaust, I suspect that it's true. No one's ever going to forgive me for this. I shouldn't expect any sympathy from anyone. Not even myself.

21

MURPHY

Murphy storms into the house, slamming the door shut after him. A crack of light appears down the hallway. Two dimple-chinned little faces give him a disapproving look before disappearing back inside the room. Alma waddles out of the kitchen wiping her hands on the sides of her velour sweatpants.

She looks at her husband, throws her hands in the air in disbelief, rolls her eyes, and heads back to the kitchen. He notices the word JUICY stretched across the seat of her pants as she retreats. So many insults come to mind that he can't choose just one to amuse himself with.

"Where's Heather?" The voice carries from the kitchen.

Murphy follows his wife, grabs a beer from the fridge, and pops the can open.

"Well?"

He lets her wait, impatient eyes rolling in her head like a mad cow while he takes a long swig.

"She's not coming." He wipes his mouth on the sleeve of his uniform.

"What do you mean, she's not coming? I told you to make her come over."

"She's not coming, and she's not welcome in this house. End of story."

Murphy knows he's declaring war with this statement. He welcomes it. For once he's got the upper hand and there's nothing she'll be able to do about it. Her face turns red, puffy fists digging into recliner sized hips.

"What do you mean, she's not welcome here? This is *my* home. She's a member of *my* family. I've invited her over for a dinner that *I* cooked. And you think that you're just going to stand there and tell me she's not welcome here? And what? That I'm just going to accept it?"

Alma speaks each word separately, slowly, her voice seeping through the walls until the entire house is infiltrated with the sound of her anger. The commotion has drawn the two boys from their room. They stare with curiosity from the doorway. Alma beckons to them as she waits for Murphy to answer her. They glare at him with sour faces, eyes full of contempt from beneath the safety of her heavy arms.

"After you hear what I have to say, you will. Boys, go to your room."

"No." She tightens her grip around them. "They can stay. There's nothing you can tell me that you can't say in front of them."

"Yeah, there is. You don't want them hearing this."

"It's not like they pay attention to anything that comes out of your mouth anyways, so just hurry up and spit it out. Standing there all puffed up like a rooster ready to crow when you're really just a pompous pig."

"That girl is a baby killer." Murphy watches the color drain from her fleshy face. "That's right, Alma. So, before you go sitting all high and mighty on whatever elephant you've found to carry you, think about that. Heather was out in those woods last night killing her own baby. Flesh and blood she shares with *you*. And the chief is out there right now. Chances are, she's gonna find Heather's filthy little secret and by the end of the week everyone in this town's going to know that you're kin to a no good, white trash, baby killer."

He looks on with glee as she swats the boys toward their room and settles her girth onto one of the kitchen chairs.

"And this is *my* house, Alma. *I* pay the bills. *I* paid for that dinner you cooked for your baby killing whatever the hell relation she is to you. What I don't think is mine are those two little brats you're raising to hate me, so if you've got a problem with something, feel free to take them and get the hell out."

Murphy can't remember the last time he felt so good. Or that he had stood up to his tyrant wife, the Tyrannosaurus She-rex. Things are going to be different from now on, he vows. The power has shifted and is finally back in his court. He turns to leave.

"Wait. Don't go."

Alma's voice is soft, contrite. Her fingers wrap around his arm. He stares down at them until she drops her hand. He gazes coolly into her scared eyes.

"What?" he asks.

"What are you going to do now?"

"I'm going to call the chief and let her know what's going on. Then, if she doesn't need me for anything, I'm going to sit down and have my dinner. Is that all right with you?"

Alma nods. She wrings a dishtowel between her fists, still staring at Murphy.

"Is there something else you wanted?"

"I was just wondering, um, can I get you another beer, honey?"

I call the staties while Steve drives us into town. Detective Campden makes his displeasure about the situation known. That I failed to make sure he heard me when I told him about Heather's appearance at last night's crime scene is a grievous error, despite the fact that it was in my report that he obviously didn't read. He doesn't say much about me recovering the baby's body from the woods. That's a job no one wants.

Campden tells me that his people are still at Hensley's Funeral Home. I tell him that I'll drop off the remains I've collected there. This keeps us from having to deal with each other, which makes us both happy.

I've just told Steve where we're headed when my phone rings. I'm surprised to see that the call is from Lieutenant Murphy. My stomach clenches as I answer.

"Chief Riley."

"Yeah, Chief, it's me, Dale. Listen, I've got something to tell you that you're not going to be happy about, but I've got to tell you anyways."

"Go on."

"I had Heather McGillis with me earlier when you saw me

out on the logging roads. I told her to duck down and hide. Don't know why I did that."

There's silence while he thinks of what to say next.

"Why was she out there with you, Murphy?"

"Aw, hell, Chief. She's one of Alma's cousins or something. When I told Alma about her being out there last night, she got all kinds of worried and told me to bring Heather over for dinner tonight so she could find out what happened."

"That doesn't explain the field trip."

"Alma's a difficult woman, Chief. She gets something in her mind, she doesn't let up until things go the way she thinks they should. I wanted to get to the root of what happened with Heather before I brought her over, make sure that she didn't say anything that would get Alma started on some kind of crusade."

I hear a series of hard swallows and know he's chugging some liquid courage.

"And what did you find out?"

"That girl's in a world of trouble, Chief. Told me she was out there having a baby last night. Said she wrapped it in plastic and put it in a tree like she was telling me about some homework assignment. Didn't understand why I'd be so upset."

"Is she at your place now?"

"Hell no, she's not welcome here. Last I saw, she was on her way to her momma's house."

"You know why I was out in those woods tonight?"

"I can guess that I do now. Did you find anything?"

"I did."

"Shit. I was hoping she was lying."

"Nope, no such luck."

"What do we do now?"

"Turn it over to the staties. I'm taking the baby's remains over to the funeral home now. You got Campden's card?"

"Yeah."

"Give him a call, tell him what you told me. She's a minor,

so the confession probably won't hold up in court, but it'll give them an edge after they get a child advocate over here and haul her in for questioning."

"Sure thing."

"Thanks, Murph."

"Chief?"

"Yeah."

There's a long pause before he says, "Thanks for under-standing."

"Sure. No problem."

But there is. There's a very big problem. Because my lieu-tenant's voice was loaded with the sentiment of what he really wanted to say to me. And judging from the tension and guilt that his tone was rife with, a thank you wasn't it.

23

HEATHER

The house is strangely quiet when I get home. No crying baby. No blaring TV. Not even the thumping clunk of the crappy old dryer tossing wet clothes around. I can't remember it ever being this silent before, and it scares me.

"Momma?"

She doesn't answer, but I hear a chair scrape across the floor in the kitchen, so I know someone's in there. When I find her, she's got her chin in her hands. I can tell she's been crying.

"Momma, what's wrong?"

I get down beside her, my knees on the floor. I pull her hands down from her face, hold them in mine, but she still doesn't look at me. I've never seen her like this before.

"Where's Penny?"

This seems to wake her from her trance. She turns her eyes toward me, but I don't think she's really seeing anything, just staring blind.

"They took the baby."

"What? Who?"

"The police."

"Well, that's kinda a good thing, isn't it?"

"I suppose so. Told them to do what they had to do, so long as they didn't take you, too."

With that she suddenly focuses on me. Her eyes go hard, and she squeezes my hands tight in hers.

"You don't want to go nowhere, do you? You want to stay here with Momma, right?"

"Of course I do, Momma," I lie. "I wouldn't leave you," I lie some more. "Why would you even ask that?"

"That lady cop, she was snooping around here. Went in your room. I think she was looking for a way to take you from me, too."

I feel my eyes go wide. Momma notices and her eyes enlarge too. Her nostrils flare as she searches my face. A tear slides down my cheek. Momma recoils like I've slapped her.

"What've you done, Heather?" Momma's voice is distant, cold.

"Momma, I... we didn't need another baby in the house. And I told the daddy, honest, but he didn't want it, either. It decided to come last night so I went out into the woods and I... I left it there. Tell me it's okay."

She's looking at me like I disgust her. I don't understand.

"I only did what you do."

Momma stands so suddenly that the chair tips over and hits the floor with a noise like the crack of a whip. I crawl closer to her, but she puts her hand out to stop me.

"You ain't never seen me kill no babies," she whispers. "I ain't ever done nothing to hurt a baby except take my pills, and everyone know that I need those pills. If my medicine done poisoned a child I didn't know I was carrying, can't nothing be done but a momma laying her little angel to rest, but I ain't never harmed one hair on one of their heads."

"Momma, I didn't—"

"—Get out." Her arm shakes as it points toward the door.

"No, Momma." I shake my head, tears streaming down my

face. "Please, Momma, I'm scared. I need you to help me. What if they try to send me to jail?"

She turns her back on me and shuffles out of the kitchen. I listen to her slippers slide down the hallway. The door to her room clicks shut. I've never felt so empty or so alone or so lost before. There's only one thing I can think of to do, only one way I might be able to save myself now. I grab my backpack and leave.

24

MAGGIE

As far as I'm concerned, I'm off duty for the night. I'm sitting on Steve's back deck with a glass of wine, enjoying the view while he grills a couple of steaks for dinner. The dogs keep a close watch on the cook from my feet. The horizon is a wash of rose and violet, blending together like watercolors as the sun melts from the sky.

The unusual warmth of this last week is coming to an end. The leaves are in their final stages of goodbye. In another couple of weeks their gem tones will be browning on the ground, with snow soon to follow. It makes me think of how fragile life is, how temporary, and I shiver. A chill wind rushes off the lake, but it's more than that. It's what the night has yet to bring.

I sip my wine and herd the dogs inside as Steve pulls the steaks off the grill. His eyebrows rise as he takes in the set dining room table—a rarity for us. He sits and I pour us both another glass from the bottle on the table. I'm usually not much of a wine drinker, but I'm not sure how hard it's going to be for me to find the words tonight. And it has to be tonight.

We make random small talk as we eat. He likes to talk about the stock market and the weather. I like to talk about world news and my garden. He tells me the DOW is up. I tell him that a few pumpkins have survived the deer this year and might make it to Halloween. We hide behind the chatter, both of us knowing it's a smokescreen.

When we finish eating, our plates get pushed to the side and we look at each other. I'm feeling anxious and would love an excuse to back out right now. Steve takes my hand in his and I know I have to move forward.

Anytime I've thought of talking about my past, I could never figure out where I'd start. Tonight, it's simple. I start at the beginning.

"The name on the evidence box? Brandon Riley? He was my brother."

Steve's eyebrows shoot up. I've always said I was an only child. It was mostly the truth.

I trace a scar on Steve's knuckle with my thumb, the faint white line barely visible. But I know that just because what you can see doesn't look painful, doesn't mean there's not a world of hurt beneath the surface.

Most pain dulls eventually. Whether the ache itself gets weaker or the threshold for pain grows larger, I don't know. The saying goes that time heals all wounds. But not mine.

I drain my glass before continuing. Because saying the next part makes it real.

"What happened... I didn't just lose my brother. I lost everything. My career. My family. My self-respect."

I feel like a jellyfish, a boneless, gelatinous mass that just wants to puddle on the floor under the table. Before I can, though, Steve has me in his arms. He carries me to the couch and cradles me on his lap as I cry, squeezing me so tightly that I cannot fall to pieces. He holds me together, and I suspect that this is what family is, what love is.

I'm a hiccupping, snotty mess and he really should let me go, but instead he holds me some more. He strokes my head, kisses me, loves me. But how will he feel when I finish the story and he knows the whole truth?

Suddenly, the dogs jump up, barking frantically as they run to the front door. Steve shushes them but they ignore him.

"Probably the wind," he says, but we both know it could be something more.

I withdraw from his embrace and stand on shaky legs. He gives me a long look and a kiss before we go see what the dogs are fussing about. As Steve looks out the peephole, I'm praying that it's not a bear. I'm too worn out for that.

"Oh, shit."

His tone chills my blood. I can tell by his expression that he doesn't want to tell me. Strangely, though, I already know. Because it's the last thing I need to deal with tonight.

"It's Heather McGillis. She's over across the street, pushing her bike down your driveway."

25

MURPHY

Murphy is almost to the front door when Alma stops him. Her red, puffy eyes look up at him pleadingly. He doesn't have any kindness left to show her at the moment.

"Where are you going?"

"Out."

"When will you be home?"

"Later."

"I thought you were going to stay for dinner? I gave the kids their plates in their room. I thought maybe we could eat together? Just the two of us?"

"Maybe another time."

"Dale, I—"

"—Now's not the time, Alma. I've got things to do."

He leaves the house without a glance back. Climbs into his truck and heads down the road faster than he should, needing to put as much distance between them as possible.

His talk with the state detective had been odd. It was obvious from the way the man spoke that Campden still has a problem with Chief Riley. He'd made no attempt to conceal the contempt in his voice. On the other hand, he'd been more than cordial to Murphy, inviting him to have breakfast with him and Detective Robbins in town the next morning so they could get an early start on the day. As he drives down the dark stretch of vacant highway, he tries sorting his feelings about it all.

He pulls off onto a potholed dirt road, his head jarring with each deep rut the truck lurches over. Realizes too late that he should have brought something with him—food, beer, porn—anything to make him a welcomed visitor. His headlights catch random sets of eyes glowing at him from the trees on either side of the lane. No matter how many times he makes the trip it still unnerves him.

Pulling up in front of the hut, he regrets his decision to come out here. Especially tonight. Debates turning around, saving the task for another day, but then the front light flicks on and it's too late for him to retreat. He climbs down from the truck, again wishing he hadn't come empty handed. The door opens before him.

The old man leans in the doorway using the butt of his rifle like a cane. He fixes Murphy under the shrinking gaze of beady eyes half hidden under his drooping brow, gives a slight nod, and disappears inside the hut, leaving the door open. Murphy wrinkles his nose against the stench from the outhouse and hurries inside.

The old man has his back to him, crouching before a small stone fireplace. He adds some kindling and slides a metal grate over the flame. He sets a cast iron pan onto the grate.

"You're in time for supper if you're hungry." The withered voice crackles like the fire.

"I'm not."

Jack Murphy turns to face his son, his wrinkles deepened by the shadows. His eyes shine in the firelight like a demon about to claim a soul. "You never did like my cooking. Not that I blame you. A man's got no place in the kitchen."

Murphy swirls the words inside his head like a sip of wine,

trying to find a way to use them to frame the questions he's got to ask. "You could always get yourself another woman."

The answer is a sound like a crow cawing.

"More trouble than they're worth. Besides, you know I'm still a married man. Too old to be a sinner now. Not enough time before I meet my maker for him to forget."

"Did you ever look for her?" The words rush out of Murphy's mouth before he loses his nerve. "Try to find her? Maybe she didn't leave, maybe something bad happened to her and she couldn't come home."

"Son, that ship sailed a long time ago. It's best to leave the past where it belongs."

"Did you ever even try?"

Jack shoots to his feet with a speed that belies his years. He raises his shriveled face into Murphy's, aggression squeezing out of his cells as his face contorts into an angry growl.

"Thirty years. Thirty years that woman's been gone, and you're still obsessed. Ain't you ever gonna let it go? No, I never looked for her, I didn't need to. I knew she wasn't never coming back."

For the first time in his life, Murphy stands his ground against his father. For thirty years he's been backing down, letting it go. This time he needs answers.

"How?"

"What?"

Murphy isn't sure if his dad doesn't know what he's asking, or if he can't believe that he's talked back.

"How did you know she wasn't ever coming back?"

He sees something foreign flash behind his father's eyes. Something he's never seen there before—fear. Jack turns away and busies himself with poking the fire.

"I said, how did you know she was never coming back?"

"I didn't. I just figured a woman don't go through all the

trouble of leaving just to tuck tail and come home." His tone is high, his words rushed.

He knows his father is lying. He crosses the room in one step and spins the old man roughly by the shoulder. The whites of Jack's eyes flash, his pupils darting desperately around the room.

"What aren't you telling me?" Murphy's voice is low, controlled, even though his body trembles with rage, his hands clenched into fists by his side.

"Nothing. I don't know nothing more about it than you do."

"You're lying."

"Dammit boy," Jack pokes a bony finger into Murphy's fleshy chest. "I'm your father. I'm the one done raised you, kept a roof over your head and food in your belly. But do you ever show any gratitude? No. You just go on fussing over a woman you ain't never gonna see again."

"But how do you know that? How do you know that I won't ever see her again?"

"Is that what this is all about? You think you're gonna find your *mommy* after all these years? You're a bigger putz than I thought." Jack smiles maliciously up at his son. "Have you really spent all these years tricking yourself into believing you'll see that woman again?"

Murphy feels sick to his stomach. Seeing the truth in his father's eyes, he backs away from the old man, toward the door. The cold night air is a shock as he flounders his way outside. He hears his father following him.

"Didn't it ever strike you as odd that she didn't take none of her stuff with her, boy? What kind of a woman takes off and leaves every single pair of her shoes behind, huh?"

His father's laugh reaches him through the closed truck door. The sound follows him down the dark dirt road. As he turns onto the highway, Murphy knows the ghost of that laugh will haunt him for the rest of his life.

26

HEATHER

Chief Riley's Jeep is in the driveway, but the lights are off, and she isn't answering. The temperature dropped with the sun and now it's freezing out. I don't have a jacket, I don't have any money, and I don't have anywhere else to go.

I sit down on the porch steps and cry. Of course she won't answer. I wouldn't let me in either. If she wasn't a cop, she'd probably call them to come get me off her doorstep.

I'm scared and I'm lonely. I hate myself and what I've done. But, mostly, I just want someone to tell me that I'm not the worst person in the world.

I'm not sure exactly when everything went so wrong. Probably when I met that guy at the motel.

He was nice, and cute, and smart, and from somewhere that wasn't Coyote Cove. He told me I'd really like the city he was from and that I should go back with him. I don't remember the exact name of the town, but it was real close to Boston, so I know I would have loved it. I liked him and I really wanted him to take me with him, so I let him do what he wanted.

He didn't take me with him, though.

Luckily, I'm not one of those stick figure girls. A baggy t-shirt and a slouch were enough to hide my growing belly. I didn't gain as much weight as most of the pregnant women I've seen, but then again, I never knew when Momma was pregnant either. I guess we've just got a frame that carries it well. Thinking about Momma makes me cry even harder.

I've lifted my head to wipe my nose on the shoulder of my shirt when I see Chief Riley standing halfway up the driveway looking at me. I wonder how long she's been there, watching. Sniffing, I wipe my eyes. There's no telling what she's thinking with that blank look on her face. After what seems like a long time she comes closer and sits down on the step, leaving as much distance between us as she can.

Her face is red and puffy, her eyes bloodshot, like she's been crying too, although I can't imagine what she has to cry about. Then I think it must have been from the horror of finding my baby and I make some strange kind of wailing noise and start crying again.

"Heather." Her voice is gentle, almost like she doesn't hate me. "Heather, stop crying so we can talk."

I try really hard to get a hold of myself, only it's like I'm broken because new waves of sadness just keep bubbling up and bursting out. I try holding my breath to see if that makes me stop, which it kind of does. The flood subsides with gasps and hiccups. She looks at me for a moment and then stands up.

"Come on, let's go inside." Chief Riley offers me her hand.

The gesture is more than I deserve. It's more than my own Momma could offer me. I reach up and grab her palm before she can take it away, hold on to it like it's a life preserver, the only thing keeping me from drowning in a stormy sea.

Her skin is warm and soft except for the callouses at the base of her fingers. Her grip is strong. She pulls me to my feet like I'm a child, which I guess I kind of still am, but not a small one. Unlocking the door, she flicks the light switch on and moves aside to let me pass. I double-check her face to make sure she isn't changing her mind, and then step inside.

I really like her house. It's not as fancy as I imagined, or as spotlessly clean, but cozy and inviting. It has a lived-in feel like it's a place where people laugh and play and make good memories. I wish I had grown up in a place like this.

The chief beckons for me to follow her. We end up in the kitchen. She hands me some paper towels, turns a kettle of water on, and leaves me there by myself like she trusts me.

I look around, eyes drawn to the pictures on the fridge. Most are of a pair of dogs, but there's one with her in it too, and even though it's a happy picture there's something about her eyes that make me think she's sad. When she returns, she hands me a soft blue sweatshirt that's the same color as her sad eyes.

She makes us each a cup of cocoa. I can't remember the last time I had some, which is a shame because it's real good and quickly warms the chill right out of me. We sit in silence for a few minutes, just thinking and sipping. I feel calmer than I ever remember feeling before. Finally, I'm ready and I break the silence.

"I'm so sorry, Chief Riley. For everything. I shouldn't have done what I did, only I didn't know it at the time, I thought it was okay and that it's what Momma did but it's not and now she hates me just like everyone else and I came here 'cause I don't have anywhere else to go and you let me in but why would you want me here, no one actually wants me but you're so nice and now you're being punished for that by having to be around me."

I watch her face, waiting for her to agree with me and ask me to leave. Instead she says, "Call me Maggie."

"Huh?"

"Heather, I can't claim to understand how you could have possibly done what you did, and I in no way approve of it. But I also understand that you're alone and you need a friend right now, and my friends call me Maggie."

I feel myself just blinking at her like she's some kind of magical creature. I want to stop but I can't. At that moment I know that there's nothing she could do that I wouldn't forgive her for.

"But what about my baby?"

"You did a horrible thing. I think you realize that now. What I need to know is why you didn't before. Why did you think it was okay to kill your baby, Heather?"

The look on her face isn't disgusted. Her tone isn't judgmental. She's simply asking for me to tell her my story. Maggie is being a friend. So, I tell her everything.

I tell her about my childhood and about Momma, about desperately wanting out of this tiny little town and the guy and his promises and finding out that I was pregnant. I tell her about Penny, and not wanting to bring another baby into the house, and about what I'd seen Momma doing. Maggie listens the whole time without interrupting, her expression compassionate, which is so much more than I deserve.

When I'm done, she makes me another cup of cocoa. She asks me if I like frozen enchiladas and then she sticks a box in the microwave. It's the fancy kind, organic.

"Heather, do you think that you could help me find where your mother put those babies?"

"I don't want to cause any trouble for Momma." I shake my head in time to the whir of the microwave.

"You can't be concerned about that now. You've got to put yourself first, like she did when she turned her back on you tonight."

I consider this while she puts the tray of food on a plate and sets it in front of me. She passes me silverware and a napkin.

"Would you eat some salad if I made you one?"

"Potato or macaroni?"

"Lettuce. You should have some vegetables with your dinner."

"I'll try it."

Maggie doesn't press me for an answer. She makes me a salad that looks just like it's in a picture on a restaurant menu, and then she sits beside me while I eat. Finally, I find myself nodding.

"Yes. I could help you find where Momma put those babies."

Maggie looks at me with relief in her eyes. It's so strange that she wants to help me. She clears her throat and I know she's got more tough questions for me.

"I'd like to take you over to Memorial Hospital tomorrow and have you checked out by one of their doctors. Just to make sure that you're okay. Would you be willing to do that?"

I nod. My eyes get all watery because I'm fighting off tears again. This time it's not because nobody cares, but because somebody does, which feels a lot better. She sets a box of cookies on the counter next to me.

"I'm going to go make up the guest room."

I look up at her in surprise. Maggie pretends not to notice.

"I've got some clothes that might fit you. I'll put them in the room. We can stop by your mother's place tomorrow and pick up some of your things if you'd like." She stops as she's walking down the hall, sticks just her head around the corner so we can see each other. "This isn't going to be easy, Heather. But I'm going to help you in any way that I can."

She seems to want to say more but instead she pulls her head back around the wall, the sound of her footsteps growing faint as she walks away. I think about her words, and for the first time, I know that I'll be okay. There's someone in this world who thinks I'm worthy of a friend. Sometimes, that's all you need.

27

MURPHY

Murphy can't go home. He doesn't want to deal with Alma. And he knows he can't go kill some time at the local bar either—a couple of beers and who knows what'll come out of his mouth. This isn't something he can just blab about to anyone.

It crosses his mind to go talk to the chief, but he can't. Not yet, anyways. So he ends up finding his way to the last place he expected to go.

He hasn't been here since he moved out when he was seventeen. His dad left shortly after that, opting to move to the even more remote shack in the woods he occupies now, like a hermit crab finding a new shell. He's out on the very edge of the town limits, near the logging camps. His dad had been a foreman for one of the lumber companies until he took early retirement at sixty-two, right around the time Murphy graduated high school.

His dad had been older than everyone else's. He'd been in his forties when he married Murphy's mom, who was almost twenty years his junior. When he was younger, Murphy had thought that was why his mom was always so unhappy. It wasn't easy being the son of a cranky old man, must have been hard being his wife, too.

Once he was older, though, Murphy realized the truth. His dad had sucked the life out of his mom. Jen Murphy was vibrant and intelligent and headstrong, with sharp green eyes and a laugh that could soothe the most savage beast—except for his father. Jack Murphy wanted a subservient wife whose place was in the kitchen, but instead of finding a woman who agreed with those terms, he'd chosen instead to find the most willful woman he could and try and break her.

His mother had told him about the way his father had been in the beginning—a charming man who had enjoyed engaging in a lively debate. Jack Murphy had encouraged her wild streak, had fed it, even, until he and Jen were married, and she was pregnant. Then his true personality had emerged. No matter how hard his father had tried to beat her spirit down low, Jen had defiantly held her head high.

He smiles, thinking about what a formidable woman his mother had been. Jen had done her best to teach Murphy about respect and equality every day, even though Jack did his best to erase those lessons every night. He feels ashamed of all the resentment he harbors toward Chief Riley. He knows that it's an offshoot of his abandonment issues from his mom.

Only, his mother had never really abandoned him, had she? She'd stood up to Jack when Murphy wanted to play the piano instead of football, sneaking Murphy into town and doing laundry and ironing for Mrs. Hanson and her family in exchange for the lessons.

She'd defended Murphy and the suckling pig he had raised for the county fair when Jack ordered Murphy to slaughter the animal after it came in second. He'd broken into tears at the thought. In angry disappointment, Jack had insisted that he witness a man doing his job, grabbing an ax and marching into the backyard, Murphy sobbing at his heels.

Jen had driven the truck into the yard between Jack and the pig pen, tossed the pig in the bed, and driven it to safety. Jack never found out where she'd taken the pig, joking for the next few years about it having been bear bait after she turned it loose in the wild. Murphy never told Jack that he could visit the pig at its new home whenever he wanted.

The derelict house before him sags on its cracked foundation, the middle bulging under the weight of the secrets it keeps. The wood is rotten, the shingles crumbling. It looks like he feels.

He gets out of the truck and grabs the shovel that's still in the back from the night before. The ghosts of memories hang everywhere, cold currents on the wind gliding past him, rubbing up against his ankles like a cat. Acid splashes up his throat as he walks over the decaying remains of the fence that had once divided the front yard from the back.

He stands in front of the nectarine tree and stares at the bare, curving branches. He remembers the day he'd come home to find it planted in the yard. It was the same day his mom had left. Somehow, on some level, he'd known.

He sticks the spade into the soil, puts his boot on the top and pushes down. He hears the grass ripping, feels its futile resistance against the blade as he shovels the first mound of dirt away from the tree. His father had made such a fuss every year when it fruited. Always swearing it was the best he'd ever tasted as he consumed every last piece, not a single one going to waste, though Murphy himself had never tried even one of the nectarines.

He digs obsessively, the smell of damp earth hanging stagnant around him despite the breeze. Having weakened its tenuous hold on the earth, he kicks the tree over with a grunt, shreds of fabric clinging to the roots, his mother's skull grinning up at him from the dark, rich dirt of her grave. Sinking to the ground, he wraps his arms around his knees and weeps.

28

HEATHER

When I wake up, I'm in a soft bed with clean sheets that smell like some kind of flowers. I rush to wash because I don't want Maggie and her boyfriend, Steve, to think I'm some kind of lazy person who sleeps late. I try not to use too much hot water because I don't want to seem greedy. Before I leave the room, I turn back and make the bed because I don't want to appear messy. Honestly, I don't want either of them to think anything less of me than they already must.

I have a feeling that Steve wasn't thrilled with me staying with them last night. Not that I could blame him. He didn't say anything, but I could see it in his eyes, not in the way he looked at me, but in the way he couldn't.

I follow my nose to the delicious smell of bacon and find him cooking. I stop, preparing to retreat, but he sees me. To my surprise he greets me with a smile and beckons me to one of the stools at the island.

"Maggie's out walking the dogs. She'll be back in a few minutes. How do you like your eggs?"

No one's ever asked me that before. "I don't know."

Steve is piling pancakes on a plate. He stops, his hand hovering over a heap of bacon.

"You aren't a vegetarian, are you?"

I shake my head, my mouth watering. He adds a large portion of bacon to the plate and sets it in front of me. I hear the front door open and moments later the click of claws as the dogs race into the kitchen. Maggie is close behind them. Steve hands her a plate and she sits next to me.

"How'd you sleep?" Maggie asks me.

"Fine, I..." Steve pushes some eggs out of a pan onto my plate and Maggie's, and then leans against the counter and starts eating his own. "Thank you." I don't want them to think I have bad manners.

The breakfast is the best I can ever remember eating. At one point I realize that I forgot to pick my fork back up after eating a slice of bacon. I catch myself tearing the pancakes, dipping them into the lake of syrup on my plate and shoveling them into my mouth. I look up, and Maggie and Steve are watching me. I'm horrified, convinced that they must think I'm a huge pig, but they just smile and continue eating.

When I'm done, I offer to do the dishes. Maggie says they can wait, tells me we've got to get started on the drive to Memorial Hospital over in Lincoln right after she makes a quick phone call. I watch her vanish down the hall, then slide out of my seat to the floor.

The dogs rush over, tiny paws pinning me to the ground while they clean the maple syrup stickiness from my face. When they finish, they give me kisses just to kiss, and hugs just for hugs.

Realizing I'm squealing, I struggle against the wiggling bodies to sit up, glancing over at Steve. He's smiling. I relax, letting the dogs push me back down.

There's always such a fuss over the secret of happiness, but it's right here, in my arms, licking my face. Maggie must be the smartest woman I've ever met. I wonder how my life would have been different if she had been my mother.

29

MURPHY

Murphy sits across from the staties, watching them chew their breakfasts. He's managed to pull himself together enough for the meeting after a couple of hours of sleep on the couch and a long, hot shower. All he really wants is to talk to the chief and get her help with his mother's remains, the open grave covered by nothing but a few sheets of rotten plywood that he'd torn from the porch. That, and for Chief Riley to help him find a way to fry his dad.

"You sure you're not hungry?" A mouthful of eggs rolls around inside Campden's mouth as he asks the question. "State's paying."

Murphy nods. "I'm good."

Campden nods back and shovels in another forkful. "Anyways, I wanted to talk to you here because we've run into a wall with the case. We're waiting on the report on the trace collected from the body. Hopefully that will shed some light, but the lab's so backed up we might not have any help from that angle for weeks. We still don't have a clue where the actual murder took place yet. Got nothing from the motel room. Of course, it doesn't help matters any that your chief keeps sticking her nose in, contaminating all our evidence."

Murphy wants to reach across the table and dunk the man's face into his plate of runny eggs. He wants to mention that it's because of the chief's quick thinking that they were able to recover any trace evidence off the body at all. Instead, he bites his tongue and keeps still.

"That's another reason I wanted to talk with you. We could use the help of a good local officer like yourself. I'm certain that you've got a lot to contribute. But I want to keep this between us men. There's no need for Chief Riley to inflict herself upon this investigation any more than she already has."

Murphy feels his eyes widen. He covers it with a sip of coffee, his gaze flicking from Campden's face to Robbins's. Robbins has Murphy fixed in a hard stare. He looks away quickly, busies himself with adding another packet of sugar to his already too-sweet coffee.

Campden rises nosily from the booth, one hand cradling his small potbelly. "Gotta hit the head."

Murphy focuses on the mug in his hands, avoiding Robbins's gaze. Robbins looks over his shoulder, watching as Campden vanishes into the restroom.

"I'd like to thank you for your patience. I know how much of a jerk my partner is."

Murphy eyes him warily.

"And, honestly, I think the only way we're going to close this case is with your chief's help. With a history like hers, I can't imagine not bringing her in on it, but Lou's old school. Still thinks women should be kept barefoot and pregnant. Just being in the same town as a woman like your boss makes him insecure as hell."

Robbins absorbs Murphy's questioning look.

"Don't tell me you don't know?" he asks, leaning across the table, closer to Murphy.

"Know what?"

"Chief Riley's history?"

Murphy shakes his head.

"You mean you never even googled her?"

Murphy's eyes narrow. He can tell that the detective thinks he's an idiot. That he's just a small-town country cop who's probably as sexist as his partner.

"I never went digging into her past," Murphy says in his own defense. "Prying seemed disrespectful. I judge people by their present. That's good enough for me."

"Then maybe I should tell you that your boss is kind of a big deal."

Murphy grins at the man. "You don't need to be a detective to figure that out, Sherlock."

Robbins grins back. "Listen, before Lou gets back, here's my card. He's going to go skirt chasing later. I'd like to meet up with you when he does. With the chief, too, if she's free."

Murphy takes the card and slips it into his shirt pocket without looking at it. He gulps hard as he smiles and nods with no intention of following through. The last thing he wants is to waste time rendezvousing with a statie while his mother's bones lay exposed and waiting.

Detective Robbins checks over his shoulder again before fixing Murphy in a shrinking stare. "Maybe the three of us can figure out how to explain a personal check from you on the victim's bank statement."

The blood leaves Murphy's face. His knees knock together under the table. With everything else that had gone on last night, he'd forgotten all about that piece of the puzzle.

30

MAGGIE

My phone rings. I struggle to get it out of my pocket one-handed. The fingers of my right hand feel squished and damp inside of Heather's tight fist. Her face is pale and worried. Her lower lip has a raw spot from where she's been chewing on it.

Caller ID lets me know that it's Murphy. Heather gives me a desperate look as she anticipates what I'm about to say.

"I need to take this." I give her hand a squeeze and then extract my fingers from her grasp. "It'll be okay. I'll be right back."

I leave her sitting alone, twisting the dingy neon friendship bracelet she wears tighter and tighter around her wrist. I briefly wonder who gave it to her, who that friend may be, because she could certainly use them right now. She looks so young and lost, so out of place in the large leather chair that faces an oversized desk in a cramped physician's office, where we've been waiting for a consult for the last half hour. I give her another reassuring smile before I slip out into the hallway to take the call.

"Hello?"

"Hey, Chief, it's Murphy. We've got trouble."

This is the last thing I need to hear. Leaning my back

against the wall, I flex my hand, trying to restore it back to normal. Each of Heather's fingers have left a crimp mark on my own.

"How bad?"

"Depends on which issue."

I curse inside my head. It's a string of words, actually.

"How about least to worst?"

"Gotcha. The staties are getting restless, looking for trouble. They want me to help them beat the bushes a bit, but they want you kept out of the loop. Well, Campden does. Robbins wants to meet with you and me later today. He, uh, well. It's complicated."

"How complicated?"

"He found a check I wrote the victim on his bank statement."

"He what?"

"Listen, I know how it probably sounds, but it's not what you think. The guy was a private investigator. I hired him to find my mom. I was going to tell you, really. It just, there was never a good time."

I swallow down a knot of anger and draw a deep breath to control my temper. "What'd you tell him about it?"

"Nothing. Campden came back first. But like I said, Robbins expects us to meet with him later."

"And there's worse news than that?"

"I dug up my mom last night."

"What?"

I'm sure I must have heard Murphy wrong.

"Guess the joke's on me, huh? I hire a PI to find my mom, he turns up dead, I'm a suspect, and the whole thing was doomed from the start because it turns out she never took off. She's buried in my old backyard. I found her last night after talking to my dad."

"Murphy, I'm so sorry."

"It is what it is."

"I still wish you'd found a happier ending."

"Yeah, well, turns out that she never left me behind, so at least there's that."

"But your dad?"

"Yeah."

"How do you want to handle it?"

"I want him to pay for what he did."

"Do you think he killed the investigator?"

I hear Murphy whoosh air on his end of the line.

"Honestly, Chief, it never crossed my mind until you said it just now. But, yeah, I suppose he could have. He's getting old but he's still the meanest old coot there ever was."

"So maybe that's what we tell Robbins tonight?"

"Yeah. Maybe."

"I'll be back this afternoon. I'll meet up with you then and we can discuss strategy. I'm really sorry about all this, Murphy, I truly am. I'll do everything I can to help."

He clears his throat. I can see him red-faced in my mind.

"Thanks, Chief. Since the staties don't have anything else going on, they're turning all their attention to Heather McGillis. Girl's gone missing. Her mother kicked her out last night."

"She's with me."

The phone line is so silent that for a minute I think the call must have dropped.

"What?" Murphy's tone is cold and disbelieving.

"I've got her over at Memorial Hospital right now. It wasn't murder, Murphy. She didn't kill the baby. We were wrong about that. Listen, I'll fill you in on the details later, you have enough to worry about right now. If the staties give you any trouble about Heather, tell them she's in my custody and they'll have to take it up with me."

"She didn't do it?" I can tell by Murphy's voice that he's

thinking out loud. "Chief, I was real rough on the girl yesterday. I thought... I didn't know..."

"It's okay. You focus on what you need to, I'll take care of this."

"Yeah, okay. If you need anything, let me know."

"Same here."

I end the call and stare down at the phone in my hand. The picture we had all painted of Heather in our minds—the teenage girl who had ruthlessly killed her newborn baby in the woods—has changed dramatically. The doctor, a middle-aged woman with a stern expression, accentuated by a deep frown line between her browns, had gone from treating Heather with curt contempt at the beginning of the appointment to an almost motherly concern by the end.

The exam revealed that Heather had never passed the after-birth. The physician performed a DNC, during which another discovery was made. The fetal end of the umbilical cord was a withered stump but showed no signs of having been severed. In all likelihood, the baby had been stillborn. It seems like a simple enough concept, but Heather genuinely appeared to not understand what the doctor was telling her.

The more time I spend with the girl, the more I suspect that she might be developmentally challenged. It could be a lack of sophistication, that Heather is simply a sheltered country girl, but she seems awfully immature for her age. The doctor seconded my proposal and arranged for a psychiatric evaluation to assess Heather's mental acuity.

I see the psychiatrist round the corner at the end of the hall, and I know the truth is close at hand. The papers clutched in the doctor's fist could very well change the course of Heather's future. I cross my fingers that it's for the better.

31

HEATHER

Maggie comes back into the room and for a moment all I feel is relief—until I see one of the doctors enter right behind her. This has been one of the scariest days of my life. First, the exam by the 'woman's doctor', which Maggie explained to me and said was perfectly normal, but I don't see how that's right. Maggie said she goes every year, but I don't understand why a smart woman like Maggie would do something so uncomfortable if she didn't have to.

It ended up being a good thing, though, because there was part of the baby left behind inside me. The doctor took it out and gave me antibiotics so I wouldn't get an infection. She said it was dangerous for it to still be in me, but I didn't even know it was there.

The other good thing is that the doctor said she doesn't think I killed the baby. She thinks that it may have been born dead. She asked me a bunch of questions, but I'm not a doctor so I don't know how I can be expected to know the answers.

I can't remember if the baby was crying when it was born. I can't remember if he was even breathing. He was kind of blue, but I figured I would be too after going through all the fuss it takes to be born. All I remember is feeling horrible and ashamed and needing to get the whole thing over with and behind me as soon as possible.

The woman's doctor then called another doctor who asked me a bunch of other questions. Maggie stayed right by me the whole time. She seems to know the reason behind all the questioning, and I trust that she wouldn't let them trick me into getting into any more trouble, so I'm guessing that it's all to help me, but it sure doesn't seem like it.

Maggie sits back down beside me. She smiles. I grab for her hand before the doctor can get settled. I'm so grateful for all of her help and that she's here for me, but it also makes me feel kind of hollow that my own momma isn't.

The doctor clears her throat and I know I need to pay attention, but my mind is racing in every different direction, and I just wish I could go outside and go for a walk. Maggie squeezes my fingers, so I do my best to focus and pay attention because I know she wants me to.

"We have the results back from the tests we had Heather take earlier. Heather, do you ever remember your mother or your teachers saying anything about a disability?"

"Momma has a disability."

Maggie and the doctor exchange a look.

"Have you ever been told that *you* have one?" the doctor asks.

I shake my head. A forgotten memory surfaces just then, so I add, "My first-grade teacher asked Momma to come in to talk to her once. After that Momma said not to listen to anything the teachers had to say and not to let them waste her time with any more meetings."

The doctor nods. She's youngish, maybe only ten years older than me. Her bangs sit on the frames of her glasses. It's odd looking.

She turns to Maggie and says, "I'm confident that Heather

is suffering from an intellectual disability that, while not severe enough to keep her from knowing right from wrong, may interfere with her ability to properly understand the consequences of her actions."

Maggie looks at me like this is good news.

"I don't understand," I tell Maggie, not the doctor.

"What the doctor is saying is that there's a medical reason that... doesn't make what you did okay, but it will help people to understand that you didn't mean to do something wrong. It means that you may get in less trouble for what you did."

My arms are around Maggie before I even realize that I jumped up to hug her. Both of our chairs almost tip over. In this moment, for once in my life, things are good.

32

STEVE

Maggie and I watch Heather out the back window, playing with the dogs. It's easy to see the child trapped inside the almost-grown body shining through as she romps around the yard. I feel a bit of peace knowing that the kid before me won't be going to jail.

"I hate to leave you." Maggie's eyes find mine. I can see the relief etched in the tiny worry lines that have formed between her eyebrows. She looks tired.

"I wish you could stay home and rest." I stroke her cheek. Her skin feels like velvet beneath my fingertips.

"So do I, but I've got to help sort this Murphy thing out. If the staties want to be difficult, they can take him into custody as a suspect for the murder. A charge like that could end his career even if it turns out to be unwarranted. I can't let that happen."

"I know you can't." I kiss her. Our lips linger. "So then, you're sure that Murphy had nothing to do with your victim?"

"I sure as hell hope not."

I stare at her, waiting for her to add something that will make me feel better about the situation. Something to the effect that she's positive her gun-carrying lieutenant, who she's about to go meet, isn't a killer. But that's not what I get.

"It would be foolish of me to assume anything. I'll believe what the evidence supports." Reading my expression, she adds, "People can only surprise you if you let them. So no, he doesn't have my complete trust right now. Only you have that."

Maggie pinches my chin between her thumb and forefinger. I've always told myself that she's never done this to any other man before, that it's only ever been me. Maybe one day I'll ask if I'm right. Until then I'll just enjoy being the focus of her attention. I'll take whatever spare seconds she'll give me.

"Are you sure you'll be okay?" Maggie gestures toward Heather.

"We'll be fine. I'll make spaghetti and rent a kid's movie off cable."

"Modern-day superman."

She kisses me. I know she's having a difficult time leaving. I want to pull her close, but the victory of knowing that this is where she wants to be will have to be enough for a while. I suppose I'm learning to be less selfish in my old age, even if it means sharing my woman with the world.

"I love you," she says.

My sacrifice has been rewarded. I return the words and watch her leave, knowing that if I could relive a version of this moment every day for the rest of my life that I'll be the happiest man I can be. I just wish I could shake this feeling of dread that something's going to try and snatch my happiness away.

33

MAGGIE

The bags under Murphy's eyes have shadows like I've only seen in pictures of cult victims. He seems to have aged twenty years since I saw him the previous day. Even the frame of his body appears older, his shoulders slumped under the weight of bitter truth.

When our eyes meet, and I see the pain behind his, I want nothing more than to give him a hug and promise him that everything will be all right. But I'm not a hugger, and I can't lie to him.

Instead, I give his shoulder a squeeze. I sit next to him at the wire patio table behind the boat-tour hut on the lake. An icy breeze blows off the water. I pull the collar of my jacket higher, wishing I'd worn a hat and scarf.

No one is around. It seems an ideal setting for a clandestine meeting, like we should be actors on the set of a spy movie. The water sloshes roughly beside us, drowning out all other sounds besides the low whisper of Murphy's voice.

"It never sat right. I never believed that my mom left and didn't take me with her. I think maybe a part of me might have suspected, but I guess I just wouldn't be honest with myself and face the truth. I mean, here I am, a forty-two-year-old man, a cop for Christ's sake, and I hired a private investigator to look for my missing mommy. How sad is that?"

I see the emotion brimming over behind Murphy's brown eyes, can feel how thin the ice is at the edge of his composure. I swear that I can even hear the tears of the lost little boy, who thought that he had been left behind, within the shaky timbre of Murphy's voice.

"I don't think it's sad at all, Murph. I think it would have been sadder had you given up all those years ago without even trying. Sometimes it's not easy to face the truth. You knew that your mom loved you. Even though it hurt to believe that she had left you behind, it left hope alive that you could maybe see her again someday. And it made it possible for you to go on living with your father until you were old enough to be on your own."

Murphy's mouth rises a little at the side. "I want to find a way to prove that my father did it. I want him to go to jail."

I nod, although I know that it may be impossible to prove the case after so many years have passed. Circumstantial evidence isn't going to be enough to get a man in his eighties prosecuted for murder.

"Tell me about the investigator."

"Not much to tell." Murphy drags a hand down the side of his face while he thinks. "Found his business card in the bathroom at the Loose Moose one night, so I looked him up online. He had a decent enough website. Seemed to be familiar with the area. So I figured, why not?"

He shakes his head. "Thinking back, I probably should have known better, but at the time... I just wanted to see my mom again so bad. So I paid him a $250 retainer. Filled him in on the details—the last time I saw her, everything I knew about her and her side of the family, any friends I knew of. He said he'd look into it. That was about two weeks ago."

Murphy stares out over the lake and shudders, his voice

dropping as he says, "Four days ago he called me, said he might have turned over the right rock, that he had a lead to chase down and he'd be back in touch. Two days after that you found him dead. I didn't even know he was in town."

I study his profile. He seems to be telling the truth, but so do some politicians. And the pieces are falling together too easily. Something about it is just too, I don't know. Convenient. Contrived.

"You really think it's possible your dad might have had something to do with it?" I ask.

"I was hoping we could get a warrant and head out to his place to find out."

"I could help with that."

Both of our heads swivel at Robbins's unexpected input, the sound of his approach concealed by the push of the wind against the lake. He towers over us like a teacher busting a card game at lunch. Robbins sits, fixing Murphy in his crosshairs for a long moment, and then looks at me.

"I didn't catch everything, so you'll have to fill me in. You think your father had something to do with our victim's death?"

Murphy stares blankly at Detective Robbins. His jaw tightens, eyes growing hard.

His eyes slowly tear off Robbins and turn to me. He nods and I know he wants me to take the lead on this conversation. He's been worn too thin—he doesn't have the patience to deal with a stranger's inquiries. He needs to know that the person fighting for justice for his mother is on his side.

"Lieutenant Murphy says the victim was a private investigator he hired to look into finding his mother. She disappeared about thirty years ago. Last night, Murphy discovered her remains after a talk with his father. It's only logical that he be a suspect for the murder of the man who was digging into his past crime."

"Do we know for a fact that the remains Lieutenant

Murphy recovered were his mother's?"

I shake my head. "At this point, identification is circumstantial. I have a friend who's a forensic anthropologist that I'd like to invite in on this case. I've actually already called her about the McGillis situation. She should be here tomorrow."

Robbins's eyebrows jump. I realize I haven't just stepped across the line but leaped miles over it. I've crunched the staties' toes under the heel of my boots, and I don't care.

This is my town. My refuge. It's been polluted, contaminated with murder, tainted by scandal, and if I don't do something soon it will change the face of Coyote Cove forever. I need to sweep the trash into a nice tidy pile, with no loose ends for the state detectives to take with them when they leave.

"Heather McGillis has been found intellectually disabled. There's concrete evidence that the baby she left in the woods was stillborn. There's also reason to believe that she was mimicking behavior she observed through her mother. I asked my friend to help recover the bodies of the mother's discarded infants to help support Heather's case. No use sending a kid to jail who doesn't deserve to be there."

Robbins is still giving me that weird stare. Maybe he expects me to keep talking, to try and convince him I'm right, to keep filling the silent void with words. But I've said what I have to say. I stare back, watching the gears turning in his head as he considers his options.

He knows my background. I'm sure he knows I have plenty of connections, that I could call in some old favors and have him buried beneath a pile of paperwork for the remainder of these cases. In order to let him salvage his pride, I don't state these facts.

"Lou is going to have an absolute fit," he says. "But I guess that'll be my problem. I'll deal with him. In exchange, I want in —on everything. I'm not saying I want you to ask my permission." Robbins looks down, his cheeks reddening. When he looks up there's a new expression on his face. "I want you to teach me."

Murphy looks at Robbins with surprise. Robbins shrugs at him.

"What? I got into this job so that I could help people. So let me help. How do I go about getting a warrant around here on a Sunday, boss?"

"We might not need one."

Both men give me questioning looks. It's my turn to shrug.

"I remember when I moved here that there was a bit of fuss about your dad living out at the old ranger's hut. Then the city council decided that since there wasn't a park ranger stationed out here anymore to use it, that they'd let your dad squat there in exchange for him keeping the place up. As far as I'm aware, they never sold him the land or offered him a lease for the use of the cabin, did they?"

Murphy nods as realization dawns in his eyes. As town property, everything on the land falls under our jurisdiction.

"What about the house where you grew up? Where your mother's remains are?"

"He signed it over to me years ago. Easier to get more money from the government the less you have. I own that ratty old truck of his, too."

The way Murphy springs to his feet, like a wolf spotting a lamb, makes me a little concerned about bringing him along. Robbins catches my eyes and I know he's thinking the same thing. I also know that he understands that Murphy is coming anyways.

I stand. I'm exhausted, I'm cold, and the last thing I feel like doing is driving to the outskirts of town to search a run-down cabin for some evidence. Except for the cold part, it feels like old times. It's a familiar irritation, like the one, tiny little place that rubs on your otherwise most comfortable pair of shoes. And I can't deny that I kind of missed it.

34

MURPHY

Murphy hops out of Maggie's Jeep before it makes a complete stop. He hears Chief Riley and Detective Robbins jumping out and scrambling to catch up behind him as he marches up to the front door and tosses it open. Jack Murphy startles' awake in the chair near the fire where he'd been napping.

"What are you doing here?" he asks, squinting at his son like a stray cat just walked through the door.

"What's the matter, Pops? You don't like my company?"

The old man shifts his weight, straightening his back. His hands rest lightly on the chair arms, like he could spring into action in a second's notice. There's a feral quality to the energy radiating from his withered frame. His nasty look moves from Murphy to Chief Riley.

"Didn't know you brought company."

He fixes Maggie in his beady stare. Standing, he closes the distance between them, his head tilted at an angle as he approaches.

"You're that lady cop." Jack Murphy looks her up and down, his face contorting into half-snarl, half-lecherous leer. "Can't say I was proud to hear my son was working under some woman, but then the boy hasn't given me many reasons to be proud. But now it makes sense. Have to say, I wouldn't mind working under you for a bit myself."

Robbins clears his throat from the doorway. Jack flinches, spinning to face him.

"Don't know who you are. Can't say that I much care to." Jack eyes Robbins suspiciously. He turns to glare at Murphy. "So, whatcha gone done now, boy?"

Murphy's clenched fists hang by his side. He looks at his father with disgust. Jack turns and points at Robbins.

"My boy tell you that he was out here last night? That I told him I was an old man, not getting any younger, and the time's come for me to make things right with my maker? That I can't keep his evil secrets anymore? Did he bring you here so he could confess to killing his momma all those years ago?"

Chief Riley jumps between them as her lieutenant lunges at his father. She keeps a hand on Murphy as she addresses Jack.

"Actually, that's the first I heard about that. As far as I knew, your wife left you. If you'd like to file a report, start an investigation into the matter, you're free to do so—after you answer our questions. The reason we're here today is to find out what your involvement was with a Mr. Chase Gibbons. Mr. Gibbons's body was discovered the night before last, out on the old logging roads. It appears that he met with some foul play. And all the evidence led us here, Mr. Murphy."

Jack looks at Chief Riley, his face puckered like he's sucking on a sour candy. He ends the standoff, his body shaking with a silent laugh. "Bullshit."

"What kind of tires do you have on your truck, Mr. Murphy? Can you account for your whereabouts Friday night?"

"Never said I didn't go for a drive." Jack Murphy bares his teeth. It looks like he's snarling. It's supposed to be a smile.

"You also didn't say at what point during the night you

came into contact with the victim," she says. "There was trace evidence on the body. And let me remind you, Mr. Murphy, that with your son being an officer of the law and all, his DNA is already in the FBI's database. When a sample is entered that contains so many shared markers that it's obviously a familial match to someone registered in the system, that partial match shows up in the search results."

"Well, if you get a match, it's not from me. I got my share of tail in my younger days. Little Dale there could have a whole army of half-siblings that we don't know about."

Maggie straightens to her full height, looks down her nose at the old man, challenging him. "I think we'll have a look around just the same."

"The hell you will. I don't give you permission. You need to get the hell off my property. Immediately."

It's Maggie's turn to smile. "You, Mr. Murphy, don't own any property. This land and all improvements on it are owned by the town of Coyote Cove. Your son and I have complete authority to do as we please. Detective Robbins here is from the state police. He's going to make sure that there's no conflict of interest in this investigation."

The energy goes out of the elderly man, leaving him slack, like a sail without wind. He sits in the chair next to the fire and crosses his arms, watching the flames flicker in the fireplace.

Robbins looks up from his phone and says, "My tech is turning off the highway now. Something you want to tell us before she gets here? No? Any secrets you have are going to be short lived."

"You all won't find nothing."

Lieutenant Murphy squats down in front of the chair, out of striking distance. "We'll see about that, old man."

35

MAGGIE

Even though it's daytime, scant sunlight filters through the thick canopy of trees overhead as we wait for the forensic technician to turn on her alternate light source. She flicks the switch, and as I spray the area with luminol, the bed of Jack Murphy's truck flares blue.

Bridgette Parsons and I exchange a nod. Although I'm pretty confident, I run a Hemastix over a brightly fluorescing area. The stick turns green, confirming the presence of blood. We set to work swabbing samples from where the glow is the densest, closing each in its own vial.

Bridgette decides that the truck should be tarped and towed to the state crime lab. As she covers the bed of the truck, I collect the dirt from the tires for later analysis. Robbins observes from the doorway, keeping one eye on Jack. Murphy stands nearby, peeling bark off a tree, lost in thought.

"What's up, Murphy?"

He looks at me, and I can tell he's trying to work something out.

"The old man doesn't drive much anymore. He might have made it to the logging roads to dump the body, but I can't remember the last time he made it into town. I bring most of the supplies he has out here."

"What are you thinking?"

Another strip of bark loses its grip as he tears it off the tree.

"I'm thinking if he did kill him, then he did it somewhere out here." Murphy gestures to the woods.

"Makes sense." I lean against a pine trunk, waiting for him to continue his train of thought.

"Gibbons was what, just shy of forty? He looked to be in decent shape, was a pretty good-sized man. My dad couldn't have taken him in a fair fight. He would have had to get the drop on him somehow."

I nod encouragement. Robbins is all ears, holding his position by the door.

"If he drugged Gibbons, doesn't make any sense to have stabbed him. There's plenty of cleaner ways to kill a man once you've got him down. There's no sign of a struggle inside the cabin. Help me out here, Chief."

"Hey, Bridgette, did the ME take casts of the wounds?"

Bridgette looks up from taping plastic over the bed of the truck. "Yeah, why?"

"Did he make any preliminary remarks?"

She leans her arms along the side of the truck bed, over an area she's already sealed. "He said the victim suffered from two sharp-force trauma wounds. He mentioned that the width and depth of the wound appeared proportional. And something about the lacerated soft tissues indicating a chop wound, maybe? I don't know, the body stuff is beyond my expertise. Sorry."

"No, that's perfect. Thanks."

Bridgette smiles and returns to sealing the truck bed.

"What are you thinking?" Murphy asks. He steps toward me, away from the tree he's been peeling. When his body moves it reveals a scarred section of pine. The gouges look fresh.

I point toward the marks. "Looks like Jack was trying to sharpen his machete."

"He doesn't use it much. The last time any bushwhacking was done around here was when he asked me to do it. Don't know where it's gone to, though." Murphy turns, checking the ground near the base of the tree. "I always put it back when I'm done with it."

"But wouldn't that cause a pretty big mess? And wouldn't Gibbons have seen something that big coming at him?" Robbins calls from the doorway.

"Yeah, if he could see it." Murphy stares at something behind me. I look over my shoulder, following his gaze to the outhouse. Even from a distance I can see the gaps between the wooden planks, can hear the steady hum of eager flies. And I can smell the stench of something rotten.

"You've got to be kidding me." I hear Robbins say it, but I know my lips just mouthed the same words.

Murphy straightens and then hesitates. He nods at me and then heads toward the toilet, stopping along the way to grab a pair of gloves from the box Bridgette has on top of her toolbox. Robbins collects Jack from his chair and walks him out to join us.

I hang back. This is Murphy's moment. It's also an experience I believe I can live without.

Murphy flings open the door of the latrine without hesitation. Even from my forty-foot distance, I'm almost bowled over by the smell. Dried blood is a dark stain against the aged gray wood. Arterial spatter has painted the entire interior. We have our murder scene.

36

HEATHER

I'm playing outside with the dogs when I hear the car door close. Thinking it's Maggie, I run into the house and to the front to greet her. Only, when I get there, it's not her that I see approaching through the window in the door.

I bolt into the kitchen, hoping he didn't see me, wondering where Steve is. When he knocks, I fight the urge to run and hide under the bed, instead sinking to my butt on the floor under the kitchen sink, burying my face into the dogs' fur.

Steve doesn't see me as he passes to answer the door. He must think I'm still outside. I make up my mind to sneak back out, to run and hide, but I'm too late. By the time I stand the man is already in the house, and he's brought someone with him. They see me.

The woman comes over and introduces herself. She holds out her hand to me, but all I can do is stare at it. I can't hear a word she says.

Her smile is kind. She's soft and plump looking, with feathery gray hair, and she smells like powder. Still, when she puts her hand on my shoulder, I want to hiss and bite.

Steve talks to the man, his voice getting louder, his hands

flying wildly through the air. The man keeps shaking his head. Steve looks at me, his expression a mix of sympathy and guilt. I drop my shoulder, ditching the old lady's hand and move beside him.

"You need to speak with Chief Riley about this." Steve addresses the old lady now. She nods her gray fluff in an understanding manner, but Steve and I both know she's not really listening. "If you truly care about Heather's best interests, then you'll let her stay here. Give her a chance to feel a bit of stability in her life."

They're trying to take me away. Panic surges through my brain. I may never see Maggie again.

"The child is a minor who has been turned out by her mother and is wanted for questioning about her role in a heinous crime," the detective states. It sounds overly dramatic, like he rehearsed the words on the way over here, or stole them from some bad TV show. The old lady just nods along with whatever he says.

"*The child* has spent a long day at the hospital, and she needs some rest. Not to mention that her physical exam revealed that the baby almost certainly wasn't born alive, which you would know if you were looking at the evidence instead of trying to ruin a kid's life. And while we're on the subject of the inadequacies of your investigation, the child in question has been found to be intellectually disabled, which further weakens your case."

Steve stands up straight and puffs out his chest, showing the detective that he's a much larger man. I've seen roosters do the same thing. The bigger one usually wins. I wish I had the guts to cheer him on.

"That all may be true, but I have jurisdiction here and the situation's gonna be handled as I see fit. Now, I've had Ms. Johnson drive all the way up here on a Sunday so that the suspect could have a child advocate present during questioning, and it's not my intention to waste either of our time."

Ms. Johnson has stopped nodding. She shifts her bulk so that she's sided with me and Steve. "Detective Campden, if what he says is true, then additional measures need to be taken. If Heather here has been found mentally incompetent for her actions, the entire situation has changed. Personally, I'd be uncomfortable proceeding without speaking with the physician who provided the diagnosis. It's in the child's best interests. I'm sure that you would agree." She's giving him a disapproving look over her glasses.

I want to stick out my tongue and taunt the detective but know that I shouldn't press my luck. Instead, I just keep my eyes wide and serious like I know what's going on and I'm shocked by his behavior, like Steve and Ms. Johnson.

"Heather," Ms. Johnson is looking at me now. "Would you like to stay here another night while we sort things out?"

I nod as fast as I can. "Yes. Very much. I like it here."

The detective rolls his eyes and mutters a word I've only said a few times out loud to myself, kind of trying it out. It seems to make Ms. Johnson very upset.

"Well, we are *done* here, Detective Campden. I will contact you when I'm ready to proceed. Heather, it was a pleasure to meet you. I look forward to seeing you again."

Then she's gone, leaving a cloud of powder scent behind her. Steve crosses his arms across his chest and gestures with his head for the detective to follow her. The detective gives him a nasty look with narrowed eyes, his face pinched up like a rat, and then he's gone too. Steve follows him to the door, locking it behind him.

I feel kind of nervous because now that they're gone I expect Steve to be mad at me for being the cause of so much fuss, but when he turns around he's smiling.

"Glad that's over with," he says, like the whole thing was just some kind of bad joke. "Now, how about some spaghetti?"

I love spaghetti. I'm about to say so when Steve asks me to be in charge of feeding the dogs, which is an even bigger thrill than spaghetti, because I love the dogs, too. As I'm pouring the food into their bowls, my cheeks sore from my wide smile, I decide to add Steve to the list of things that I love. Nobody's ever stood up for me before like he and Maggie have. It would be pretty perfect if they let me stay here with them forever.

37

MURPHY

Murphy watches his father closely as Robbins leads him over to the outhouse. Jack moves stiffly, back bent at an odd angle, sidling sideways like he's part spider. He suddenly looks every year of his age.

He stops when the smell hits him, nostrils flaring wide. His eyes flash, too much of the whites showing as they flit nervously around the group. His steps are reluctant as Robbins tugs him forward, like he's being led to slaughter. The old man's face trembles when he sees the gore inside.

"I have no idea how that happened." Jack looks imploringly at Murphy. "You've got to believe me, son. I ain't even been out here in months. I've been shitting in a hole out back. Honest. Come on 'round and I'll show you."

"And I bet you have no idea how the blood got in the back of your truck, either?" Robbins asks.

Jack looks at him, stunned. "What blood?"

"You said yourself that you were out on the logging roads, Mr. Murphy." Maggie addresses him calmly, her face expressionless. "Would you care to tell us what you were doing out there?"

"Rick Hodges and his brothers go out there hunting. Sometimes they call me to give their dogs a lift home when they've got the bed of their truck full of game. Pay me in meat. But that's all I do. I ain't never even had one of their kills in my truck, only the dogs. I haven't done anything illegal."

Murphy snorts. Jack looks at him, eyes wide.

"Okay, boy, I killed your momma. I admit it. Didn't mean to but it happened and I'm the one who's gonna have to pay for it in the hereafter. It was an accident. I know that don't make it no better, but I'm sorry, always have been but I was too stubborn to say it, even to myself. And I was angry that you were so stuck on her, even after she was gone. A boy should look up to his daddy like that, but you never did, not even after I was all you had left. My pride has always been my downfall, but I'm telling you, I didn't kill anyone else, and that's the God's honest truth."

"Well, you can tell that to the walls of your God's honest jail cell, because you, Jack Murphy, are under arrest by the state of Maine." Robbins retrieves a pair of handcuffs from a case on his belt and latches them around Jack's thin wrists.

"Dale, you've got to help me. Tell them I didn't do it, boy."

Murphy turns his back on his father, facing the woods. He does his best to drown out the sound of his father's voice begging him as Detective Robbins leads his father to the car and puts him in the back.

"Okay if I put him in the holding cell back at your office?" he asks Maggie.

Keys jingle as Maggie tosses a set to Robbins.

"State tow truck should be here later tonight. I'll meet it in town and lead him out here if that's okay?"

Murphy hears Maggie respond to Bridgette, hears the sounds of Bridgette's van as the engine starts and she sets off down the long dirt road, hears the pine needles crunching under Maggie's boots as she comes up behind him. Murphy knows it's time to leave. He's done what he came here to do. Make a killer pay.

38
MAGGIE

When I get home, feeling tired and drained, all I want to do is take a hot bath and go to bed. I sneak in as quietly as I can. Heather is curled up on the couch with the dogs. Steve is sitting at the kitchen counter, working on a laptop. For a brief moment, I consider this way of life. I'm old enough to have a daughter Heather's age.

I don't know why this thought pops into my head, but I shake it free. Rush out of the room before any other uncomfortable thoughts can take root. Steve looks up and smiles as I enter the kitchen. He sees my face and hands me his beer.

"How were things here?" I ask.

His smile vanishes and he shakes his head. "Detective Campden came out here with a child advocate. They tried to take Heather."

I feel adrenaline surge through my body. The nerve of that little...

"After I explained today's events, the advocate agreed that it would be best for Heather to stay here until she had spoken with the doctors. Campden was not happy."

"They're going to take her eventually." I watch Steve's face closely for his reaction. "They'll want to place her in a foster household that's equipped to deal with her special needs."

"I know." Steve nods. He doesn't look too upset. "I just didn't want to turn her over to that little pipsqueak. I don't like his attitude. It was disrespectful, him going behind your back instead of including you."

I grin. "Were you defending my honor?"

"Well, yeah. I guess so. Is there a reward for that?" Steve grins back.

I lean forward and kiss him. My tension melts away. I open my mouth to invite him to bath time, when a rustling from the living room draws my attention and I notice that Heather is watching. I don't understand how couples deal with children in the house full-time. Strange as it seems, raising a child strikes me as a single person's endeavor.

I see by the look in Steve's eyes that he is aware of what just transpired—the twist of events that wordlessly took place. There's a promise in his expression to make up for lost time at a later date. I kiss the top of his head, wave to Heather, and head for my bath alone.

Steve is a good man. I'm fortunate to have found him. I hope I'm lucky enough that he'll stick with me when this is all over. But first we have to get through tomorrow.

39

HEATHER

I like Maggie's friend. I can't remember the word she called herself, but I know that it means that she's a bone doctor. Her name is Linda, and she has long black hair that's braided down her back. She was already here when I woke up. She brought blueberry muffins.

Maggie and Linda discuss their "game plan" while Steve and I work on the muffins. I guess there's something else for her to do while she's in town besides digging up Momma's babies. I don't pay much attention until I hear that I'll be coming with them to Momma's house. I don't want to see her, and it's boring over there. I'd much rather stay here and play with the dogs, but I don't say so.

If that mean little man from last night comes back, I want to be with Maggie. It's not that I don't trust Steve to run him off again, there's just something about Maggie that makes me think she might pick the guy up and toss him right out the door. I definitely want to be around to see it if that happens.

The drive to Momma's house is quicker than I thought it would be. We wait in the Jeep out front until another car shows up. The other state detective gets out, and for a moment I feel real nervous because this one's bigger and I don't think Maggie could pick him up and throw him, but he's smiling and Maggie's smiling, and they seem to be friendly, so I don't worry too much.

I watch from the back seat at he goes and knocks on the door. Momma answers. He hands her a piece of paper that she balls up without looking at it. I can tell she's angry. Her face turns red, and she gets the same look she does when I break a dish.

He tries to guide her away from the house, but Momma shoves his hand off her arm. He steps aside and gestures for her to lead the way. She marches ahead of him to his car. I duck down as she glares toward me.

Maggie waits until Momma is settled in the back seat of the other car before she opens the door for me to get out. She and Linda are waiting for me to take them to the right spot, which makes me feel real important. I lead them around the side of the house, through the backyard and a short way into the woods, until we're standing before a row of rocks stretched out in a line.

Stone walls are common in the woods. This is not a stone wall, though. Each rock in the row is a tiny little grave marker. I point to the one on the end.

"That was the last one."

I've been trying to remember how long it's been since I saw Momma carry this one out to the woods, but I'm not that good with time. I do know that my baby was already in my stomach when it happened. I tell this to Maggie and Linda.

"Thank you, Heather. You're a brave girl, helping us like this." Linda smiles at me and I smile back.

Maggie adds her smile and says, "This is going to take a little while, and it's probably going to be really boring. Is there something you want to do while we're working? Maybe go watch some TV? Or pack some of your things?"

I nod and head inside, relieved that I won't have to be there when they pull that tiny little baby out of the ground. It gives me the shivers. Poor little baby, alone in the dark like that. That's why I put mine in a tree. As I settle on the couch and turn on the TV, I think about how Momma never did understand much about the dark.

40

MAGGIE

I lay out a tarp while Linda sets up her equipment and gets to work. As I drive tent stakes through the eyeholes to keep it from flapping up in the wind, I can't help but think about what it's going to look like later in the day, dotted with tiny infant bones. This is a part of the job I don't miss.

Linda dumps dirt into a screen, making shallow swipes with a trowel. Every so often she stops to take pictures. I watch as a form emerges. Like with an archaeological ruin, Linda peels back the layers of soil until the still figure is pedestalled on a mound of earth. She photographs, takes measurements, and draws a sketch before she lifts her find out of the shallow hole and moves it to the tarp.

She stares down at the still form for a moment, shaking her head. "This one is way too fresh for me. It's going to have to go to a medical examiner."

I move to her side. "No observable abnormalities."

"None at all," Linda agrees. "And it looks like there's an awful lot of dirt in the mouth. I'm wondering if the ME will find soil aspirated into the lungs."

Linda returns to work in the baby graveyard while I pull out my phone and text Robbins. Let him make the call to the medical examiner's office. I hope Mary McGillis overhears what he's saying so she can start sweating about her future. Dirt in the lungs would mean that the baby was alive when it was buried. This little town is filling up with murderers, fast.

By lunch there are four individuals on the tarp in varying states of decay. The last one is represented entirely by bones. Linda's face is smeared with dirt and sweat.

"That's all the markers," she says, referring to the line of rocks Heather had led us to. "But I have a feeling that if we ran a GPR around here we might find more."

I weigh the idea. I'm sure the staties could get a ground penetrating radar unit out here, but I doubt they'll think it's worth the effort considering we already have at least four charges lying on the ground in front of us. Linda's sharp. She's probably drawn the same conclusion.

"I'm going to bag the remains, and then we'll head to the next scene. Is there someone who can take possession over them for now?"

"My lieutenant is on his way," I say. "And Detective Robbins has someone coming out from the state to collect the fleshed remains. Would you like to examine the bones at their facilities or have them taken to your lab?"

Linda and I have known each other for about nine years. We met when we were both living and working in Florida. She now lives about a six-hour drive away in Massachusetts. It's funny how people spread like seeds in the wind. How something from your past can cycle around full circle until it's right back in your face, staring at you from the present again.

"I'd like to use their lab if they'd be willing to extend me the courtesy."

Linda is also unfailingly humble and polite. She is one of less than a hundred and fifty board-certified forensic anthropologists in the United States. Most forensic institutions would jump at the chance of hosting her, yet she always acts like expecting them to do so would be an imposition.

"I'll ask Robbins to check, but I'm sure they'll be fine with it. Did you want to stop and grab some lunch?"

Linda shakes her head. "I have some granola bars in my bag. It's easier for me to stay focused if I wait to eat a heavy meal until I'm done digging."

I remember this from our Florida days. We only got the chance to work together on a few cases, but we always kept in touch in between. Linda is more than a colleague. She's a friend. One of the few I've ever had.

The sound of heavy steps crunching through the leaf litter draws me from my thoughts, before I get sucked down the rabbit hole of my past. I greet Murphy, introduce him to Linda as he joins us. Judging by his sallow skin and dark-ringed eyes, he's had another sleepless night. Not that I can blame him.

He sinks heavily onto a large rock and stares at the bags laid out on the tarp. After a moment, he glances up and catches me watching him. He gives me a curt nod, then returns his gaze to the grim scene before him, dismissing me onto the next task at hand.

I guide Linda around to the front of the house, leaving Murphy to his thoughts. We find Robbins leaning against the side of his car, on the phone. He waves, ends the call, and approaches.

"What's the verdict?" I ask, gesturing toward the car where Mary McGillis's head is leaning against the passenger window as if she's sleeping. "Do we have enough to charge her?"

"I had Sue check to see if a family burial ground on the property was ever registered with the town clerk. She said no, so right now we have Mary for improper disposal of human remains. That should keep her off the streets for the next few days."

"I can have my report done before then," Linda says. "I

imagine the ME will have a good idea of what he's looking at by that time, too."

"I appreciate that." Robbins gives his phone a little raise toward Linda. "And I checked with headquarters, they'd like to offer you full privileges at the Skowhegan lab, so that should help move things along. I've got a transport unit coming soon for Jack Murphy, figured I'd put McGillis in it too as long as you didn't think it was a bad idea."

"Won't hear me complaining," I answer. "I texted Steve, he's on his way to pick up Heather. Would you be able to stay until he gets here?"

"Not a problem. What about—" Robbins nods toward the back, where Murphy is keeping watch over the recovered fetal remains.

I'm hesitant to leave my lieutenant alone right now. He's understandably distracted, but the evidence needs to be handled properly down to the letter. An oversight in the chain of command could jeopardize the charges against Mary McGillis. "How long do you think it will be before the ME arrives?" I ask.

Robbins consults his watch. "Shouldn't be long now." But he must have picked up on my hesitation, because he's quick to add, "I'll stay here until he arrives and takes possession, too. Handle the transfer."

"You sure you don't mind?"

"Nah. Not like I have any other plans. It'll actually make things easier. I'll have the transport unit swing by to pick McGillis up and then the ME van can follow me from here to Murphy's old place."

"Thanks, Hal, I appreciate it."

"Anytime."

Linda and I get into the Jeep. I turn the key and the engine sparks to life.

"That guy out back?" Linda's voice is soft, as if she's afraid of being overheard. "Is it his mother that we're about to...?"

"Most likely."

"And he's the one who discovered the remains?"

"I'm afraid so."

"Wow. That could really mess a guy up, huh?"

I don't respond as I pull out onto the road. Linda and I both know more than our fair share about misery and trauma and the darkness we've chosen to face. It's our jobs. Technically, it's Murphy's, too. But that doesn't make it any easier, especially when it's personal. There's a fine line between managing and malfunctioning. I've been on both sides of that line.

We travel slowly down back neighborhood streets to our next stop, passing front yards filled with kids' bikes, toddlers' power wheels, and mothers' flowerpots. It seems a perfect example of family life, untouched by evil and sin.

I wonder how many of the doors we're passing have ugly secrets lurking behind them. I wonder at the nature of human perseverance, about what breaks us and what makes us stronger. I wonder about what's going on in the brain behind Murphy's thick skull. It's possible that he's stronger. But I have a feeling that he's irreparably broken.

41

MURPHY

Last night, when Murphy got home, Alma had been waiting for him. She didn't say one word, just put a beer in one of his hands and a hot plate of food in the other. He'd wanted to reach out to her. Had wanted to hold her and let her hold him and maybe even make love until the world felt like a better place. Instead, he'd taken the food and eaten it in the garage, sitting on a cinderblock in front of a space heater.

At one point he'd seen Alma out of the corner of his eye, watching him through the window in the door. Again, he'd wanted to make some kind of gesture, some movement toward humanity. But he just kept staring at the coils inside the heater until they glowed bright, fiery orange. Like his anger.

Murphy had never wanted to be like his dad. He'd always aspired to be a loving father and husband. He had failed. And he could feel that failure rotting inside him like something from his father's outhouse.

The truth is, no matter how hard he fought it, he'd always been able to feel that little bit of evil just under the surface of his skin, his father's DNA, dormant, perhaps, but lying in wait for its moment to attack. Maybe he'd kept people at a distance for that very reason. Maybe they'd kept the distance on their own, sensing the foulness that filled his soul.

Murphy had spent the night in the garage, sequestering himself from the rest of the population for the benefit of humankind. He relived all of the most influential encounters with his father, the top-one-hundred countdown. Memories had played in his brain throughout the night. Try as he might, he couldn't come to terms with what was happening.

His father was a wicked man, of that there was no question. Jack Murphy had stolen the one good thing from his life. He'd made a career of mistreating his son. Of making sure Murphy was aware of all his shortcomings, doing his best to make Murphy feel unworthy of being a part of the human race.

But of all the crimes Jack Murphy had committed, the murder of Chase Gibbons was not one of them. Anyone who looked hard enough into Jack's beady eyes, two hard little shards of black coal, would see the truth. And that scared him.

In the morning, Murphy passed the boys in the hallway as he was leaving. They had flattened themselves against the wall, bare, thin shoulders pressed hard against the floral-sprigged wallpaper to avoid contact with the man who they knew as dad. Their wide eyes followed him until the door was shut between them.

They'd been terrified of him, like Murphy had been of his own father. The one thing he had tried to avoid in life had happened despite his best efforts. Murphy was now a carbon copy of the person he hated most in the world. His dad's life was his life. His father's future was his own.

Now, standing in the McGillis's backyard, he stares down at the line of small bags on the tarp before him. Each one represented a life that had been saved from interaction with him. Each had been spared the pain and suffering of life. Yet, each might also represent the sin of murder. His father's future was his own.

He'd never been much of one for hunting, had only ever killed turkeys before, and even that had been at his father's insistence. He'd never felt the desire to take the life of another creature. It had never seemed fair for the decision of life and death to lie in his hands. And yet he'd done it anyways.

The old adage is true—the apple doesn't fall far from the tree. In the whole nature versus nurture debate, doesn't nature always win? You can't teach a tiger to be a lamb. You can't make them change their striped fur to wool.

He feels his own stripes now, the ones he'd denied for so long, burning their way to the surface of his skin. He can't hide who he is any longer. He can't deny what he is.

His father is being charged with a murder he hadn't committed. And he's doing nothing to stop it.

It's only a matter of time before the cycle of life repeats and Murphy finds himself facing the same situation. Innocent or not.

His father is a killer. The man had murdered his mother. But did that mean he deserved to pay for a crime that was not his own?

And if Murphy just stood by and let it happen, would that mean he deserved it when God, karma, or even one of the sons he had raised as his own decided it was his turn?

How could he pretend to be a better man than his father? He'd been the one to point the finger at Jack Murphy. The one to find the evidence that framed him.

What's happening now is all his fault.

He doesn't forgive his father, could never forgive the man who stole his mother from him and cut short the happiness he had once felt. But that's all in the distant past. And hadn't Jack paid for that already, suffering through decades of a miserable, isolated existence where even his own son couldn't stand to be around him?

The present is another story.

There is no way to rewind time, no way to reverse this. His father would go to prison for a murder he did not commit. And because of that, one day, it would be Dale's turn to even the scales. Unless he does something to stop this.

But what?

He looks up and notices Heather's face peeping at him from one of the back windows of the house. He spends a long moment studying her face. Raising a leaden arm, he waves. Heather bends her fingertips back at him.

His dad didn't kill Gibbons. He can't let him take the fall for a crime he didn't commit.

Murphy feels his lips curve into a smile. He gestures for Heather to come out and join him. Heather smiles back and then vanishes from the window.

42

MAGGIE

The excavation at the Murphy's old house is much more labor intensive than at Mary McGillis's. Tree roots have disarticulated the body, distributing the bones over a larger area. Scraps of cloth—shreds of jean, what looks to be flannel from a shirt— are seeded among the jumbled ruins of wood, rocks, and soil.

I sieve the dirt as Linda dumps it onto the screen. A collection of remains grows on the tarp—a long bone, a few ribs, a half-dozen vertebrae, a cranium, and a mandible. Linda takes a few pictures and adds a humerus to the assortment. I remove what I suspect is a phalange from the screen and add it to a growing pile that will need Linda's expert eyes to identify.

As usual, Linda digs in silence, but something about the way I keep catching her glancing at me makes me think she wants to talk. I would appreciate a little conversation myself. My skin keeps getting an eerie, creepy sensation, like an army of spiders is marching across my flesh, and I'm abnormally anxious. I know it's because I'm out of practice. I've been out of the game too long and now I'm just psyching myself out, spending too much time in my own head with spooky thoughts.

"Your lieutenant," Linda's voice sounds strangely distant

even though she's peeking her head over the edge of the deepening hole. "You sure he's going to be okay?"

"You know as well as I do that there's no guarantee about those types of things, but he's never given me cause to worry before. Why?"

"I don't know. I can't quite put my finger on it, but there was just something behind his eyes. Or maybe something that wasn't there that should have been. I can't shake the feeling that something bad is coming."

"Said the woman digging up the dead body."

Linda flicks the dirt off the fingers of her glove in my direction. "Seriously. Can you really tell me that you don't have a nagging feeling in your gut?"

I can't. I've been trying to ignore it, but all those neurons that line my intestines have been screaming danger all day. I've been trying to repress the memory of the last time I felt like this, but something about seeing the fear pinching Linda's forehead into a map of worry lets it resurface.

"Help me up." Linda holds her hand out to me. I see her holding tightly to a clump of grass at the edge of the hole with her other hand. She's already lifted her leg for leverage. I stand and give her the boost she needs. Once she's out, we face each other, our eyes communicating in the wordless exchange that sometimes occurs between women. When our hearts and minds confess what our words can't.

"I haven't felt this way since—"

"Neither have I." I cut her off before she can say it.

Linda bends, pulling up a corner of the tarp. She starts rolling it around the bones we've collected. I pull the rotten sheets of plywood that Murphy had scavenged back over the hole. Linda never leaves a job until it's done. Abandoning a grave is simply unheard of to her. If she's this nervous, then I know we're in for one hell of a storm.

When she has the tarped bundle of bones nestled under her

arm, we return to the Jeep. I press the lock button as soon as the doors are closed. We buckle our seatbelts and look at each other.

"Now what?" she asks.

"Now I take you back to your car and you get out the hell out of Dodge."

"What? I can't just leave. I haven't finished yet."

"Yes, Linda, you *can* leave. And you will."

I feel the tears in my eyes as I look at her. The irony is that even though Linda and I aren't that close, not compared to most women and their best friends, we are close. We're closer to each other than to almost anyone else, and in our worlds that attachment is one of the few things we've got.

When you're an extreme introvert whose personality separates you from 99.9 percent of the rest of the population, that thin thread that links you to another can feel like the only thing connecting you to the rest of humankind. It's a lifeline.

"I've almost gotten you killed once." I bite the inside of my cheek as I struggle with the rest that I have to say. "Please don't put me through that again."

Linda shakes her head no. I put my hand on her arm and make her look at me. Maybe we're just being dramatic by behaving like some impending disaster is looming on the horizon like an apocalypse. Or maybe we've learned from our past mistakes, and this is how wisdom and experience are displayed through actions and reactions.

"Neither of us would have made it last time if we hadn't been together." She tells me a fact I already know.

"It won't be like last time."

"How do you know? You can't be sure."

"I can be sure. Last time, it was personal. I was too close to play it safe."

"Maybe you don't realize it yet, but it's personal this time too, Maggie. You care about these people."

"That's true. And there are a lot of people counting on me here. But this time it's not my baby brother."

I let that hang in the air between us.

"If you get killed, I'm gonna be pissed. You're the only friend I get a Christmas card from."

"You're the only friend I have to send one to." I grin. Mainly because I know I've won this one small battle. "Also, when whatever happens is over, I'm telling Steve everything."

Linda's eyes flit across my face. I'm not sure what they're looking for. The next thing I know she has her arms thrown around me in a hug.

"I'm so happy for you." Her words are muffled against my shoulder.

I'm always surprised by how well Linda knows me. It's like she was born with the secret decoder that everyone else I've ever known in my life never bothered to order from the back of the cereal box. Steve has never needed the decoder because he simply accepts me as I am. And now that I've become accustomed to the strange, uncomfortable wonderfulness of having someone share my world with me, I want to embrace it.

"I really think I should stay."

"And I really think you should leave while you can." I roll my eyes up, peer at her from the tops.

"This is silly. We've just spooked each other. Reliving memories like ghost stories and making something out of nothing."

My phone rings. Even though I'm sure it was on vibrate, had been feeling the gentle pulse against my leg all day as emails and texts came through, the shrill tone fills the car, causing both Linda and me to jump. I have never wanted to answer a phone less.

43

STEVE

I stopped to get gas. It's an ordinary, everyday task that you don't think twice about. You need gas, you're passing a gas station, so you stop and fill up. I didn't want to do it on the way home, with Heather in the car, so it made sense to get it on the way to pick her up.

I pull up in front of the McGillis house maybe five minutes later than I would have if I hadn't made the stop. Detective Robbins is leaning against his car, eyes focused on the cell phone in his hand. Someone sits in the back of his black Nissan. I can't see who, but I can guess.

I get out and walk over to the detective. We haven't met, but I know who he is. I also know that he's being an ally to Maggie, going against the partner he has to deal with full-time to work with her on this case. For that, I'm grateful. The man has earned my respect and I'd like to introduce myself.

He looks up as I approach, slips the phone into his pocket and smiles.

"You must be Steve." He crosses the last few steps between us and extends his hand.

We shake and make two minutes of small talk. Maybe three.

I think I can hear Mary McGillis snoring from the back of the car. Other than that, the neighborhood is silent. The air has that super clean lack of smell that happens when the temperature drops quickly, like any odor gets frozen and falls to the ground. My new friend Hal tells me that Heather is waiting inside, watching TV.

I head into the house to get her. The interior is dark and chilly. It smells like stale crackers and dirty socks. I feel bad for stopping for gas and leaving Heather in this place a second longer than she had to be. It doesn't matter that she lived here until two days ago, that this is the place she knows as home, and she probably doesn't realize exactly what a depressing hovel it is. I feel bad just the same.

The front door opens onto the living room. There are no lights on, just the flash of the TV, the screen filled with teenagers talking in front of a row of lockers, a stereotypical ponytailed cheerleader and a jock in a letterman jacket. There's no sign of Heather, besides the blue sweatshirt she left the house with this morning abandoned over the arm of the couch. I recognize it because it's Maggie's.

I walk further inside, noticing the piles of debris that line the junction where the walls meet the floor. The yellowed wallpaper is covered with smears and marks. The glass on the framed pictures is covered in a thick layer of grime. A dirty diaper is balled up and discarded in the middle of the hallway.

I reach the kitchen, but Heather's not there. I feel myself getting anxious. I don't want to be in this house anymore.

"Heather?"

As impossible as it seems, I know from the way my voice bounces off the walls that I'm alone.

"Heather?"

I call her name again and again as I knock on doors and fling them open, searching the small house until I've been through the whole thing. I realize I'm still calling her name when Robbins bursts through the front door.

"What's wrong?" He looks spooked.

"I can't find Heather. She's not in the house."

Robbins brushes past me, doing the same search that I've just completed until he comes full circle and joins me back in the living room.

"She's not here." I know I've already said it, that it's become quite obvious to us both, but I'm still trying to wrap my head around it.

"Well, she didn't come out the front. Maybe Lieutenant Murphy saw her." Robbins crosses to the sliding glass door hidden behind a curtain. Pulling the drape to the side he stops and looks at me. "It's unlocked."

He says this with relief, like it explains everything. He vanishes behind the curtain, and I rush to catch up with him. By the time I do he's standing at the far end of the backyard, staring at the woods. I jog over to his side. There's a haunted look in his eyes that makes my stomach immediately feel sour.

"Maybe she just went for a walk?" I say the words even though I don't believe them.

Robbins's voice cracks. "It's a little more complicated than that."

"Heather?" I call her name, hoping that she'll miraculously appear before Robbins can say what's on his mind. "Heather!"

"It's no use," Robbins says as I repeat the call for the fourth or fifth time. He puts a hand on my arm to get my attention. "We need to call Maggie."

I feel myself shaking my head. None of this makes sense to me.

"Huh? Why?" I'm still scanning the trees for a glimpse of Heather walking back toward us.

"Because Heather isn't the only one missing."

Now he has my attention, every ounce of it, as I turn to face him, trying to ignore the expression on his face that perfectly matches the pain lancing through my gut.

Robbins gestures to the tarp laid out on the ground. For the first time I notice the bags lined across the middle. I think my subconscious purposely missed this detail.

He clears his throat and says, "Murphy was out here, keeping a watch on the evidence. It's not just Heather. Dale Murphy's missing, too."

I don't know what to do with this information. My mind struggles to deny what it could mean. I don't think I'm even aware that I've dialed Maggie until the ring of the phone against my ear drills into my brain with the refrain—I stopped to get gas.

44

MAGGIE

Linda and I both stare at the ringing phone in my hand. Steve's calling. This can't be a good thing, because Steve never calls. Steve texts—he's a texter. I don't think I've ever actually heard the sound of Steve's voice over the phone.

Linda gives me a nudge. "Aren't you going to answer?"

I know I should. I comfort myself with the fact that if Steve is calling, at least he's alive. Then it occurs to me that someone else could be calling from his phone to let me know that he's not okay, and that's why a call is coming from his number. I end my pointless head games and answer the call.

"Hello?"

"I stopped for gas."

The voice is Steve's, so at least there's that.

"Okay. And?"

"And Heather's gone."

"What?"

Steve's words rush out and I realize that he's blaming himself for something that is essentially my fault. I was responsible for Heather. It was my job to keep her safe.

"Steve, stop, wait. You've done nothing wrong. There's

nothing you could have done differently. I'm sure that stopping for gas had no impact on the situation."

Linda looks at me, her head cocked to the side as she tries to figure out what's going on from my end of the conversation.

"Is Detective Robbins there?"

"Yes."

"And he's aware of the situation."

"Yes."

"What does he think happened?"

"He says that Murphy's missing too."

"Murphy? Does Robbins think he has something to do with Heather's disappearance?"

Linda gasps softly in the seat next to me.

Steve says, "Yes. Maggie, we need to go look for her. I have a really bad feeling about this."

Linda and I shoot worried looks at each other like a volley of lit arrows during a medieval siege in a movie.

"Steve, we all want to see Heather back safe and sound, but you and Robbins can't go look for them yet, do you hear me? I want you and Robbins to wait for me. Okay?"

"Maggie, we're wasting time."

"Steve, do you have a gun?"

"What? No."

"Well, Murphy does. So I want you and Robbins to wait until I get there. Okay? Promise me?"

Steve reluctantly agrees.

"Put Robbins on."

The sounds of the phone being fumbled from man-hand to man-hand transmits loudly from the phone's tiny speaker. When I hear heavy breathing sounds through the line, I know that Robbins has possession of the device.

"Robbins?"

"Yeah?"

"Don't go looking for Heather and Murphy yet, okay? I'm

on my way. I'm going to call my reserve officers in on this. We need to do this right."

"Gotcha."

"So you're going to wait?"

"We'll wait."

"Okay, I'm on my way."

I hang up the phone and give Linda a brief, wide-eyed look of disbelief. A moment later we're traveling much too fast down the narrow residential road. And even though my mind is a blinding snowstorm of worries, there's one that stands out from all the rest, one that shouldn't matter as much but strangely matters the most—I didn't tell Steve that I loved him before ending our call.

45

STEVE

Detective Robbins hands my phone back to me. We're standing on the front doorstep, close enough for him to keep an eye on Mary McGillis in the back of his car, yet too far away for her to hear that her daughter is missing. Even though Maggie told me that this is not my fault, I can't help but feel responsible.

Gravel grinds under tires as a van pulls up. It parks behind my car, the passenger door flying open before it reaches a complete stop. Detective Campden hops down from the vehicle and storms across the front yard. I hear Robbins cursing under his breath as the smaller detective approaches.

"Funny seeing you here." Campden glares at Robbins with narrowed eyes. "Woke up at the inn this morning and the car was gone. Front desk said you left a message saying you had some personal errands to run. This doesn't look personal to me."

The toe of his right boot taps loudly as he vents his irritation. Something about his manner strikes me as laughable. I'd be having a hard time keeping a straight face under different circumstances.

"Listen, Lou, we've got a problem."

"We sure as hell do, if you think it's all right to abandon

your partner so you can go run off and play with the locals. I don't know what the hell has gotten into you, Hal, but don't think I'm just going to forget about this when we get back to headquarters."

"Lou."

"Luckily, Sue was kind enough to lend me her car so I could get some *real* police work done this morning. Real nice that *she* was the one who had to fill me in about the suspect in custody. He's loaded in the van, by the way. The driver told me you requested that he stop at this address for another pickup. Would you care to tell me about it? Or should I just wait until you file your report?"

"Lou, I'm sorry, but we've got a serious situation on our hands right now. I'm going to need you to save your anger for another day and help out."

Campden's eyes bulge. He exhales noisily out of his nose.

"Then are you going to tell me what's going on?"

"I've taken Mary McGillis into custody for improper disposal of a body. The ME is sending a transport for the four illegally buried infants in various stages of decomposition that have been recovered from the backyard. Additional charges are pending on the postmortems."

Campden's face calms. He gestures in a "give me more" signal.

"Heather McGillis led us to the bodies. She was in the house watching TV but has since disappeared. Lieutenant Murphy was posted in the back during this time and is also now missing. We have reason to believe that the disappearances are related."

Campden's arms fall to his sides as his eyes close. I can see his lips moving but can't tell if he's praying or cursing. He squeezes the bridge of his nose, shakes his head from side to side, and then looks up.

"This is bad." He glances toward the black Nissan with Mary McGillis inside. "She know yet?"

"No."

"Let's keep it that way."

He whistles, the shrill call tearing through the air like a missile. The driver of the van looks up. Campden nods and points toward Mary in the car.

I watch as the driver knocks on the rear passenger window, then opens the door. He speaks with Mary for a moment. She climbs out of the car and follows him through the backdoors of the van. A minute later, the driver reemerges and gives Campden a thumbs up. Campden returns the gesture. As the van starts up and drives away, I ponder the ethics of keeping Mary McGillis unaware of the possible danger her daughter is in.

"You."

It's not until I feel the finger jabbing into my bicep that I realize Detective Campden is talking to me.

"You know this Murphy character?"

"Me? No, not really. Vaguely. Why?"

"Because this morning after I found out Robbins and your woman arrested his father last night I went out to his house. He wasn't there but I talked to his wife. Picture she painted—well, it doesn't look good. Not for him or anyone he decided to take off with."

"How's that?" Robbins casts a sidelong glance at his partner.

"She says he's become completely withdrawn and uncommunicative."

"Sounds like a normal marriage."

"She said there was a look in his eyes she's never seen before. Described it as the look people in the movies get when they've been possessed by some kind of evil."

"I don't think we can take a comparison to a horror movie too seriously."

"No, I agree. What I did take seriously was that she was spooked enough that she was packing herself and her two kids up and was getting ready to take off."

"You ever hear anything about her leaving him before?"

I shake my head. "I'm not really in on any of the town gossip, but that's something I think Maggie might have mentioned had she known."

"Yeah, Sue had never heard any rumors either. So, I'm guessing that whatever you and *Chief* Riley did last night pushed the guy over the edge."

Robbins has fists made like he's planning to use them. I step between the two detectives, a palm held toward each, and say, "Now wait a minute, Detective Campden. I think you better make sure you have all the facts before you go slinging accusations. Your murder victim is someone Dale Murphy had hired to track down his mother. Murphy dug up her remains night before last. Did it on his own, after a conversation he had with his father. Considering the circumstances, he suspected that his father may have had something to do with the investigator's murder, too, and he asked Chief Riley and Detective Robbins to accompany him on the visit."

"Doesn't sound like the kind of information you should be knowing about. Seems this town's chief should learn a little discretion with her pillow talk."

Something in me wants to get aggressive with the man. I want to point out that he would have been there too if he hadn't been such a sexist asshole. I have to stop myself from poking him in the chest to accentuate my point.

"The fact of the matter," I say, fighting to keep my voice from being too loud, "is if something in the man broke, the only thing you can blame it on is his own unfortunate life."

Detective Campden gives me a hard look. I return it, holding my ground, refusing to back down. Finally, he breaks eye contact, turning his head to spit.

"Guess you're right. That's a lot for any man to deal with."

Before I can respond, a motorcade of pickup trucks comes into sight down the road.

"What the hell?" Campden heaves a deep sigh.

"Must be the reserve officers. Chief Riley said she was going to bring them in on this," Robbins explains.

"Did she, now?"

We watch in silence as the pickups pull off to the sides of the road, rowdy men hopping out, joking loudly. They proceed to suit up, pulling leaf-patterned sweatshirts on and tightening the laces on their boots. Campden heads off to meet them, Robbins and I following close behind. I recognize Chet, the guy from the gas station, as he unlatches the tailgate on his truck and slides a long, black trunk to the end.

"Chief here yet?" Chet asks.

"Nope." Campden stretches to peer into the bed of the truck. He watches with interest as a couple of the guys strap on knives. "Looks like you fellas are getting ready to do some hunting."

The guy who sold me my lawnmower at the local hardware store grins. I think his name is Frank. His teeth are widely spaced and stained dark, nicotine brown. "That's what we got on our hands, ain't it? A manhunt?"

"The Chief tell you that?" the detective asks.

"Naw, Sue said there were some missing people you all needed help finding. She had us bring the arms locker so we figured they must be dangerous types."

"Did she mention that one of them was Dale Murphy?"

Frank exchanges looks with a couple of his buddies and then snickers. "No shit? Ole Murph went off the deep end? What happened, he figure out those boys Alma has him raising ain't his?"

A chorus of chuckles erupts. Campden turns and gives me and Robbins a look that plainly says these guys are a bad idea.

Chet unlocks the arms locker and flips the lid. Grabs a clipboard from inside, logging names next to the numbers corresponding to those etched into the butt of the sidearms, as the men start arming themselves. Robbins grabs one and hands it to me.

"You ever handled a gun before? You know what you're doing?" Frank's grinning at me with his scummy teeth.

"Yeah."

"You sure? Cause shooting a real gun is a lot different than that pop gun daddy let you play with when you were a little cowboy."

These morons are starting to give me the creeps. Part of me wants to remind the guy that it's his buddy that we're arming up to find. The other part knows better than to bother. I just want to find Heather.

"Yeah, I know. I've done it before." I drop the clip, check to make sure it's loaded, and then pull back the slide, chambering a round.

"'Course, you got yourself a woman who can take care of the dirty work for you. Maybe we should just find you a nice stick. You really shouldn't carry a gun unless you're prepared to use it. Shooting a man is a lot different than squishing a bug on your kitchen floor."

Frank and all his pals grin at me, toothy and toothless smiles wide on their insipid faces. I notice that even Campden and Robbins are smirking. I know I shouldn't let them get to me, I know I should just keep my mouth shut and walk away, but I don't. I can't. Damn male pride.

"Yeah, I know. I've done that too." I turn and walk away, toward the house. I know I just exposed a chapter of my past that I've fought hard to keep under wraps in the years since I moved to Coyote Cove, but, strangely, I don't care. I just keep strutting away, head held high.

46

MAGGIE

There's a cluster of men wearing hunting fatigues loitering out front when Linda and I get to the McGillis house. I immediately regret the decision to have Sue call the reserve officers, but we'll be able to cover more ground, faster, with their help. Linda's nose wrinkles and I know she's not loving the situation either.

"It's not too late for you to leave."

I hold the car keys out to her, let them dangle in the air like a fishing lure.

"No, I'm coming."

There's nothing I can do but sigh and keep moving. The men turn when they catch sight of us and watch us approach. A few nod, a few say, "Chief." Lou Campden looks at me like he smells something bad. I try not to roll my eyes as I look away. I don't see Steve anywhere.

"Thanks to everyone for coming. I want to do this the quickest and safest way possible. We'll spread out and do a line search. Know who is on your left, who's on your right, and keep them in sight at all times. We'll move at a pace that everyone can maintain. If you see anyone, radio it in. Please, don't approach anyone on your own. Guns are to remain holstered at all times unless there is an immediate threat of danger, which means a hostile gun is being aimed. Grab whatever you need, we leave in five."

As I turn to Robbins, I hear a can crack open behind me. I tense.

"It's soda," he assures me.

I nod. "Where's Steve?"

"He's waiting in the house."

I check the weapons locker that's open on the tailgate of a truck. Three guns remain inside. I take all three, scribbling my name next to their numbers on the sign-out sheet. Checking the first one, I pass it to Linda.

"Just in case."

She nods and tucks it into her waistband. I check the other two as I'm walking to the house. Lou jogs a few steps to catch up with me.

"That boy toy of yours doesn't look ex-military."

I'm annoyed by the term but ignore it.

"He's not."

"He was definitely never on the job."

That seems pretty obvious to me, too. Steve lacks the kind of dark, scarred quality that most cops seem to wear like a badge. What isn't obvious is Lou's interest.

"That's right."

"Hmm."

"Listen." I stop to face him. Linda and Robbins give us a wide berth and continue to the house. "We don't have time for games. What's this about?"

"He said he's shot a man before."

I'm shocked that Steve shared that much of his past. It's more than he's ever shared with me. Glancing back at the boisterous crowd around the truck, I can only guess what prompted the confession.

"Yes, that's right, too."

"Well?"

"Well, what? This isn't something you need to know the details about."

"Bullshit. We've got a potential hostage situation on our hands right now, and I need to be able to trust the people I'm heading out there with. Now, those boys back there, they're harmless, all talk. But I know a man admitting to the truth when I see it, and I saw it. So, please," the look on Lou's face is sincere, "it never has to go beyond the two of us."

As much as I want to deny it, I know that Lou has a valid point. I would expect the same courtesy from him. I tell myself that I'm not betraying Steve, that it's not something that needs to be kept a secret, even if it's something he's never been able to talk to me about. There's plenty I still haven't confided to Steve myself.

"His name is Steve Winters."

"Why does that sound familiar to me?"

I speak the headline that went national. "Botched Beemer Burglary in Boston?"

Recognition dawns behind Lou's dark eyes.

"He's the guy from that attempted carjacking? Some guy attacks him, pulls him out of his car, he shoots the perp with his own gun? A clear case of self-defense, all on security camera, only the carjacker ends up being just seventeen and the innocent citizen gets raked over the coals and dragged into court for a murder trial? That was him?"

His expression morphs into something different, a mix between disbelief and regret. He swallows hard, his Adam's apple straining against the thin skin of his throat.

His words are soft. His voice would be a whisper if a man like Lou Campden did such a thing. "He got a bum deal there. Did what any law-abiding American should have done. Next, the bleeding hearts will expect citizens to lie down and let themselves be killed so the criminals don't get arthritis in their trigger fingers from trying too hard."

"I'd appreciate it if you didn't say anything."

"Roger that. But I want you to know that I'm proud to be out there by his side."

Our tender moment lasts a nanosecond before we're jarred back to reality by the approaching whoops of our search team. I jog into the house to find Steve and Linda before we get going. Temporary truce with thorn-in-my-side Campden or not, I still have a really bad feeling about this.

47

HEATHER

I'm surprised when Mr. Murphy waves to me, and even more so when he smiles. I thought he hated me. I've never been able to stomach people being mad at me. Used to drive Momma crazy, the way I'd come up with lists of nice things I could do to make someone like me again. I'm so relieved that he isn't angry with me anymore that I don't think twice when he waves at me to come over. I wonder what he wants, but then I realize I don't really care. Anything to get me out of that house.

It's chilly out, and I instantly regret not bringing the sweat-shirt that Maggie let me borrow, but I'm already halfway across the yard before I remember it, and I figure we won't be too long out here. So I continue across the patchy grass and dirt to meet him, arms curled around myself, goose bumps raising the hair on my arms like I'm a cactus.

He doesn't say anything as I get closer. He doesn't wait for me, either. He steps over the low stone wall that runs along the back of the property and enters the woods.

I pause, looking back at the house. I really think I should tell someone where I'm going. But I don't see Maggie or her friend Linda anymore, which is strange.

When I turn, Mr. Murphy has stopped. He smiles again as he gestures for me to follow. Maybe Maggie and Linda are in the woods and he's taking me to them. I pick up my pace, climbing over the wall and walking through the trees after him.

He's moving too fast for me to catch up, but he stays within eyesight. Every ten feet or so he pauses and makes sure I'm still coming. My head starts to spin—I'm not sure what we're doing here, and I wonder if everything's all right. Mr. Murphy seems a little tense.

I've always liked Mr. Murphy. I've never had much experience with father figures. Momma never really let men hang out around the house when us kids were home, but sometimes Alma would come over or invite us to her place and Mr. Murphy always seemed to treat his boys real well. Sometimes he would help Momma out and make some repairs around the house. Now, though, this walk into the woods makes me think I might need to adjust my view of him.

It's getting darker and colder the deeper we go. I try to guess what time of day it is, whether the sun will be setting soon or not. I'm staring up, trying to see the sky through the leaves above, so I don't notice the fallen tree trunk in front of me until my foot catches it mid-step and I go flying through the air, landing on my stomach.

I'm not hurt, but something about the way I hit the ground knocked all the air out of me. I roll onto my side, trying to catch my breath. The sound of crunching leaves comes closer and then I'm staring at the toes of Mr. Murphy's scuffed boots. I'm relieved that he came back for me.

"I'm okay," I say, even though he didn't ask.

I push myself onto my knees and elbows, trying to get the strength to stand up, when I feel myself being lifted into the air. A strangled yelp escapes my mouth as he picks me up, one hand grabbing the back of my pants, the other the back of my shirt. I'm gasping for air as he sets me roughly on my feet. I stumble,

THE GIRL WHO LIED   173

trying to keep my balance, wiping at my eyes with the backs of my hands, trying to hide the tears that squeezed out.

When I look at him, he's a little blurry, so I wipe my eyes again. I wish I hadn't. His gaze is dark and narrowed and he's breathing heavy. His teeth are showing, but I don't think he's smiling. I take an involuntary step backward, shocked by his expression.

"I... I'm sorry. I didn't mean to."

He grunts in response. I don't know what it means.

"I'll be more careful. I promise."

He just keeps staring at me and now I wish I hadn't followed him into the woods. I wish I knew where we were going. I wish Maggie was here with me right now.

"I'm okay, we can keep going."

Mr. Murphy sets off again without a word. I scramble to keep up with him, doing my best to be careful and not trip again. His steps are loud in the otherwise silent woods. Something about the stillness around us makes me think that we're alone out here. I'm starting to worry.

48

MAGGIE

The reserve officers crash noisily through the woods, like they're trying to flush out their prey. I can't help but wonder if that's what we're doing—hunting. I mean, what is it exactly that we're expecting to happen? We find Murphy and Heather, and then what?

We have a happy reunion? Or a standoff?

I have no idea what to expect, especially after Lou filled me in on his meeting with Murphy's wife, Alma. Alma seems to think her husband has lost his mind. Taking off into the woods with Heather would certainly confirm that, but what if we have it all wrong?

What if Heather took off into the woods and Murphy followed her to keep her safe? What if they're not together? Or even in the woods? I'm driving myself crazy, more questions springing into my mind with each step.

I look around and see the same tension, the same uneasiness that I'm sure is clear on my own face. All these people from different backgrounds and we all jumped to the same conclusion. That's the thought that makes the wave of nausea in my stomach splash up into my throat. All those neurons in all those guts and they're all shouting the same message—that a teenage girl is in danger.

In a way it feels like Brandon all over again. My heart has already made the decision that Heather is family. I think even my brain is onboard. Maybe it's because we're both misfit daughters of disinterested parents. Or maybe it's that we've both had to face the loss of a younger sibling. I haven't had the down time to work out why I feel such a connection to her yet. Now I'm wondering if I'll ever get the chance.

Like with Brandon, I feel helpless. I feel like I failed in some way. I try so hard but it's just never enough and I can't understand why that is.

The memory of the day I lost my little brother is ingrained in my brain unlike anything else. I can recall the moment with such perfect clarity that it's more than just reliving it—I am literally transported through time and space to that exact second of my life. The beginning of the end.

It was my first day off after nine in a row on the job. I woke late. I'd thrown on an old UF t-shirt and a pair of jean shorts in anticipation of working in the garden after breakfast. I sat on the back porch, my knees pulled up, my toes curled around the wicker edge of the chair. My laptop played the morning news.

The breeze was gentle but warm, carrying the promise of a scorching day and the aroma of my new cinnamon-bun flavored coffee. My eyes were closed as I chewed a bite of English muffin, relishing the taste of the butter lathered into the nooks and crannies. I stopped chewing when I thought I heard the newscaster say my brother's name in her slightly clipped tone.

My eyes flew open and landed on my mother's tear-streaked face, the image grainy on the computer screen. The paper plate with my breakfast flew off my knees as I scrambled toward the laptop, grabbing it in an attempt to wrest the truth from it. My dad's face appeared next. I sprang from my seat and dashed inside to call my parents.

But no one answered.

They never returned my calls. They never spoke to me again. After their little boy was gone, they never again acknowledged that their little girl had ever existed.

Maybe they felt that, as a detective, I should have been able to do more. And I tried, I really did. But it wasn't my case. All the clout I usually had at the department was worthless. Everyone knew this one was personal. All the smiles and nods enraged me like a bull drawn to a red cloth. No one took me seriously.

What happened to Brandon became my obsession. I couldn't let it go. Even after I lost everything—my family, my career, my confidence in myself—I still couldn't drop it. And the truth is, I still haven't. And I never will, not until it's done, even if it means losing everything I have all over again.

That's where my mind is as we walk through the woods, searching for Heather and Murphy. My eyes tired and dry, my sinuses burning with tears left unshed. My chest tight with tension. A lump lodged in my throat that doubles as I see the freshly gouged wood on the tree trunk that lays across the path and the damp, mussed leaves on the other side where someone had fallen.

I can no longer keep a veil of denial drawn tight over my eyes. I can't keep telling myself that searching the woods is simply procedure. There is no longer any need to tell myself to stay calm when we find nothing, calmer still when I discover Heather waiting on my front doorstep when I get home, because that isn't going to happen.

Staring at the neon threads of Heather's friendship bracelet peeking out from beneath a pile of dead leaves, reality smacks me in the face like a 1980s soap-opera star. There's no denying the truth. Heather is out here, and she's in danger.

49

MURPHY

Murphy may not have thought things through very well. He doesn't have a plan, just some vague ideas blowing around inside his head like leaves in the wind. It's too late to change his mind, and he can't keep leading the girl deeper into the woods forever, so he knows he needs to work something out quickly.

He wonders if anyone has noticed they're missing yet, figures they probably have, that they're probably already on his trail, hiking into the woods looking for them. Maybe he should get rid of the girl. It would make the hike quicker, easier.

It would also destroy any leverage he has that he may need later. He listens to Heather thrashing through the brush behind him. She's disposable—he has no feelings about her survival other than how it can help him achieve his purpose.

But what is his purpose? Murphy still has no idea what he's hoping to achieve. He only knows that his father is being charged with a murder he didn't commit, and that he can't let that happen, although he isn't quite sure why. By all means, his father is a murderer who deserves to be punished.

Yet, Murphy is drawing some dangerous parallels between his father and himself. If his father is framed, one day he could be, too. On some level he realizes that his paranoia has grown beyond stable levels, that it's developing a life of its own and has become the driving factor behind his actions. He just doesn't care. Someone needs to pay for that PI's murder besides his father.

Murphy freezes as this insight dawns on him like the sun on a new day. That's it. What he wants is for someone else to confess to the crime his father is being wrongly charged with.

He turns his head to the side. A pair of worn sneakers stumble into view. The gray shoelaces are untied and the left one is fraying. He slowly lets his eyes travel upwards, skimming over the baggy jeans with dirty knees, the loose t-shirt, pale arms with the hair on end, a puffy face with pink, flushed cheeks.

This sloppy mess of a child is the only tool he has at his disposal. He watches her teeth chatter, her breath emitting little clouds of exhaust with each pant, feeling nothing other than satisfaction. If anyone cares about her welfare, they'd better be smart and give him what he wants.

50
MAGGIE

Knowing we're on Heather and Murphy's trail, we pick up the pace. I do my best to remain casual, to not betray the emotions welling up inside me, but I can't deny that for me this is more than just personal. This is my chance at redemption.

I glance over at Linda. She's the only one who knows how far off the deep end I went after losing Brandon. The only one who knows the lines I crossed, lines that almost got us both killed. Lines I'd gladly cross again. I wonder if she suspects how close I am to that same place right now.

Every step I take, every leaf that crunches under my foot is a promise to myself. I had sworn long ago that I would never let the tragedy of a child's loss strike so close to my heart again. I had refrained from having my own children, had avoided making friends with kids. I had shunned any connection of the type like an infectious disease. Until now.

And this time, I'm here, right in the middle of it. This is my jurisdiction. Whatever happens, it's on my shoulders. Any fault or blame will solely be my own.

There is only one way to survive this. Saving myself means

saving Heather. Two fates curiously intertwined. I'm a little concerned about how it's going to turn out.

Mr. Murphy stops and I'm finally able to catch up. He's giving
me a weird look as I stand beside him, trying to catch my breath.
Even though I'm freezing, I'm starting to sweat from the hike.

A wide smile spreads across his face. I grin back in relief.
Maybe he's just having a difficult day and needed a break.

"Are we going to stay here for a while?"

"Yes, we'll rest here. I need to concentrate on the plan if
we're going to win this game, anyways."

"Game?"

I didn't know we were playing a game, but the look on his
face means I'm just going to go along with whatever he says.

"Yep."

"Who are we playing against?"

"Chief Riley and the staties."

"What kind of game is it?"

Mr. Murphy's head cocks to the side as he looks at me. It
seems like he's taking a long time to answer. Then the corners of
his mouth twitch. He gives me a wink like we're co-conspirators.
He has no idea how deranged he looks.

"Have you ever heard of those murder mystery dinners?"

"Kind of like Clue?"

"Uh-huh."

"I've always wanted to go to one of those. I saw an ad for one that a tourist left in their room once, but Momma told me it would just be a waste of time."

"I knew I picked the right partner. You and me, we've got this in the bag." He taps his fist against my shoulder. "We are *so* going to trick everyone else and win this."

My insides squeeze, there's a twitch behind my eyelid. There's no one I trust more than Maggie, and I know that she wouldn't have suggested a game when she's just dug up all Momma's babies. I'm so scared, and so cold, but I know I have to play along. It's just me and Mr. Murphy out here, and if he wants me help him "win" then that's exactly what I plan to do.

"What do we get if we win?"

"Hot fudge sundaes."

"What do we have to do?"

"We have to act."

My smile disappears, my lower lip jutting out. I quickly tuck both my lips around my teeth inside my mouth.

"What's the matter?" His voice isn't angry, but it isn't happy anymore, either.

"I'm not good at acting." This *is* me acting. I'm so good, he doesn't even realize it.

Mr. Murphy nods slowly. "Then how about I do all the talking? You just act really scared and pretend I'm the bad guy. Do you think you can do that?"

I take a moment before I answer. "I can do it." I use my most serious, adult voice.

"That's a girl. I knew you could. Now give me a few minutes to think about how we're going to do this and then we'll get started."

I grin, but I don't feel anything but nerves. I'm going to play the best scared girl anyone's ever seen.

52
MAGGIE

The temperature has dropped so low that the chill manages to make its way through my thoughts. As soon as I register the stiffness of my icy fingers, I immediately wonder if Heather is warm enough. I'm betting she's not dressed for the weather. It seems like just one more straw of failure placed upon the stack on my back. I wonder at what point in my life I became unable to do anything right.

I shove my icy hands into my pants pockets. My fingertips brush against the woven threads of Heather's friendship bracelet. I tell myself that each step is bringing me closer to helping her, but my thoughts are playing devil's advocate.

Unbidden images of what could be happening to her right now keep intruding in my mind. I used to have a much better grip on my imagination. Now it runs wild like a cheetah through grasslands.

I do my best to focus on what's in front of me, here and now. The seriousness of the situation is etched clearly across my companions' faces. We've walked miles. It seems like it's been hours, but I refuse to check my watch. Confirming the length of time Heather has been gone will only make me feel worse.

When a child goes missing, a clock starts. Great strides have been made in the reduction of abductions each year, and, of those that do occur, the recovery rate has skyrocketed since the inception of the National Center for Missing and Exploited Children and its affiliated programs. Despite all this, there are ugly realities that cannot be denied.

Statistically, 76 percent of abducted children who are killed are dead within the first three hours. An overwhelming 89 percent of murdered kidnapping victims will be killed within the first twenty-four.

I've been trying to convince myself that this is all simply a misunderstanding. That Murphy just wasn't thinking clearly and that his intentions were misconstrued. With all the time that has passed, though, and the miles that we've covered, knowing that we're indeed on their trail, but that they are still moving away from us, is making it impossible for me to see the situation in a positive light.

A noise shatters the fragile glass of my thoughts. The banging is loud, echoing through the frigid air of the woods. I stop mid-step. A look down the line confirms that we've all frozen in place. The hammering repeats again and again. I break into a run and race deeper into the woods, praying that I'm not too late.

53

MURPHY

Murphy has found the perfect spot. Heather's legs are bound by his belt. He's put his jacket on her backward and knotted the arms tight around her so she can't free her limbs. Most remarkably, the girl believes it's a game and is having fun. He had to pull the collar of the jacket up to hide her face.

Using a fallen branch, he hits a tree over and over to draw his pursuers to the spot he's chosen for the showdown. The thick oak is half-rotted. He can stand within the cleft in its trunk and hold Heather in front of him. What Heather doesn't know yet is that the other hand will be holding his police-issued firearm to her head. They will have no choice but to meet his demands.

Between each beat of the branch he listens to the sounds of the woods. Stillness reigns between the throbs of his makeshift drum. He's shocked when Maggie makes it so close, seen before she's heard. The rest of the searchers lag behind, racing to join her.

Murphy lets the branch drop and pulls Heather in front of him. He removes his gun and aims it at her temple. He knows that Heather has seen the firearm when her frame goes rigid. He feeds off her fear, using it to fuel him.

"Murphy, don't. Please. You don't have to do this."

He's surprised by Maggie's voice. It's thick with desperation. He can hear the emotion barely constrained within the tone. It makes him feel powerful. He tightens his grip. Heather shudders with sobs under his hand. The kid has finally figured out that it isn't a game.

"Lieutenant Murphy, drop the weapon and put your hands in the air."

Murphy looks at Detective Campden from under lowered brows. He feels the corners of his mouth curling upward. The sound of his own laugh catches him off guard. Both of the staties have their weapons drawn and aimed at him. Heather whimpers, her trembling worsening.

"Come on, Murphy. Let's figure this out. What is it that we can do to make things better?"

He focuses his attention on Maggie. She has both hands empty and held in the air. She takes a step closer.

"Don't," he warns.

She freezes. Her eyes dart between his and Heather's.

"Talk to me." Her voice is calm now, smooth. She has a small, hopeful smile on her face. "What can I do to help?"

Murphy snorts and rolls his eyes. Heather flinches at the sound. He jerks her roughly back into place as his human shield.

"What I want—" he begins, surprised by the tone of his words. His voice sounds foreign, like it's not his own. Like it belongs to a madman. And maybe it does.

For the first time, he notices the expressions on the faces around him. He grew up and went to school with a lot of these guys. He's hunting buddies with almost all of them. He can't think with their judgmental stares focused on him. "I want all those guys to go away."

Maggie waves her reserve officers back.

"Wait! No. Don't leave. Walk out fifty paces and then lay down on the ground."

"Just do it," Maggie mutters to them. "Please."

She watches them start their retreat and then turns her focus back to him.

"Murphy. Dale. Can I come closer? Can we talk, just you and me?"

"No and no."

"Then help me out so I can help you. What's the next step?"

"The next step is for you to drop the charges against my father."

"I'm sorry. I don't think I can do that."

He moves the gun under Heather's chin and jabs it into the tender soft spot there.

"Dale, wait. You're a cop. You know I can't get an accused murderer released just because I ask. It's not that simple."

"Then get him released by doing your job and finding the real killer."

"Wait. I don't mean to intrude, but can I interject here?"

His head swivels toward Detective Robbins. Robbins holsters his weapon and holds both hands out to Murphy.

"I want to help you, Lieutenant, but I don't understand what's going on here. You said yourself that your dad was a murderer. You said he killed your mother."

"He did," Murphy says, exasperated. He lowers the gun from Heather's chin. "But he didn't kill Chase Gibbons."

"But how do you know that? You were there. You were the one who found all the evidence."

That's what has upset Murphy the most. That he was the one who caused this, same as if he'd killed the PI and framed his father himself. But he hadn't.

Someone else had known who Gibbons was. Someone else had known he was in town. The real murderer.

"All the evidence that was planted for me to find."

The words hang in the air, a fly luring the statie into the spider's web.

"What are you saying?"

"I'm saying, my dad was framed. I know he's a miserable old bastard who killed my mom and deserves to rot in hell. But he did not kill Chase Gibbons. Someone went to a lot of trouble to make it look like he did, though, and I'm not going to let it rest until I find out who and why."

"I hear what you're saying, and I understand. I promise that Detective Campden and I will do everything within our power to get to the bottom of this, but it's going to take some time. I need you to let the girl go."

"Bullshit!"

Murphy's roar rips through the woods like a crack of lightning. He grabs Heather by her hair and yanks her head back, holding the gun to the hollow in her throat. The whites of his eyes flash wildly. Heather's muffled cries carry over to the detectives.

"Wait, Murphy. It was me. I'm the one who framed your father. I'm sorry."

54

STEVE

I did *not* want to leave Maggie behind. Linda had given one feeble tug on my sleeve, looked at my face, and then been kind enough to let me make my own decision. The reserve officers, however, hadn't been as nice.

I couldn't make a fuss, couldn't risk causing a scene that might make the situation worse, but I also couldn't just turn around and leave the woman I love within shooting range of an unstable man with a gun. Chet and Frank each grabbed one of my arms and half-carried, half-dragged me toward where the others had gathered.

Realizing that we hadn't truly gone fifty paces, an idea begins to take shape in my mind like a boat drifting out of the fog. I lay on my belly among the leaves, the rich scent of dirt and decay stinging my nostrils, threatening to make me sneeze. I give one a small toss into the air and watched it float a short distance in front of me before it settles back to the ground.

"Any of you have a gun that can make the shot?"

My question is met with wide eyes and disbelieving stares, but I know I can't be the only one thinking it. These guys are hunters. They *like* to shoot things. It's what they do in their spare time for fun. And I'm the weird one?

"Steve, you've got to trust Maggie. She'll work it out, she always does. The best thing you can do to help is to let her concentrate on keeping safe instead of worrying about you."

I hear Linda's words, I see the validity in her reasoning, but for some reason it just doesn't sit right with me. Or anyone else. Apparently, wisdom from a woman isn't this group's favorite thing.

"Waste of time. That tiny statie will cap him before you can." Chet pokes at the brim of his hat with one finger. It settles back onto his head at an angle.

"Thirty says he'll do it in the next five minutes." Frank flashes his tarnished grin at the group.

"I'll match that, but say five to ten minutes. Give things time to heat up a little more." Chet bites his lower lip and wiggles his eyebrows at Frank.

"Fifty says the chief will do it. We all know she's got the biggest pair in town. Isn't that right?" Some chubby guy I don't know slaps his hand against my back.

This is the moment I realize that Linda is right. All I can do is sit tight and pray that everything goes well with whatever negotiations are taking place, because if these guys aren't kept out of the situation, someone will definitely get hurt.

55
MAGGIE

"I'm so sorry. I never meant for any of this to happen."

I feel every eye on me, boring deep into my flesh as I take a faltering step toward Murphy, then another. My hands are raised over my head. He's lowered the weapon away from Heather, holding it awkwardly, not sure where to point it. I take a third step forward, which is enough for him to swing the gun toward me.

"Maggie?"

"I'm sorry, Murph, I really am. I never meant to hurt you."

His expression changes like a slideshow—confusion, anger, disbelief, suspicion—finally settling on doubt.

"But how? Why?"

"Take me instead of Heather. I'll tell you everything you want to know."

"This isn't some game. You can't just tell me what you think I want to hear and have this all be over with." He turns the gun back on Heather. I've moved too fast.

"But it's true."

He makes a guttural noise of doubt and shakes his head.

"Yeah, right. Little miss super cop killed a guy and blamed my father. Do you really expect me to buy that?"

"Your dad is a sexist, good-for-nothing piece of shit. Who better to pin it on? Why wouldn't I choose him?"

This grabs his attention. I can tell by the way his head cocks slightly to the side that he's considering what I've said. I keep going while I have an edge.

"I realize the man is your dad, and I'm sorry about that. But I'm not sorry that I framed him. Maybe it's because you're too close to the case, maybe it's that he's the only parent you have left, but everyone in town knows what you've just figured out. Hell, when I moved here four years ago and first read the file on your background check, I knew. It was obvious. The personality type, the history of domestic violence—a man like your dad doesn't just let his wife leave. Not without repercussions."

The gun drops to Murphy's side. His other hand is still on Heather's arm, but the grip is weak, the purpose forgotten.

"So yeah, when I needed someone to pin a murder on, your dad seemed an ideal candidate, given his background as an actual killer."

His forehead furrows, his eyes shifting restlessly as the thoughts filter through his head. I take another step forward.

"But why? Why did you kill Chase Gibbons?"

I close my eyes and take a deep breath, channeling the strength and courage to continue. When I open them, the world seems duller, like I'm seeing everything from behind a curtain.

"Chase Gibbons is the reason I left my home and my family and my career and moved to this tiny corner of the country."

I move another step closer and lower myself onto a fallen log, sinking with defeat. I'm sideways now, Murphy to one side, the staties to my other. All eyes are on me, waiting for me to explain. It looks like Lou Campden's gun has shifted slightly away from Murphy's position, closer to mine.

"He murdered a kid. It was my case. All the evidence was

there, there was no doubt that he didn't do it, but he got off on a technicality. They let him go free."

I cover my face with my hands, elbows on my knees. Through my fingers I can see that Heather has slowly shifted away from Murphy. If she can manage to get just a little more to the side, I can risk a shot.

"He what? I don't understand."

"What's there to understand?" My hands drop from my face as I angrily spit the words in Murphy's direction. "He's a child killer. It was my job to make sure he got put away and didn't do it again, and I blew it. So when you *invited* him here, into this town, my town, what was I supposed to do? Just turn my cheek and let him walk away again? Pretend that I didn't know who he was and what he did?"

"I... I didn't know."

I have Murphy's complete attention now. Heather is leaning almost entirely to his side, her shoulder propped against the tree, her feet bound too tightly for her to move any further without hopping.

"That's right, you didn't know." I tear into Murphy with a verbal fury I didn't know I had. "But you do know that your dad is a murderer. That whatever he gets dealt is the justice he deserves. But you couldn't just leave well enough alone." I jump to my feet, facing Murphy. The weight of my gun is heavy on my hip.

"I couldn't let that bastard Gibbons go, knowing what he'd done. I couldn't live with myself if I'd done that. It was him or me. Everything would have been fine if you could've just left things alone, but you didn't. And now my life is ruined *again* by the same worthless bastard. But at least you finally get my job, huh?"

"No, wait. That's not what I wanted. Jesus. Maggie, I'm sorry."

Murphy's forgotten all about Heather. He leaves her against

the tree and starts walking toward me, hands out in supplication, the gun held loosely atop his right palm. Halfway to me he stops. His head turns from me to the staties, moving back and forth between us, seeming to realize his mistake. His grip tightens on the gun, the weapon turning in his hand toward me.

The crack shreds air, then flesh. My ears ring as I watch Murphy's knees buckle. He looks at me. His mouth opens and then shuts. His eyes move down, toward the hole ripped in his chest, before he slumps onto his side on the ground.

Detective Campden runs to the body to secure it. Detective Robbins runs to me. I know from the location of the wound that if Murphy isn't dead yet, he soon will be. I see Hal's lips moving, know he's speaking to me, but I can't hear him. I shake my head, point, and say, "Heather." I stand on shaky legs, leaving him speaking to air as I walk over to Murphy's limp form.

I ignore Detective Campden as I kneel beside Murphy. I take his hand in mine. It's lifeless.

He wasn't my friend, not exactly, but he was something. He deserved better than this. It's impossible to always keep the internal demons in check, especially if you're dealt a hand like me and Murphy. Eventually, the evil within manages to wrestle its way to the top and gain the advantage.

I've been lucky so far. I've always managed to get my sanity back before the demons have been loose too long. But who knows what the future holds?

By the time I stand, Steve is by my side. His arms wrap around me so tight that I can barely breathe. It feels good. Right. For a moment, I'm saddened that Murphy will never have a chance to feel this way. Then I push the thought from my mind and enjoy the comfort of the embrace while it lasts.

Over Steve's shoulder, I see Heather talking to Detective Robbins, hands gesturing energetically. She appears fine, although there's blood spattered across her cheek. Then again, I know more than most people that sometimes the worst damage done to you doesn't leave a physical trace.

Steve loosens his arms. Lou Campden's face is uncomfortably close. The man obviously has no qualms about intruding on our moment. I turn to him, keeping one arm wrapped around Steve.

"That was some quick thinking back there, Chief. You did a good job. I don't think this would have turned out as well as it did if it weren't for you."

I smile and nod. I know it wasn't easy for him to say that. But if he only knew the truth of it, he'd be singing a much different song.

56

HEATHER

The very second Maggie found us, and I heard her speak, I knew I was in far more danger than I'd imagined. There was something in her tone that I'd never heard before. Fear. For me. I had a brief moment where I was thrilled—she really cared about me! It was immediately followed by terror.

Mr. Murphy held the gun to me, jabbing me in different places while he talked to Maggie and the detectives. I smelled the sweat drifting off him in waves. I watched as he sent his friends away, wondering what that meant. That's when Maggie confessed.

She really is the smartest person I know. Her words might not have been exactly what Mr. Murphy wanted to hear, but it was enough to get his attention. I used the distraction to try and get out of the way, not that I could go far with his belt wrapped around my ankles, but I managed to clear the path of the guns aimed at him. I think he even forgot about me.

I was so worried that he would shoot Maggie. I don't think they could see his finger twitching on the trigger like I could. I prayed that one of the staties would shoot him. I stared at them, trying to send the thought into their minds. And then it happened.

The blood was hot when it hit me, hot and thick, like warmed maple syrup. I felt it on my face and neck. There was a glob caught in the eyelashes of my left eye. I tried not to blink. I did my best to ignore the coppery smell, to not think about what it was that heated my skin.

Even though I told myself not to, I looked at Mr. Murphy where he lay on the ground. I knew he would never be getting back up. I tried not to remember that I had prayed for this to happen, but I couldn't help but feel like I was a bit responsible.

Detective Robbins was the one who freed me from Mr. Murphy's belt and jacket. He asked me what had happened, how he'd gotten me out here. So I told him about the game, and about wanting to play along so we stayed on good terms. I told him how I knew as soon as they showed up and Maggie spoke that we weren't playing. I told him how scared I was.

He offers me a napkin out of his pocket to wipe my face. I take it, but then run over to Maggie to make sure she's okay before I get a chance to use it. Steve is hugging her, so I throw my arms around them both. If they mind, they don't say so.

When I pull back I feel bad and apologize because I've gotten some of the blood from my face onto Maggie's jacket. She tells me not to worry about it and takes the napkin from my fist and uses it to clean my cheek. For a moment I think she's going to spit on it like Momma used to, but she doesn't. I almost feel disappointed.

I look down and see Mr. Murphy's hand, limp and so very pale against the dried leaves. Maggie puts a gentle palm along my chin and uses it to turn my head away. That's when I realize I'm crying.

"I didn't mean for them to kill him. I just wanted them to shoot him before he could hurt you."

Maggie gives me what is probably the saddest smile I've ever seen.

"Oh, honey, this isn't your fault. Murphy was sick. He didn't really know what he was doing. If he did, he never would have hurt you or me."

"He used me to get you out here into the woods, didn't he?"

"I think…" Maggie takes me by the hand and squeezes, leading me away from the body, Steve on her other side. "I think he was very sad and very confused, and he didn't want to be alone, so he brought you with him. I think maybe he was so confused that the only idea he could come up with to make himself feel better was a very bad one. There's nothing you could have done to make this turn out any better than it did. You did the exact right thing."

"I did?"

"You did."

"It doesn't feel that way." I pause to look back over my shoulder at Murphy. Maggie gives my arm a soft tug, pulling me forward so I can't.

"That's because there was a sad outcome. But it would have been much sadder had you been hurt, too."

"I shouldn't have prayed that they'd shoot him. That was wrong."

Maggie stops. She looks at Steve and he nods and walks on ahead of us. She slides a hand around the back of my neck and leans her forehead against mine. This is probably the most comforting thing anyone has ever done to me in my life. When she speaks, Maggie's voice is such a soft whisper that I'm the only one who can hear her.

"Heather, I was praying they'd shoot him too."

I feel myself draw back a bit in surprise.

"You were?"

Maggie nods.

"Were you scared?"

She nods again. I can see the tears building in her bloodshot eyes, her lower lip quivering, and I know it's true.

"But you still did it? For me?"

I hug Maggie tighter than I've ever hugged anyone before, even Momma.

"What's going to happen to me, Maggie?"

She strokes the back of my head as my tears dampen the shoulder of her jacket.

"I don't know, sweetie. But I'm going to do everything in my power to make sure it's as good as you deserve."

I look at her for a long moment, this woman who has so much faith in me. Who risked herself for me, who has shown me kindness in a way that I haven't earned.

She pulls away and wipes the last of the tears from her eyes, puts an arm around my shoulder and steers me forward again, out of the woods. And I feel something I wasn't expecting. Something more than just relief.

57
STEVE

I don't want to let Maggie out of my sight. I try to give her some space to talk with Heather, but honestly it takes every iota of willpower I have to put ten feet of space between us.

When I heard the gunshot, my heart stopped. I've heard the phrase before. What they don't tell you, what you don't know unless you've experienced it yourself, is that it truly feels as if your heart ceases to beat. Your breath catches in your throat, your entire body goes rigid, and there's an odd stillness in your chest that threatens to linger until you find out what happened and determine whether you want to go on living or not.

Seeing Maggie standing there, pale and unsteady but alive —there's no way to describe the feeling I had. Every ounce of gratitude and relief I contain bubbled up inside me. My heart could go on beating.

I'm not exactly sure what happened, although I'm guessing tons of time will be spent going over every minuscule detail in the near future. What is clear is that Maggie is a hero. That she talked Murphy down long enough to get Heather out of his sights. I have a feeling she did that by putting herself in his sights instead, but I don't want to think about that just yet.

58

MAGGIE

I've kept the same fake smile plastered on my face all evening. It was there when we drove to the trading post and bought a couple of frozen pizzas for dinner. It stayed there when we walked the dogs while waiting for the pizza to cook. I wore it during dinner and for a brief bit of small talk afterwards.

I used it while saying goodbye to Linda as she left to return to her room at the Luxe Loon Bed and Breakfast in town for the night, before heading to Skowhegan in the morning. Now Heather is settled on the couch watching a movie, and I've used it to convince Steve that I'm well enough to be left alone long enough to take a shower.

I'm thankful for the door that separates me from the rest of the world. Like a shield in battle, it provides the protection I so badly need. For the first time ever, I turn the lock.

Standing in front of the bathroom mirror, my hands clutch the sides of the countertop in tight fists. The granite is cold and unyielding as I stare at my reflection, my lips still curled in a lie. Slowly, my frozen features begin to fall, melting like ice. My knees buckle. Sinking onto the side of the tub, I turn on the shower to drown out the sound of my sobs.

Tears flood down my face in a torrential downpour. Although I'm holding myself, I can't stop shaking, the tremors racking my body like seizures. Acid burns my throat, and though I fight against it as hard as I can, I find myself on my knees before the toilet, hot bile erupting like lava from a volcano.

When I'm spent, I lean back against the side of the tub, struggling to catch my breath. I pull my ponytail off the back of my sweaty neck and let the porcelain tub cool my skin. None of it makes me feel better. I'm not sure if there will ever be any feeling better, or just this new state of being, full of fake smiles that hide a hollowness that feels like it's rotting my core. Maybe I'm being dramatic, but maybe I'm not.

The world has changed forever. A new wrinkle has been etched into the surface of my brain. The image of Murphy's blood-leached face floats through my memory and I find my arms thrown around the toilet again. With each body-racking spasm I hope that the evil inside me will find its way out, but it remains firmly lodged where it is.

I pull myself up onto legs that feel foreign, shaky, and weak, like they belong to someone else. I shed my clothes like they're the skin of this other person, thinking maybe I can wash this unclean feeling off. Stepping into the shower, I pick up a bar of soap with a hand that looks too small and frail to be mine, and I wonder—will I ever feel like myself again? Or did a part of me die with Murphy?

59

HEATHER

I want to do something nice for Maggie. When I wake up, I hurry to get dressed and take the dogs out so I can get started. I've decided to make her breakfast. The problem is that the only breakfast I know how to make is a bowl of cereal. But that doesn't seem good enough. So, I'm considering eggs, because they go well with toast and I'm pretty sure I can make toast, when I hear the thud of car doors shutting from around the front of the house.

Fear surges through my body. Visitors never mean good news. I want to run and hide in the woods, but the dogs have already taken off around the side of the house and I feel that I have to protect them. I took them out, they're my responsibility. Reluctantly, I follow their path.

The detective who shot Lieutenant Murphy is crouched down, petting the dogs, a pair of paws propped up on each knee. The term traitor comes to mind, but I can't fault the dogs for taking his attention. And he might not be an enemy anymore. I'm not sure yet.

I look from him to the other detective to the powder-scented lady who's supposed to help me as I linger in the shadows at the corner of the house, watching them just kind of standing around like they don't know what to do with themselves. I think maybe that's a good thing.

The detective catches sight of me so now I have to join them. Detective Robbins is okay. He was real nice when he untied me yesterday. I remember noticing that he has the longest eyelashes. I cross over to him, giving the other detective as much space as I can.

"Morning, Heather. How are you feeling today?"

His voice is friendly, and I think that he really wants to know. His eyelashes are just as long and thick as I remembered. I notice little gold flecks in his brown eyes while he stares at me, waiting for an answer.

"Okay. Better."

"I'm glad to hear it. Is Maggie home?"

I know they know she's here, but I don't know what to do. I don't think she would like it if I let them in the house while she was asleep.

"She's still sleeping. She's real tired from yesterday, you know."

"I bet she is." He looks from me to the other detective and back. The smaller statie is still crouched down with the dogs, his back to us, but I can tell that he's listening to everything we're saying with those big ears of his.

"Heather, do you think you could go in there and wake her up for us? I hate to be rude, and I'd love to let her sleep, but we've got a lot to get done today and we're in a rush to do it."

I feel the eyes of the little old lady on me. It makes me nervous.

"Yeah, sure. I'll go get her."

I turn and jog around the side of the house before they can say anything else. When I reach the back, I call to the dogs. I listen for the jingle of the tags on their collars, so I know they're coming, then wait just inside, sliding the door shut and thumbing the lock as soon as they're through. I lower the security bar and pull the curtain closed, then lean against the thick glass like this will help keep them out.

I really don't want to wake Maggie and Steve, but I can't see any way around it. I trudge down the hall, stare at the closed door for a long moment before I tap against it. It's just my initial knock, the one where I practice and work up my nerve for a real knock, a louder one, but Maggie somehow hears it.

"Just a minute, Heather."

Maggie is either the world's lightest sleeper or she was already up. Only a minute passes before the door opens and she joins me in the hall. I stumble back at first sight, and then stare at my feet, trying to cover my reaction.

Her face is puffy and red, her eyes bloodshot, swollen, and darkly ringed. Her hair has dried funny, and I think she may smell like alcohol. I saw a character in a movie that looked like this once. She was a homeless person who had lost everyone she loved in a car wreck. I think it was on Lifetime.

"The staties are here with that lady who's supposed to help me."

I can tell by the emotions that ripple across Maggie's face that this is the last thing she wants to deal with right now. I feel real bad since it's my fault. They're only here because of me.

She blinks and her face returns to an expressionless shield. Then she smiles at me. I can tell she's acting, but she's doing a real good job of it. That smile could fool a lot of people. But not me.

"Oh, goody." Maggie takes a deep breath and sets off down the hall. "Have you eaten yet?" she asks me.

"Not yet."

"You want me to make you something really quick?"

I feel horrible because I was supposed to make her breakfast today. I shake my head and mumble, "Cereal."

She nods and sits on the bench by the door, tugging on her boots and lacing them up.

"Maggie? Is there anything you want me to do? To help?"

"Thanks for the offer, but it's probably best that I handle this."

I think that for a moment the smile she wears is real. Then she's standing and pulling her jacket on, and I know her expression's back to being a mask. I watch her disappear out the front door, wishing that there was something I could do. But there's not. So, instead, I feed the dogs, pour myself a bowl of cereal, and settle onto the couch in front of the morning TV.

60
MAGGIE

I pause at the door, taking a moment to prepare myself for what I'm about to face on the other side. I draw a deep breath, then swing it open. The first thing I see is Lou Campden's sourpuss face. Not exactly an ideal way to start the day.

"Morning, Chief. I'm sorry about waking you up so early. Wish I could have left you alone today, given you a break, but unfortunately we've got a lot to do to wrap things up and get out of your hair, and I need your help with some of them. I apologize."

Campden's tone is sincere, but he can't meet my eyes. I nod, fingering Steve's house keys in my jacket pocket.

"Why don't we head inside and get to work then."

"We'll have more privacy if we use Steve's place." I gesture toward the house across the street and walk in that direction. I stop when I realize no one is following me. I turn to look at them. I really don't want to let these people into my home, where I live my life and hide my secrets in the basement.

"He won't mind?"

"He'll mind less than having to be polite before he's had a cup of coffee."

The older woman with the detectives smiles. "I can understand that. And hopefully that means there'll be coffee fixings at his place, too?"

I give her a conspiratorial wink while trying to place the region of her slight southern lilt. "It's stronger than what I have."

"Fantastic."

She ignores the staties and walks beside me.

"Delores Johnson." She extends her hand.

"Maggie Riley."

We shake while walking. Her palm is soft, the skin fragile, but her grip is firm. I unlock the front door and let her inside, then lead the way to the kitchen. I have a pot of coffee brewing by the time the detectives join us. I wonder what they were privately discussing that took them so long.

"Chief Riley..."

"Maggie, please."

"Maggie." Delores smiles warmly. I can tell by the slight pinching around her eyes when she continues that she doesn't want to say the words she has to speak.

"I'm afraid the state has determined that Heather should be removed from her current situation."

Delores holds a hand up, asking me to be patient and hear her out. I'm so tired that I do. I busy myself pouring us each a mug of coffee while she speaks.

"I understand that you and Heather have formed an attachment. I find it commendable and must say that it warms my heart. In almost forty years of working for the Office of Child and Family Services, I can count on one hand the number of times an officer of the law has gone to the measures you have to help a child like Heather."

She covers my hand with her own and gives it a soft squeeze. "By opening your home, you've paved the way for the girl to form trust bonds. You have no idea just how much your actions have benefited her. But you aren't able to provide her with the environment she needs. We feel it's best that she be moved to a state-run halfway house for girls like her."

"What do you mean by 'girls like her?'"

"Special needs girls. Not necessarily problem teens. She won't be going into the criminal rehab system. She'll be entered in the life skills program. She'll learn how to take care of herself, handle her finances, how to budget, basic health and nutrition information. She'll also be provided with job training. The place where I've recommended Heather be sent to, it has an outstanding record of preparing girls like Heather for a success-ful, independent life."

There's really nothing she's said that I can argue with. It sounds ideal. It would be selfish of me to fight to keep Heather here, dependent on me, when she has the opportunity to learn to be self-sufficient.

"How long would she be allowed to stay?"

"The cut-off age for this program is twenty-one. Heather would have years to find her footing. When the time comes, she'll be assisted with finding affordable housing. Many of the girls end up living together for a while. Some even go to college."

"Would I be allowed to have contact with her?"

"Of course. Maggie, I understand that this is hard. And I want you to know that there is a *long* waiting list for this program. We're talking years. I've bumped Heather to the top because of her relationship with you. I feel that she will utilize the program and get all she can out of it. I believe Heather could have a very bright future."

I look at Robbins and Campden. Robbins shrugs.

"We've got nothing to do with this," Campden says. "Delores here called first dibs on your time this morning. Hal and I are just waiting for you two to settle your business before we get to our own."

I turn back to Delores and give her a long look. She holds my eyes. I search her face silently, then, with a heavy blink, I concede.

"May I be the one to tell Heather?"

"Of course, dear."

"When did you want to take her?"

Delores bites her lip and I know that means she wants to be on the road already. I consider my options.

"Will you guys be okay here on your own for a bit?"

Robbins looks at Campden before answering. "As long as there's still coffee in the pot, we're good."

Nodding, I stand. Delores jumps to her feet, impressively spry for an older woman. I follow in her powder-scented wake as she leads the way out of the house. As soon as the door is shut behind us, she turns to me and says, "I'm glad we have this moment alone. It might not be my place to say it, but those two are up to something. Been overly smug all morning. If you want my advice, don't trust them an inch."

I smile weakly as I reply, "I wouldn't even dream of it."

61

HEATHER

A door creaks open down the hall. I listen to the sound of bare feet slapping against the floor. A moment later, Steve stumbles into the living room in a groggy fog.

"Where's Maggie?" he yawns, stretching.

"She's with the staties. I think she took them to your place."

I watch his reaction carefully. His eyes flash wide for an instant, and then he seems to relax. Or pretends to, at least.

"How long have they been over there?" he calls from the kitchen.

I can hear him making coffee. I could have done that. That should have been what I did for them this morning. Oh well.

"I'm not sure. Maybe a half hour? A little less?"

I imagine him nodding in the kitchen, jaw tensed tight. I wonder what it is about the situation that upsets him the most—being left out or them being in his house. The rush of cereal hitting against ceramic is followed by the refrigerator door opening and closing. Silverware clinks as Steve grabs a spoon. A moment later he appears again, a bowl in one hand, a cup of coffee in the other.

"Any idea what's going on?"

"They had that old lady with them. The one who was here the other day. I'm guessing that they're here to take me away."

I stare at the TV, bright colors flashing before my eyes. I feel Steve studying me like I studied him a few minutes ago.

"How do you feel about that?" he asks.

I roll my answer around my head for a minute before I speak.

"Well, it's going to happen no matter how I feel about it, right? I might as well just go along with it. No use making it any worse."

My words seem to surprise him.

"Not that I wouldn't want to stay here with you and Maggie. That's what I want the most," I rush to say it in case he has any doubts. "I'm so grateful for everything you guys have done for me. Really. But I don't think that Maggie gets to make the decision on this. I wouldn't want to make things more difficult for her by being upset."

"You're very wise, has anyone ever told you that?"

I snort. "No."

"Well, it's true. You're a good person, Heather McGillis. I want you to remember that no matter what anyone else ever tells you."

I blink back the tears that have sprung into my leaky eyes. "Really?" I whisper.

"Do you really think Maggie would have let you in the house if you weren't? Much less let you stay here. Or touch her dogs. Maggie saw something in you, and I see it too. Promise me that you'll see it in yourself?"

"I promise."

I've just said the words when we hear the front door opening. Steve crosses over to me and holds out his hand. I stand and take it. The squeeze feels good, comforting. He's still holding my hand when Maggie comes in with the old lady in tow. I can tell by the looks on their faces that I was right.

I throw my arms around Maggie and hug her like I've never hugged before. I try to tell her with my embrace what my words cannot manage—that I love her, that I understand, and that if I had my choice I'd stay with her, but I know I can't. When I let her go, I turn to the old lady. A damp trail cuts through the layers of powder on her left cheek.

"Heather, this is Delores Johnson."

Maggie's voice wavers. Her hand settles on my shoulder. I lean my cheek against it briefly and then smile shyly at the older woman.

"It's nice to meet you, ma'am."

"Please, call me Delores. Or even Dee. I already have too many reminders of how old I am without my friends calling me ma'am."

Delores notices my raised eyebrows.

"Maybe I'm jumping the gun a little. But I've decided that I'd like to be your friend, Heather. If you're interested, that is. It's okay if you're not, we can maintain a business relationship if you're more comfortable with that."

I look at Maggie. Her eyes tell me that Delores is a person I can trust.

"I think I'd like to be friends." I manage to make my voice just loud enough to be heard.

Delores grins at me, a genuine smile, full of warmth. "That makes me really happy. I was just telling Maggie how much I hate to have to be the one to take you from here, but I think you'll like your new home."

Maggie nods. "Delores told me about the place you'll be staying. It sounds wonderful. She got you into a program that's all about teaching you the skills you need to be successful and independent."

I look at Maggie in surprise. She gives me an excited grin.

"But, I thought..." I thought I'd wind up in one of those places where they keep bad kids. The kind of place featured in made-for-TV movies where they don't let you have shoelaces, and the head mean girl takes all your stuff.

"Delores has confidence in you, Heather. We all do."

I know that this is true. I feel more support coming from the people in this room right now than I've ever felt before in all the previous years of my life put together. I actually feel hopeful about my future.

"I don't have much to bring with me, just my backpack."

"That's okay, dear. We'll get you everything you need."

I run to the room I've been staying in and grab my bag. When I get back, Delores holds her hand out to me. I throw my arms around Maggie and give her one last hug. Steve's palm closes over my shoulder as I do. I know I need to go quick, before any of us starts crying. Being strong is the least I can do to repay Maggie and Steve for their kindness. But I have something else in mind, too.

Looping an arm through the straps of my backpack, I bend down and give the dogs a cuddle, their soft tongues wiping away any sadness that I feel. Then I stand and take Delores's hand, let her lead me out to her car. I get in and buckle my seatbelt. Then I'm out of Maggie and Steve's lives as quickly as I came into them.

62

STEVE

"She's going to be fine."

I wrap my arms around Maggie and hold her tight, knowing this is just the start of what will be a very long day for her. She hugs me back. Her tears dampen my shirt.

"This is the best thing for her. We'd be selfish to keep her here."

"I know." Maggie's voice is muffled against my chest.

"It's just like she's going off to college, right?"

Maggie leans back and smiles at me. "Right."

"Is the program really as good as it sounds?"

"It is. It's all about teaching the kids job skills and what they'll need to know to take care of themselves. And Heather can stay there until she's twenty-one."

"See." I kiss Maggie on her forehead, her nose, her mouth. "Everything is going to work out just fine."

"Maybe."

"Are you worried about the staties?"

"Kind of."

"Do you think they're going to try and cause trouble?"

"Yes."

"Do you want me to go over there with you?"

"No."

"Then what can I do to help?"

Our eyes lock. There's an intensity between our gaze that I've never experienced before. I wonder what it is that has her so spooked. I wonder how much she knows. Her answer is one word, spoken with complete sincerity. It sends chills down my spine.

"Pray."

63

MAGGIE

I don't have the energy to explain my suspicions to Steve. It's best that he knows as little as possible, anyways. I give him one last kiss and head back across the street, trying not to look up the road where Delores Johnson's car has disappeared with Heather inside.

I enter the house as quietly as possible. When I get to the kitchen, the two detectives are sitting at the counter drinking coffee, just as I left them. If it weren't for their quick breathing and reluctance to make eye contact, I might have believed they'd been like that the whole time. Maybe, but probably not.

"So," Robbins's eyes skim mine, then shoot back to the mug in his hand. "Heather's all set?"

"She and Dolores are on the road to the halfway house where she'll be staying."

"I'm sorry. I know that must have been hard for you."

I shrug.

"Well, we all know it's for the best," Campden says. "And it'll free up our time for more pressing matters."

I dump my cold coffee in the sink and refill the mug. I add some milk and then settle across from the staties, looking at them expectantly, waiting for them to explain why they're here. Both men are still focused on their cups. The soft hum from the refrigerator is the only sound. With a sigh I make the first move.

"No offense, but I don't exactly have the patience to sit around all day while you two work up the nerve to say whatever it is you're here to say. So why don't one of you do us all a favor and speak?"

Robbins clears his throat loudly and looks at his partner. The two men exchange a glance before he turns to me. His mouth opens and closes. He looks down at his fingers as they drum on the countertop.

"For goodness' sake." Campden rolls his eyes. "Listen, Maggie. We've been talking about what happened yesterday, and we think we'd better take a closer look at the evidence against Jack Murphy before pressing charges. You see, our guys turned up some concerning stuff when they were tossing the vic's place."

I gesture for him to continue.

"Seems Chase Gibbons wasn't a real private investigator." He studies my face as he adds, "But he was a snoop. It looks like he made most of his cash by blackmailing people to keep their secrets quiet."

He looks at me like I should know where this is going.

"I'm sorry, Lou, but you're going to have to give me a bit more if you expect me to know what I have to do with any of this."

"He had piles of research on potential marks. Some of it was about you. And some was about Steve."

Now I see where this is heading. And though I suspect I know what his interest was in me, I have no idea what he had on Steve. I need to play this very carefully.

"So, you think maybe part of the reason he was in town was, to what? To dig up more dirt on us?"

"That seems likely, yeah."

"And maybe he blew his cover? Or tipped his hand? Tried to apply some pressure? Made one of us lose our temper, so we offed him? That seem likely to you as well?"

"That's not what we're saying, Maggie." Robbins has finally grown a pair and learned to talk. I'm not impressed.

"Really? Because I can't think of any other line of investigation you'd be pursuing by means of this conversation."

Campden huffs noisily and crosses his arms. "Cop to cop, you know we can't just ignore this information."

"Cop to cop, I know that you could have looked into it a bit on your own, first. That you didn't have to come running over here to what? Get a confession? I had no idea who the guy was or what he was up to. And Steve? A murderer? Yeah, right. Self-defense worked out for him so well he decided to give cold-blooded killing a try. I see that happening."

I lean against the back of my stool and cross my arms, regarding the men across from me with narrowed eyes and an amused grin. "What is it that this guy supposedly has on us that you think would be worth killing him over?"

Campden stares at the ground and stands. Robbins joins him.

"I think that maybe you should call a lawyer before we discuss that."

I can't help but laugh out loud. This seems to irritate them both.

"Yeah, that won't be necessary."

"Maggie, I really think—"

"Well, maybe that's the problem, Lou," I interrupt. "You know what they say about old dogs learning new tricks."

He looks like he just finished sucking on a lemon. I have to force myself to stay quiet, to not antagonize an easy target. But what I really want to do is sink my teeth in and draw blood.

Robbins puts a hand on Campden's arm to silence his reply. "Do you waive your right to an attorney?" he asks.

"I do."

"Mr. Gibbons's research suggested that you were responsible for a string of felonies back in Florida. He had some pretty serious charges listed."

I flinch as if slapped, not believing what I've just heard.

"You know that's crap," I say. "Completely unfounded."

"We understand that the allegations are very serious." He tugs at his collar like it's too tight.

"This is ridiculous." I've found my voice now, and it's growing harder and louder with each syllable I utter. "So, what? You're going to investigate me based on some lowlife's suppositions?"

"Yes. And we expect your complete cooperation, or we'll be forced to charge you."

"With what?" I really can't believe what's going on. It seems like a bad joke on a prank show.

"With murder."

I jerk back, unable to believe what I just heard. "Based on?"

"Based on the confession two state detectives personally heard you give yesterday."

My mind races, flying over the events of the past week. My wheels screech to a halt with the memory, out in the woods with Murphy—a desperate man holding a gun to the head of a teenage girl. A cop doing whatever she had to do, saying whatever she had to say to talk the distraught man down and keep the worst possible outcome from becoming a reality.

It was obviously a lie. They wouldn't dare leverage that to their advantage. But, apparently, they are.

64
STEVE

I can't take it anymore. The waiting, the suspense, the worry—I've had enough. Even though I know that Maggie will be upset with me, I walk across the street to join her discussion with the staties. It's my house, after all.

When I get there and go inside, it's completely silent. There's a tension in the air, kind of like static electricity during a thunderstorm, and I know I'm walking into a battle. Something bad is happening here.

I reach the kitchen and find Maggie sitting across from the detectives. Her eyes fly to my face and my gut clenches. What I see in those wide blue orbs is something I've never seen there before. Fear radiates from her like heat from the sun.

Instantly, I'm enraged. It's like some primal man switch has been flicked and my sole purpose is to protect my woman. In the back of my mind, I imagine the laugh Maggie would have if I told her that. In the front, I'm calculating how to best handle the situation.

"Lou, Hal," I nod. They refuse to meet my eyes. The hairs on my arms rise like a primitive signal of danger. I take a seat beside Maggie and find her hand under the counter. "What's going on?"

"The detectives were just explaining to me how the man I found dead was a known blackmailer and had been conducting research on both of us, most likely with extortion in mind."

I feel my jaw drop. I'm working on closing my mouth when Maggie's next words cause every muscle in my body to go limp.

"They've decided to investigate me. If I don't comply with their investigation, they're going to charge me with homicide, based on what I said to Murphy yesterday while trying to defuse the situation and get Heather away from him safely."

Moving my head to face the detectives feels like fighting through quicksand. It takes all the strength I have.

"We don't want to do that," Campden says defensively. "But we do have to investigate this. It'll go a lot quicker if we don't have to wait for warrants."

"Then what the hell are you waiting for?" Maggie snaps.

I want to tell her to calm down, to not make this any worse than it already is, but I can't blame her for being angry. She has them fixed in a poisonous glare. She points toward the door.

"Go on. Search my house. Do whatever it is you have to do to get this over with, then get the hell out of my town so I don't have to look at you anymore."

"Maggie, this isn't personal."

"The hell it isn't."

I watch their backs as they leave. Maggie scrapes the stool against the floor as she gets up to follow them. I grab her arm to stop her, not trusting my legs to hold me yet. I give her a look to let her know I need to talk with her before she chases them down. Nodding, she tiptoes silently down the hall, and peeks around the corner. She turns to me.

"They're gone."

65

MAGGIE

I can't even begin to imagine what Steve is thinking about all this. I can't imagine what it is that he has to say. I'm more than a little afraid to find out. I debate staying where I am, one eye firmly fixed on the door, half of my muscles already bunched up ready to bolt through it, but I decide to join Steve back in the kitchen so we can talk face to face.

He takes my hand in his. His eyes search mine. I'm not sure what he's hoping to find. Or not find.

I draw a deep breath, focusing my efforts on fortifying my muscles. Strong body, strong mind. I hope.

"Are you mad at me?" he asks.

"What?"

I have to fight the urge to laugh, which I'm sure would no doubt sound a bit maniacal given the current situation.

"That I came over? Are you mad?"

"No." I lean forward, touching my forehead to his. "Not at all. You had perfect timing. If you hadn't shown up, well, you probably saved me from committing an actual murder."

"Good. Remember that."

"Why?"

I don't understand why Steve is acting so weird. As much as I don't want to, I know I need to head across the street and keep an eye on the detectives. I need to try and limit their snooping, and my presence is probably the only thing to keep them from tossing the place.

"I moved your boxes from the basement."

I don't know whether to kiss him or shake him.

"Where?"

"They're in the trunk of my car right now. What's in them—it's none of their business. And I just got the strangest feeling, sitting over there, all alone. My gut told me to do it."

I decide to go with the kiss. Then I pull Steve to his feet.

"Come on, I still want to keep an eye on them."

I've already got the front door open when my memory jogs.

"The guy was researching you, too. They didn't tell me about what. Is there anything that you need to move?"

I know by the way his eyes shift hard to the left that there's something he's hiding. It might not be physical evidence, but there's something that he doesn't want me to know. Then I remember that Steve has never shared his past with me. I only know his secret because I did a little detective work. I wonder if I stopped digging too early, if maybe there was something darker concealed in his closet.

Steve takes my hand in his, kisses my fingers, and then leads me out the door.

"Just more crap having to do with the shooting." He tilts his head and gives me a knowing look from under raised eyebrows.

"You're a cop. I knew you'd find out. That's why I never saw a point in telling you about it. You knew what I was running from, what a nightmare it was. But there were some details that could... complicate things. Some facts that were never made public. Or discovered at all."

I look at Steve as if seeing him for the first time and wonder if I really know the man who holds my hand in his, or if he's truly a stranger. Then I realize that it doesn't really matter. We're both in a deep pile of shit and the only silver lining is that we're in it together.

We cross the road and stand on my front doorstep. My free hand is on the knob. He nods, signaling that he's ready, and I give it a turn.

I keep a tight grip on his hand and pull him into the house behind me. The dogs greet us, slightly frantic. We follow them to the door in the hall that leads to the basement. I might have known that the detectives would head there first. I hear a metal-on-concrete sound and the image of a shovel pops into my mind. Dropping Steve's hand, I run down the steps as fast as I can.

Robbins looks at me. He has a length of pipe in his hand that would explain the noise. Campden is crouched down, inspecting the floor.

"You have some work done in here recently?" Campden asks over his shoulder.

"A pipe burst the same day you guys came into town."

He stands. If I had to guess, I'd say the look on his face could best be described as triumphant.

"That so?"

"Yes."

"Convenient timing."

"Well, I suppose you could say that. I was with you when it happened. Steve noticed and called the plumber out. They had it all patched up by the time I got home."

His expression sags.

"You got the number of the plumber who can corroborate that?"

"Sure do."

The sound of Steve's voice from the stairs startles me.

"You can see it here in my call log, along with the date and time." He holds the phone out.

Robbins crosses to him and takes a long look at the display.

He pulls his own phone out, types in the number and heads up the stairs to make the call. I can't believe that they're going to such lengths, that they're seriously investigating us for the murder of Chase Gibbons. It's like being in an episode of one of those old shows, *The Twilight Zone* or *Night Gallery*, except a part of me feels like I deserve this, that I've brought it on myself. Because in a way, I do, and I have.

I join Steve by the stairs. There's no use watching them rifle through my belongings, looking for something to link me to the murder of a man I never met or the crimes he planned to accuse me of. It's too upsetting. I need to keep myself calm, distracted. As odd as the idea seems, I know I should eat.

"I'm going to grab some breakfast."

As low as I say it, I can tell by the tilt of his head that Campden has somehow heard. It must be those satellite dish ears of his. Steve puts his hand on my back.

"I'll go with you."

I've dragged my exhausted body halfway up the stairs when Campden says, "I'm done here for now. Mr. Winters, I'm afraid I'm going to have to ask you to stay. I need to ask you a few questions. Alone."

A sinking feeling poisons my body, gravity weighing heavily over me. I haven't just brought this on myself. I've brought this on us both. And poor Steve is paying a steep price for loving me. Now he's just as deep in this mess as I am.

66

STEVE

It wasn't so much Detective Campden's words or tone that upset me. It was the look on Maggie's face, like I'd just been sentenced to death, and she was forced to sit and watch. For a moment I wonder what she knows—maybe something I don't, or maybe what I do and hope she doesn't. Any of the possibilities that come to mind could cause that look. That's when I realize just how sticky this situation is.

I motion for her to continue up the stairs, for her to leave me alone with the detective. Tears glisten in her eyes. The knuckles on her hand that grasps the railing have gone white. She opens her mouth and I know she's going to try to insist on staying for my interrogation, so I speak first.

"Go on, Maggie. Go get something to eat. I'll be up as soon as we're done here."

I smile, do my best to make it a reassuring one. She nods reluctantly, unable to deny my request despite her misgivings. It might mean leaving me with a bully who can arrest me, but it also means leaving me with my dignity as a man. We both know it will be easier for me to answer his questions without her around to hear the answers. I wait until the door has closed after her at the top of the stairs, and then I turn my attention to Detective Campden.

"Where would you like me to start?" he asks.

It seems a pretty odd question. I have a feeling that he's trying to trap me in some way. Give me enough rope to see if I'll hang myself. I'm not taking the bait.

"How about with whatever it is you need to ask me?"

I don't think he likes my tone, but I really don't give a damn.

"What do you think it is?" he asks. "That I want to talk to you about?"

I really don't have the patience to play games. I sit down on the steps, lean my back against the wall, shrug and cross my arms. He waits a long minute until he's sure I'm not going to break and fill the silence with guilty ramblings.

"The victim, Gibbons, he did a lot of digging in his spare time. Had a whole slew of people he was blackmailing."

I feel those squinty eyes staring hard at my face, gauging my reaction. The only problem for him is that I don't react. I raise my shoulders a little, shake my head, furrow my brow like I have no idea why he's telling me this. "But you're not investigating any of them? Just me and Maggie?"

"He had some interesting thoughts about you. About the case you were involved with in Boston."

I sigh loudly to let Campden know that this is a subject that had been beat to death long before he arrived on the scene. But also, it's with relief. Because if that's what this is about, then my real secret, the dark one that wakes me up at night, tangled in sheets soaked with sweat and guilt, is still safe.

"So what spin was he planning to try? That I planned the whole thing? That I knew the kid was looking to carjack someone, so I stopped at a red light to bait him? That as the adult I'm a bad person for defending myself, for not letting the kid shoot me? That I knew the traffic camera was filming everything, so I used the opportunity to make a statement? I could go on, if you'd like, with the hundreds of theories that have already been proposed, but it would be a lot quicker if you'd fill me in on the one that you've chosen to buy into."

"Actually, I believe that Mr. Gibbons's theory was new. He proposed that you were the one to introduce the gun into the equation, not the kid."

That one is new. I do my best to cover my surprise.

"It's all on video. Have you watched the tape?"

"Not until this morning. You see, Mr. Gibbons's notes were very explicit. He wrote that the gun never appeared until after you returned to the car. I looked for myself and found that Gibbons's description was accurate. The kid's hands are empty when he pulls you from the car. You punch him, return to your vehicle, but he follows you, grabs you before you're completely inside. Hauls you back out."

His eyes narrow on mine. "There's a two-second period when both the kid's hands and your hands are in the car, hidden from the recording. It's during that time that the gun comes into play. Could have come from him, could have come from you. Or it could have come from your girlfriend in the passenger seat."

I don't like where this is headed. Nothing good can come from this conversation, so I decide to bring it to an end.

"Detective Campden, I hear what you're saying. Please understand that I am trying to be patient, but this case was closed *years* ago, and I don't understand why people want to keep rehashing the worst event of my life when the fact remains that what happened in Boston was self-defense. I stood trial and was found not guilty. I can't be charged with the same crime again. So, unless you have something else you'd like to discuss, I'd like you to stop wasting my time."

"Okay. Why were you paying Jack Murphy $500 a month?"

The lights in the room seemed to have dimmed and the walls are skewed at odd angles. It takes me a second to realize that I'm on the verge of passing out. I concentrate on my breathing and focus on his tiny figure. When I feel a bit more normalized, I say, "Excuse me?" My voice is shakier than I'd prefer, but at least I'm still conscious.

"Mr. Gibbons had proof that you were paying Jack Murphy $500 a month. He was trying to figure out what for. And, to be honest, I'd like to know, too."

Adrenaline gushes through my body like floodwater through a storm drain. I'm drenched in sweat. But I'm also sure that he's bluffing about the proof, so I force out a little laugh.

"Had proof, or wrote that he had proof? There's a big difference, Detective."

I feel a small jolt of victory as he fumbles to plan his next move in the game. He must have been betting that I'd lose my wits with the accusation, that I'd try to defend myself instead of parrying the allegation. I seize the opportunity his silence presents and run with it.

"I understand that you have a job to do, Detective, but I need you to understand that I've been sentenced to a lifetime of persecution for something that I regret very deeply, but could not have avoided, and that was not my fault. I've not only been judged by a jury of my peers, I'll be judged by every single person I meet for the rest of my life who connects my name with that incident. Unfortunately, the world is filled with vultures waiting to pick their piece of meat off the bones of a tragedy. It sounds like Mr. Gibbons was one of them."

I pause, give him a chance to agree with me. He doesn't.

"All I want is to live my life in peace. I've done my best to keep a low profile and prevent the people in this town from knowing who I am. If, for some reason, this were to get out, say because you were openly investigating some criminal whack-job's unfounded theories about me, I'd be forced to get my lawyers involved. I find it ironic that the system you have sworn to uphold is failing me because of people like you."

He clears his throat and pulls at his collar.

"Are we done here?"

His eyes cast up, searching his mind for the answer.

"For now. I'm guessing that I don't need to tell you not to leave town, Mr. Winters?"

"Where would I go?"

I stand. It takes all my self-control to walk up the stairs instead of racing from the basement like the devil himself is after me. I need to tell Maggie about this. And hope she believes my explanation.

Because over the last three years, I've paid Jack Murphy over $15,000, and I'm pretty sure that if the staties manage to prove that fact, that it will make me look very, very guilty. Perhaps even guilty enough for them to dig up the real reason I paid Jack Murphy's demand for blackmail.

67

MAGGIE

The door closes behind me before I realize my mistake. Getting me and Steve in different rooms was part of the plan. I know this as soon as I see Hal sitting at the counter, waiting. I force myself to close the distance between us, settle onto the stool next to him and wait for him to begin.

"I want you to know that neither Lou nor I want to do this, Maggie. If there was any way we could avoid putting you in the hot seat like this, we would. But the notes Gibbons had on you? It makes you look bad. Real bad."

He stares at me, waiting for something—me to defend myself, I guess. I throw my hands up in the air and shrug.

"I don't know what you want me to say. I have no idea what the guy wrote about me."

"Well, for starters, why don't you tell me why you moved here?"

"I don't know. Because I needed to start over in a new place? Because no one knew me up here? But mainly because it's where I was able to get a job."

"What do you mean?"

I've rehearsed these lines enough times, but this is the first time I've actually used them. Here's hoping it's believable.

"My little 'break' wasn't exactly a secret in the forensic community, Hal. All my friends, every connection I had made over the years, knew what happened. There's not exactly a huge pool of opportunity for cops who derail."

I run my hands through my hair. There's more to this story, much more than what anyone who wasn't there could possibly know. Like my true intentions for moving across the country, where I lie in wait like a spider for the right opportunity to present itself.

"The detective who drew my brother's case was bungling it. I couldn't just stand by and watch."

I pinch the bridge of my nose, trying to relieve some of the tension that's building inside my head.

"You disobeyed direct orders and performed your own investigation. You used your status as a police officer to conduct unapproved interviews and searches. Seizures."

"I had nothing left to lose by then. I had already lost everything. At that point, I didn't give a damn about my career. Hell, I was getting ready to take a job as a rent-a-cop at the mall when I got a call about the application I had put in up here."

He shifts noisily on his stool and clears his throat. I look at him, which seems to be what he was trying for. Eye contact—it's a very important tool of the detective trade. I know he'll be watching closely for my reaction when he says his next piece.

"You're aware that you would lose your position here if anyone revealed what Gibbons had found out about your past, don't you?"

I swallow hard, feeling ill. There's a hollow ache in the pit of my stomach that I've only experienced a few times before. None of them good.

Because it isn't only my job that now hangs in Campden

and Robbins's hands. It's my long game, the retribution that I've spent the last four years working toward.

I slowly nod my head, eyes frozen on his face, searching for a hint, a clue to his intentions. I seem to have lost control over some of my motor functions. Blinking, swallowing, breathing.

"Hal, I had no idea Gibbons even existed, much less that he was looking into my past. Honest." The words sound choked, breathless.

"And there's no chance of me and Lou finding anything here that might suggest otherwise? Something that would force us to share what Gibbons had discovered?"

An image of the evidence box from the basement pops into my mind's eye and I draw a sigh of relief. My secret is safe. For now.

I'm overwhelmed with emotions. Love and gratitude for Steve are topping the list. Knowing that the box is not in my house, that the dirty little secret concealed within is momentarily safe from prying eyes, gives me the confidence I need. I clear my throat and say in a loud, strong voice, "Go ahead and look, Detective. You won't find anything here."

68

STEVE

Reunited with Maggie, I can tell that Detective Robbins was grilling her while Campden was interrogating me. We cling to each other like a raft in a raging river. We are the other's salvation. I know that now. I think I must have always known. The world threw us together for a reason, and this is it.

The detectives stand on either side of us, playing with their phones. It takes me longer than I care to admit before I realize that they're texting each other in our kitchen. Apparently, they can't discuss the situation in front of us.

Maggie gives my hand a reassuring squeeze. I know she would tell me this is just another ploy to make us sweat. I hate to say that it's working. Finally, Campden looks up from the screen of his iPhone.

"We've got to touch base with the lab about a few things. In the meantime, we'll need you both to remain in town."

With that, the two state detectives leave. No threats, no drama, just an anticlimactic retreat out the front door to their car. I can't say that I'm sad to see them go, but I guess I expected more. It just seems so... unfinished.

Maggie collapses against me and we stand in the kitchen, holding each other for a good five minutes, until the dogs start pawing at us to let them join in. Maggie kneels and rubs their heads. I squat and run my fingers through their wiry hair, struck by the silence. This is it—my family. This is what I have and I'm going to do everything I can to hold on to it.

"Maggie, I—"

"*Shh.*"

She puts her fingers to my lips, cutting me off. Taking me by the hands, she pulls me to my feet and leads me down the hall. I follow her into the bathroom. I feel like I'm watching a play as she locks the door behind us and turns on the shower. Some kind of drama, maybe. The mirror has fogged by the time Maggie turns to me.

"Are we taking a shower?"

I'm not sure what to think. Or how to feel. We were both just informed that we're murder suspects, and this is how she reacts? Not that it's not a great form of stress management, but this isn't the type of intimacy I had in mind. Then I notice the look she's giving me. I'm relieved to see that sexy shower time isn't what she has in mind either.

She leans forward, her mouth close to my ear, and says, "I wouldn't put it past them to have bugged the house. So we can't say anything out there that might be... incriminating, until we're sure it's not."

Maggie pulls back and looks at me, worry creasing her brow. She's biting her lip. Her hands clench together, twisting each other absentmindedly. I suspect there's something she needs to tell me. But I need to make my confession first. That way, I won't feel guilty for lying when she bares her soul.

Reaching out, I tuck a strand of auburn hair behind her ear and give her what I hope is a comforting smile. "Is it safe to do that now? In here?"

She nods. I take her by the hand and sit on the edge of the tub. She joins me, the length of our thighs touching. I put my arm around her. She rests her head gently on my shoulder. This is the way it was meant to be.

"I've never told anyone this, but somehow that guy figured it out. It wasn't the kid's gun. It was Trista's. And it was unregistered. Illegal."

Maggie knows that Trista is my ex-girlfriend.

"When I went back into the car, she had pulled it out of her purse. She gave it to me. The video isn't clear."

"But you've been tried on the case. They can't charge you again, even if new evidence arises."

"That's true. But it might make other things I've done seem more suspicious. Like paying Jack Murphy $500 a month."

I feel her head flinch against my shoulder.

"About six months after I moved to town, his truck was pulled over on the side of the road. I saw that he was an old man, thought that he might be having car trouble, so I pulled over. Turns out he was waiting for someone." I lick my lips, take a deep breath, and start lying to the woman I love. "And that he was the only person in Coyote Cove to recognize me from the trial."

"He blackmailed you?"

I nod, then realize she can't see my head.

"Yes. A monthly payment or he'd tell everyone who I was. I just wanted to keep my fresh start. My anonymity. I didn't want to be that guy who got those looks again. So I paid him. A cash withdrawal every month, left in an envelope in the hollow log by the ditch at the end of his drive."

"And the staties know this?"

"Not exactly. Apparently, the payments were mentioned in the research Gibbons had compiled about me. If they checked my financial records, they could prove I made the withdrawals.

But I don't think they can prove who I gave the money to. Jack didn't have a bank account, so there wouldn't be any corresponding deposits. I don't know if he told anyone. Our deal was that he wouldn't."

"But Gibbons found out?"

"Yes."

"Hmm. Any idea how?"

"None at all."

She shifts her cheek against my arm.

"Still love me?"

Maggie turns so her chin is propped on my shoulder and says, "Of course. It's going to take a lot more than that to scare me off. But you may change your mind about me."

"Impossible."

I give her a squeeze and a kiss. She settles her cheek back against my bicep.

A tremor runs through her body. I look to see if she's crying, but I can't see her face.

"That box you have in the trunk of your car? It contains more evidence than just my brother's case. I... did some bad things. And I plan to do more."

Her use of the present tense hangs heavily between us. The water from the shower seems to pound harder against the silence.

My thoughts are jumbling as I consider what bad things she might be planning. It doesn't really matter, only it does. Or, at least, it should. But the bottom line is that I love this woman. Nothing is going to change that.

"What's in the box?"

I can tell by her expression that she doesn't want to answer the question. She looks down, away from me. "Just some research of my own."

"So as long as we get rid of the research, and they can't

prove that I was making payments to Jack Murphy, we're in the clear, right?"

Maggie leans back, her head tilted up so she can see my face. The smile that curves her lips fills me with peace. I fix this moment into my memory for safekeeping, just in case.

"I think we just might be."

69

MAGGIE

I know Steve lied to me. But I lied to him, too. And if his reasons are anywhere near as good as mine, I'm okay with that. Besides, now's not the time to worry about our mutual lack of honesty and what that might mean for our future. Not when the staties are still in town, breathing down our necks. And not while there's incriminating evidence still in a box in the trunk of Steve's car.

"I'm going to run up to the store, grab something for dinner," I say between bites of my sandwich. I give Steve a look, hoping he understands where I'm going with this.

"Do you want me to go with you?"

"Yeah, sure, if you want. I was going to stop at Margot's on the way back, just to let her know that Heather won't be returning to work. I want to tell her in person. It just seems wrong to deliver a message like that over the phone."

"Such a sweetheart," Steve says. His eyes ask me if this is about disposing of what I alluded to earlier. I respond with a barely perceptible nod.

"I try."

"I meant Margot, not you," Steve jokes. "You'll have to tell me where you want me if I come with you. That woman makes me so nervous I can never remember where to place my own feet when I'm around her."

"You can stay in the car. It'll give me an excuse for the stop to be quick."

"Glad to serve a purpose."

I get up, cross the room, and grab Steve's car keys from the hook. I can tell by the vein bulging from the middle of his forehead that he needs this to be over with as soon as possible. Especially if he's going to relax in a room that might be bugged. When we get back, I'm going to have to look online to see if there's any way to detect a listening device, or at least scramble one. I toss Steve the keys and he catches them one-handed.

"Then you can chauffeur, too."

"My pleasure."

I shove my wallet in my pocket and give the dogs a biscuit as we leave. On the walk to the car, I pull on my uniform bomber jacket. It offers a bit too much warmth for our weather today, but it has a set of inside pockets that will serve my purpose well.

Steve deflates as he settles into the driver's seat. He sits for a moment with his hands resting on the steering wheel, then his eyes widen, and he turns toward me.

"You don't think?"

I know he's asking me if I think the car is bugged or not. It seems unlikely, but I can't rule it out. I shrug and say, "Maybe." Even though I know that's not what he wants to hear.

He exhales loudly and starts the engine. I wish there was something I could say to make him feel better. I can't help but feel that all of this is my fault. Probably because it is.

We make the drive in silence, Steve concentrating on avoiding the wild turkeys that seem intent on dashing in front of the car, and me running over my plan in my head, trying to detect any flaws. We arrive much too quickly.

Even though it's the middle of the day, the lights in the store seem too bright. A few people mill around the trading post, mostly tourists looking for the perfect Maine keepsake. We veer to the right toward the groceries, walking so closely together that we keep bouncing off each other.

"Seafood?"

Steve nods at my suggestion. He heads to the counter while I make my way to the vegetables. I select a clump of asparagus, shove them into a plastic bag and grab a container of brownies as I pass through the bakery on my way to rejoin Steve. He's settled on a pair of salmon fillets and has moved on to the wine aisle at the back of the store. A bottle of red for him and white for me and we're ready to go, except for one detail of my plan.

"Why don't we grab a box of fire logs?"

Steve raises an eyebrow, but hands me the food and wine so he can grab the heavy box off the shelf and carry it to the checkout counter. We make small talk with the cashier, a girl around Heather's age named Tracy. Her sparkle nail polish catches the light as she scans our items and puts them in a bag. She runs my credit card and we're ready to head out of the store.

I know by the way Steve tenses, his jaw popping as it draws tight, that he sees what I do. I can't say that it's unexpected. I've been waiting for the detectives to show up.

They've done a poor job of concealing themselves behind the dumpster at the corner of the store, relying on the green netting that fences the area off to help hide them. It doesn't. But I pretend like I don't see them and continue to the car.

"Here, I'll open it."

Cradling the paper bag of groceries in one arm, I reach into Steve's pocket for the keys and push the button to open the trunk. It rises into the air before us as we approach. Steve gives me a nervous look.

"We'll put the box in the trunk, so it doesn't get the seat dirty. I'll make room."

Setting my bag on the ground I lean into the trunk, swipe the lid off of the evidence box and grab what I need to dispose of. I slip it into my inside-jacket pocket, then grab the toolbox, part of Steve's emergency car kit, and step back to where the detectives can see me holding it.

"There, now there's room."

I focus on Steve's eyes, finding the strength I need to smile and pretend I don't have my own ruination in my pocket. If the staties chose now to take me into custody—well, let's just say they'd have a reason to make some of their charges stick.

Steve smiles back, his relief evident. Because he doesn't know, not really. And he can't. Not now, possibly not ever.

I step aside so he can place the box of fire logs into the trunk. I pass him the roadside kit, watching as he puts it back and shuts the lid. Then I put my bag of groceries in the back seat and strap myself into the front.

"Good thinking about putting the box in the trunk," Steve says as he starts the car, maintaining the assumption of the car being bugged. "Last time the dye marked up the interior."

"I remember."

He ignores the detectives as he pulls out of the parking lot, heading toward Margot's. I see his eyes flick to the rearview and know the detectives must be following us. His smile grows bigger, more genuine. I wonder if it's in amusement or because he thinks we're getting closer to putting this whole mess behind us.

He pulls into the motel parking lot and parks in front of the office. I hop out, holding a finger up to signal one minute in case the detectives can see, and then duck inside. The office is uncomfortably hot. Margot dozes at the desk, snoring softly, like a cat purrs.

I slip past her into the restroom. Even though I close the door, I look over my shoulder to make sure I'm alone before lowering the lid on the toilet and stepping on it. Sliding one of the ancient ceiling tiles to the side, I empty my pockets piece by piece, carefully placing each item where I can reach them when I come back.

It makes me flush with guilt. Because I'd led Steve to believe that what I had was something I'd dispose of, like papers I could shred and flush. But I can't give this stuff up. Not until the job is done.

Less than two minutes pass before I'm back on the floor, flushing the toilet in case Margot is awake, lifting the lid so she doesn't know I was in here in case she isn't, washing my hands, and slipping back out into the office to find her still asleep.

"Margot?"

Crouching down, I put my hand on her shoulder and squeeze lightly.

"Margot?"

Her eyes flutter. Then they open wide, her gaze searing into mine as she bolts up in her chair, fully alert.

"Maggie."

She relaxes a little, her expression suspicious but her body at ease.

"I'm sorry to wake you. I was just passing by, and I wanted to let you know that Heather won't be returning to work. She's in state custody."

If Margot is surprised she doesn't show it. What I do see briefly pass across her weathered face is sorrow. She nods and fumbles for her pack of cigarettes.

I let my hand fall down to her forearm. "Is there anything I can do?"

"Nope." She averts her eyes, and I can tell she wants me to leave so she can experience her feelings in peace, without having another human watching. It's the exact reaction I predicted. "These things happen. Thanks for letting me know." Margot thumbs her nose and I know I'm being dismissed.

"You know I'm—"

"Yeah, I know." Margot waves me away. "It's not like it'll be that hard to find a new girl to do the cleaning. Unless you want the job? You'd best be on your way before I put you to work."

Even though Margot winks, I hurry to take her advice. Halfway out the door, I say, "Try to wait until next week before you have someone calling me on you, huh?"

I return her wink and know by the grin on Margot's face that the old girl is going to be just fine. Especially if the detectives stop to ask her about my visit. An opportunity to unleash a bit of her wrath always seems to make her day.

Steve's expectant expression greets me when I return to the car.

"Well? How'd it go?"

"I can't say she was happy to hear it, but she'll be okay. I think Margot may have been more attached to Heather than I thought."

"But we can go home now? No more errands?"

"We can go home now."

Steve looks so happy that I can't help but lean over and give him a kiss. He catches the back of my neck as I draw away to pull me in for another. For the first time in what feels like forever, I believe that everything is going to be okay. I can't wait to get home.

70

HEATHER

I like Delores. When I ask her to stop at a rest stop so that I can use the bathroom after we've been on the road for only an hour, she doesn't complain or ask me if I can hold it—she just smiles patiently and says, "Of course, dear."

That, and she got me into an awesome house just on the outskirts of Portland. The more she tells me about where I'll be staying and the program I'll be in, the better it sounds. I couldn't have hoped for a better deal. I was willing to do whatever it took to get out of Coyote Cove.

I feel like I owe a lot of this to Maggie and Steve. I've never had someone try to help me like they did before. A part of me almost wishes that I'd found them earlier, but I know it's better this way. Still, I feel like I owe them a lot, which is why I'm going to do what I'm doing now.

Delores stays in the car and lets me go by myself, which is a huge bonus. If she thinks that it's weird that I bring my backpack with me, she doesn't say so. She's probably used to kids not wanting to let the small bag that holds everything they own in the world out of their sight.

I fall in line behind a large family on the way inside. I catch the eyes of the younger girl and smile.

She can't be more than nine or ten, but her hair is already bleached with wide blonde streaks. She's tripping around in a pair of platform shoes even though her feet must be freezing, and she's clutching her oversized purse like it's her most prized possession—it's clear that she wants everyone to notice it. Instead of filing into a stall, she heads to the mirror to reapply her lip gloss. I go to the sink beside her to wash my hands.

"I love your purse."

Her eyes light up. She takes in my worn shoes and tattered backpack and is unable to find anything she likes of mine to return the compliment. I can tell she's reluctant to talk with me because of my appearance.

"I'm backpacking across the country. I had to leave all of my cute stuff at home."

"Really?"

This excuse seems to have done the trick.

"Uh-huh. I'm trying to leave something in the lost and found at a rest stop in every state."

"That's cool."

I can tell by her tone she doesn't really think so and that I'm losing her interest.

"Where are you from?"

"Jersey."

"Really? That's awesome! I don't suppose you'd want to help me out, would you?"

"Maybe."

Her expression tells me that I've got her circling the bait. I have to get my tug just right to snare her on the hook, and I have to do it fast.

"Could you leave something at a rest stop for me? I'd be so, so grateful, and if you give me your name, I'll put it on my blog and in the book I'm going to write when I'm done."

"Really? Do you have a pen?"

Mission accomplished. I begin digging in my bag. "Yeah, in here somewhere." I use the paper towel I was drying my hands with to withdraw a plastic-wrapped bundle, bound in layers of tape, and hand it to her while I dig around some more, finally producing a marker and a scrap of paper.

"I appreciate this so much, you have no idea. All you have to do is leave the package behind, exactly as it is, in the bathroom at one of your next stops. Somewhere other than Maine. But no peeking, because that would ruin my experiment. Can I trust you to do that?"

The little girl eagerly nods her head as she presses the paper and marker back into my hand. Her name is Pam.

"I put my cell number on there, too," Pam says. "In case you want to call me when you're done. Then I can tell you where I left it, or I can help you with the book, whatever you need. And I promise, I won't look. Honest."

Pam makes an imaginary X across her heart. I believe her.

"Thanks, Pam, you are so cool for doing this. I'll definitely call you. I can use all the help I can get with this."

A series of toilets flush, which is my cue to leave.

"You'll have to come on a couple of the stops of my book tour with me," I promise as I back out of the tiled room, giving Pam a thumbs up. The girl's eyes sparkle like it's Christmas morning. I hurry back to the car as fast as I can and give Delores a big smile.

"Thanks again for stopping, I really appreciate it."

Delores reaches over, giving my hand a pat.

"Of course. Now buckle up and we'll get this show back on the road."

I fasten my seatbelt and settle in, ready to be taken to my new life. Within moments, Delores has the car back on the highway. I watch the leafless branches of the maple trees blur with the evergreens as we speed by.

It's funny. I took only a pound or two out of my backpack, but it feels tons lighter. Maybe it's because I've repaid a debt, done what I can to help Maggie and Steve to thank them for their kindness to me. It was the least I could do, considering I was the one to blame for their troubles.

But that's all behind me now. It's time to focus on the future, because mine? It's actually starting to become something worth looking forward to.

71

MAGGIE

The morning light trespasses through a flip in the blinds, stretching its rays across the room to warm a stripe on my hand. I sigh deeply, satisfied, thankful for this new day and the hope that it brings. Steve groans softly beside me as he stretches and rolls onto his side. I cuddle up behind him, wrapping an arm around his waist, and bury my face against his back.

I'm not what you would call a morning person, but I enjoy the peace that can be found in the early hours, before the chaos and disaster of the day descends. The freshness of a new dawn always seems to hold so much promise. I know that I'll have to get up soon and walk the dogs, but I want to enjoy this moment for a little longer.

I listen as a pair of birds flirt with each other outside the window, chattering a song between them. A buzzing noise joins as a backbeat. It takes me a groggy minute to realize that it's my cell phone.

Instantly, the day around me transforms. The birds' music isn't as sweet, the sunlight loses its rosy glow, even the sheets on the bed aren't as soft. The air in the room is completely still. I realize both Steve and I are holding our breath.

Rolling over, I lift the phone from the nightstand, my stomach lurching as I read the caller ID. It's Detective Campden. Sitting, I pull my knees up in front of me and hug them to my chest as I answer the phone.

"Hello."

It's not a question. My voice is dull and emotionless. I say the word like it's a burden.

"Chief Riley, it's Lou Campden."

I don't respond. I have nothing to say. I shift the phone against my head, so he knows that I'm still on the line.

"Listen, I know that I'm the last person you probably want to hear from, but I'm calling to apologize. For everything."

"Okay."

I'm sure he can hear the doubt in my voice. The word even tastes suspicious as it makes its way through my mouth.

"I know that I can be a bit difficult to work with."

Understatement of the year.

"I've been doing this job a long time. Maybe too long. And I guess maybe I was a bit unfair toward you when I got here."

The line goes silent. If he's expecting me to pardon his behavior, he can keep waiting, because it's not going to happen. After an uncomfortably long minute, he clears his throat and continues.

"Maybe if I had handled the situation better, things would have turned out differently. Maybe your lieutenant would still be alive. I know it's of little comfort, but that's a thought that's going to be with me every day for the rest of my life."

He takes a deep breath and I wonder where he's going with all of this.

"I realize that I also handled the investigation into your affairs, and Mr. Winter's, the wrong way. I know you understand that I had to follow the lead, but I didn't have to treat you like you were criminals. I guess I kind of made up my mind that one of you was probably guilty, but I shouldn't have jumped to the conclusion. That's not what a good detective does."

Steve sits up and leans his head against mine. I hold the phone so we can both listen.

"Anyways, I just wanted to say that I'm sorry. Detective Robbins and I both are. The good news is that we're on our way back to Skowhegan now, so you won't have to deal with us anymore."

"What about the investigation?"

"We still don't know for sure who killed Chase Gibbons, but we do know that it wasn't you or Steve. What we believe to be the murder weapon was discovered in a bathroom at a rest stop off the New Jersey turnpike last night."

I fumble the phone. Steve catches it as it drops from my hand and returns it to me.

"How do you know it's the right weapon?" My voice shakes.

"It was a bloody machete. Not many machetes used in murders nowadays, but that type of weapon matches the injuries that were recorded during the postmortem. It's already being processed at the local crime lab in Jersey. The initial serology report says the blood type is consistent with the victim's. We're waiting on DNA to confirm an exact match."

"New Jersey?"

"I know. Guess we were on the completely wrong trail this whole time. It must have been a transient just wandering through. Or someone who knew the victim and followed him to your town. We've still got a team at his place. They're going to reinterview his friends and neighbors, see if anyone went missing around the same time Gibbons was murdered."

"So, Murphy was right?"

"Huh?"

"About his dad being framed. He was right."

"Yeah, I guess he was. Jack Murphy is still being held on suspicion of murdering his wife, though."

None of this makes any sense. There's definitely some subterfuge going on. I briefly consider that this may be a trap, that the staties are feeding me misinformation as a ploy to make me and Steve lower our guards so they can trick us into revealing our crimes.

But I don't consider Campden or Robbins intelligent enough for that. This is simply police ineptitude at its finest. The murder of Chase Gibbons will never get solved unless I decide to do it myself, and I'm not sure I want to do that.

Maybe I just want to let the matter rest, to enjoy my life and freedom and put this whole experience behind me. Or maybe I'm afraid of what I'll discover. Linda's name catches my attention and I realize that he's still talking about Jack Murphy.

"I'm sorry, Lou, can you repeat that?"

"I was just asking for your friend, Linda's, contact information. If she can't do the rest of the excavation at the old Murphy house, I was hoping she could put me in touch with someone who could."

"Oh, sure."

I give him her number and make minimal remarks to the rest of his small talk until he gets the hint. He apologizes one last time, during which I can hear Robbins adding his sentiments in the background, and then the line goes dead. Steve and I look at each other and laugh.

"Still want to be a cop?" he asks me.

"Still want to live in Maine?"

Steve's face grows serious. I'm afraid I've upset him.

"Do you want to marry me?"

The question takes me completely by surprise. I'm not sure how to answer. I'm not even sure if I heard right.

"Are you proposing?"

"Are you accepting?"

The word flabbergasted comes to mind, although I'm sure I've never used it before. I want to say yes. I think that surprises me more than Steve's question. The last few days have been such a ridiculous whirlwind, but, at the same time, I feel like we've grown closer by leaps and bounds.

We've discovered things about each other, and ourselves, which we'd kept hidden from the world. We supported one another unconditionally, and even parented a teenager for a short while.

"The only detail I really care about is the cake," I say.

"Does that mean I get to pick the location?"

"As long as the place allows dogs."

"I wouldn't dare choose anywhere that didn't."

72

HEATHER

I have to share my new room, but other than that this place is pretty perfect. My roommate is a girl named Sarah with eyes that are way too close together and short, curly brown hair. She repeats half of what I say and forgets to flush the toilet, both of which I find truly annoying, but I understand all about having patience with someone like Sarah. My momma is a bit slow. My brother Jimmy is, too.

That's probably why I'm so good with people like that. With understanding them and how they understand things, even with pretending to be like them myself. It's not like anyone would suspect otherwise.

I never applied myself in school. I stopped talking to the people in Coyote Cove years ago. By the time I was ten I knew it wasn't worth the effort. A few words here, a few there, I don't think I've ever said anything too intelligent out loud. Now, in my thoughts, that's a different story. I've spent years living in the pretend world inside my head.

I've chatted with a few of the male guests at the motel, but it's not like any of them are going to find out what's going on and speak up. Not if it means facing the underaged girl they made false promises to, used, and left behind. Besides, it's not like I was a rocket scientist during any of those conversations. I was just more normal girl than *Forest Gump*.

Margot never treated me like an idiot. She talked to me like I was a friend sometimes, but I know she never would have told me some of the things she did had she known I actually understood everything she was saying. It was like she was giving her confession to a living, breathing doorpost that would never tell her secrets. Still, I think I might miss Margot. We had more in common than I would have thought when she first gave me the job at her motel.

I miss Maggie and Steve, too. I miss them in a way I've never missed anything before. It's like I've lost a piece of my body that I'll never get back. I figure this must be what it feels like to have a family, a real one, which is something I never expected to experience.

All in all, though, things worked out better than I could have ever imagined. I'm not worried about keeping the façade up, because in a way it's who I've been for so long. I'm more worried about when I'm finally turned loose upon the world, free to develop my own real personality.

I wonder about who I'll be by that time. I've done an awful lot of bad things already in my life. But I'm going to try and forget about all that.

I sit on the floor in front of the mirror, my back leaning against the foot of the bed, and study my reflection. Now that I'm free, rid of the small-town stench that seeps into your clothes and covers every inch of your skin with its grime, I can be anything, anyone that I want. I did what I had to do to get out. I'm not going to apologize for that.

I had just turned sixteen when I first met Chase Gibbons. I was weeding the flowerbeds down at the far end of the motel when a shadow fell over me. I glanced up, squinting into his face, but the sun was too bright, and all I could see was the dark outline of his head against the glowing orb behind him.

Looking away to stop the spots that had appeared in my vision, I noticed his shoes. They were shiny and leather and much fancier than any you ever saw around Coyote Cove, even at funerals and weddings.

"Hey, kid, can you get me a room?"

The sound of his voice was like the time I tried chocolate a tourist had left behind from some fancy sweet shop—smooth, rich, and instilling me with a desire for more. I pushed myself to my feet as gracefully as I could, which was pretty much an awkward jumble of clumsy limbs making odd angles. I jutted my hip out a little, the way I'd seen other girls do, feeling both silly and empowered.

"Kid?" I asked.

He let his eyes take their time traveling up and down my body.

"My bad. You looked younger when you were digging in the dirt."

His grin was lazy, lopsided, and made my heart do some weird kind of gymnastics inside my chest. His twinkling eyes bore into me like they could see all my secrets. He reached out, curved a finger under my chin, and my skin seared with a heat I had never known before. That was it. I was in love.

Chase enthralled me with exciting tales of his private investigations. He seduced me with talk of how he drilled deep into the dark places no one wants to go to find the secrets hidden there. How once he had those secrets, he'd use them to blackmail the owner, and if they refused to pay, how he'd sell the juicy information to newspapers and magazines, mostly tabloids. This was a man who'd get paid, one way or another. This was a man who was going places.

I got Chase his room that first day, and many times after that. He'd visit regularly over the next ten months, during which I'd always lift the keys of "our" room from the office while Margot was sleeping behind her desk. He thought it best if he kept a low profile while he investigated the cases that brought him to town.

It never once occurred to me the damage I could cause to the lives of the people Chase had targeted. I only thought about the life we'd live after I proved to him how useful I could be, after I made myself indispensable and he took me away from Coyote Cove.

Every time I suggested that he take me with him, he swore up and down that he would the very day I turned eighteen. He'd stare into my eyes in that way he had that made me feel like the only girl in the world, everything else melting away, taking all my cares and worries with it. Who knows how long it would have gone on if I hadn't gotten pregnant?

I knew months before I told him. I recognized the signs, could feel it happening, but I just couldn't bring myself to say the words. I figured if I waited until it was too late to get rid of it, then he'd have to take me with him. Or maybe I knew how it was going to turn out and I was just delaying the inevitable.

Late summer and early fall, I spent all of my free time at the transfer station, watching as people dropped off their trash and recycling. Waiting for the right people. The right trash. Then shifting through their stinking bags of garbage, searching for the proof that Chase so desperately wanted.

I met him at the motel, this time in a room he paid for because he had a client in town he planned to meet with. Maybe it was how secretive he was about who he was working for, or maybe it was just the deviation from the norm, of him not staying in our usual room, but something about this visit didn't make me as happy as I normally was to see him.

Chase let me in and then took the only chair, which I

thought was strange, because he normally sat next to me on the bed. He wore a plaid flannel shirt and had bought a pair of boots so he would blend in better with the locals. I teased him about them, but he didn't laugh.

I asked him who his client was again, but he wouldn't share. He seemed restless, bored even, like he had someplace else to be. But when I held out the crumpled, stained slips of paper, I suddenly had his complete interest.

He flipped through the stack, his eyes lighting with delight. I'd just presented him with a potential goldmine, the proof he needed to corner his next victim. Four bank slips, each in the amount of $500, all of which could be traced to Steve Winter's checking account.

I told him then, while his face glowed and his eyes were bright. I told him and watched the smile slip off his face and a storm cloud descend over his features. I told him, and he told me there was no way that he could be the father.

There was no one else besides him, no possible way he could not be the father of the baby that stretched my belly further every day, but he'd have none of it. I was devastated. I felt like I'd been stabbed in the heart. The whole life I'd envisioned for us swirled down the drain of some dirty toilet.

I have no idea how I recovered and switched gears so fast. Maybe it's because I've learned to always have a contingency plan. It might be that part of me was expecting his reaction and had subconsciously planned the next step. I'll probably never know for sure.

What I do know is that I'll never forget the look on his face when I told him that Jack Murphy was expecting us so he could go on the record about the bribes he'd been receiving from Steve every month. It was the break Chase had been waiting for, ever since he'd overheard the evil little man running his mouth in the town bar. No one else had paid what he was saying any attention, but Chase sure had.

The greedy sparkle returned to Chase's eyes, but a look of disgust distorted his mouth. Lips that were soft and plump and perfectly shaped grimaced at the idea of getting in the car with me. I know that's what it was. And I know that, had Chase Gibbons survived the night, I never would have seen or heard from him again.

73

MAGGIE

The sun sinks low in the sky, a fiery blaze of tangerine spreading along the horizon as I watch Steve play at the water's edge with the dogs. I sink into the embrace of the wicker chair, curl my legs up under me, willing my body to relax. I'm trying to focus on being in this moment, but my mind can't help drifting.

The dogs bark, telling Steve to stop teasing them and hurry up and throw their toys. They race into the lake after the Frisbees, splashing through the water. Any day now it will be too cold for that. The temperature will plunge, the edges of the lake will freeze, and the snow will fall, a film of white veiling the world in a cloak of purity, hiding all the darkness.

But the darkness is still there, simmering beneath the surface. It would be foolish to think it's not.

Jack Murphy was framed for murder. I'm certain that phrase will haunt me until the day I die, along with the image of my lieutenant lying dead in a pile of leaves, and a half-dozen other ghosts who make their home among my memories.

My brain picks at the mystery of who murdered Chase Gibbons like a scab, refusing to let the wound heal. Because none of it makes sense. I can't believe what Detective Campden said, that an outsider killed Gibbons. The odds of a stranger just happening to choose Jack Murphy to pin the crime on are simply too great. Which means that a murderer may still be in my town.

I could argue with myself about whether Coyote Cove is still "my town" or not, but the truth is, it doesn't matter. Regardless of how I feel about this little burg, whether I will continue to call it home or not, a murder was committed on my watch.

I imagine the way the machete looked, the surprise of the person who discovered it in the bathroom of a rest stop off the New Jersey turnpike. It just doesn't jive. The machete is the weapon of choice for a very select few killers. I doubt any of those slaughter-types would bother framing someone for one of their kills—or would even want to.

No, the machete was a weapon of convenience, not choice. Chances are that the killer found the weapon close to where the murder was committed; perhaps resting in the very tree we saw the chop marks on, where it was kept. The more I consider the case, the more I'm convinced that it was not premeditated. My instincts are screaming crime of passion.

The killer will be someone who I can connect to both Jack Murphy and Chase Gibbons.

The easiest place to start would be to figure out who even knew that Jack Murphy lived in the ranger's cabin off the industrial dirt road. It wasn't the type of turnoff taken by tourists. I doubt they'd get a half mile into those dark Maine woods before visions of toothless huntsmen and banjo music played in their heads.

Most of the locals avoided Jack like the plague. Besides the town council—who voted to let him stay after he was discovered squatting at the ranger's station by the previous police chief—I'd be willing to bet that only his son and a handful of others were aware of the relocation.

I'm tracing the names of the council members with a finger on my pants legs when Steve jogs up the porch stairs with the dogs. He pauses to look at me, then continues inside. A moment later he returns and hands me a notebook and pen.

"I know that look."

I glance up at him in surprise, taking the supplies.

"Come inside when you get cold. Or finish solving the case, whichever happens first."

The way he winks, I know he understands. I should give thanks yet again to have found someone who gets me, but I'm already scribbling madly in the notebook. My brain dumps all over the pages until I've made several lists.

One with the names of members of the town council, another with Lieutenant Murphy and his friends and family. A third contains anyone who might have possibly come in contact with Chase Gibbons during his stay—the grocery clerks, restaurant staff, motel workers, gas station attendants. There is one name that appears more than any of the others. It is not a name I want to consider.

One of the oddest facts of this case is that the murder weapon was discovered in another state. Most of the people in Coyote Cove don't leave often. They host visitors even less.

I consider the timeline of the crime, putting a check next to the names of people who I know were in Coyote Cove when the murder and body dump were committed. Then I cross out any of those names if the person is still in town. Only one name remains, glaring out at me from the page like a blinking neon sign.

Closing the notebook, I lay it on the swing and place the pen on top. I draw my legs up in front of me and hug them to my chest for warmth. I know I should go inside, but I can't yet. Not until I've thought this through. Not until I know what I'm going to do.

74

HEATHER

The trip out to Jack Murphy's cabin was agonizing. We made the drive in silence, Chase refusing to look at me even once. I only spoke to give him directions. I'd never been there before, but I'd seen a map of it once while shredding old town council documents for Margot. It wasn't hard to find once you knew where to look.

I told Chase to turn off the road, onto the narrow lane that wove through the woods, sneaking glances at him while we bounced further into the dark wilderness. I was running out of time to make up my mind. But I needed to be sure. It was an important decision, one I couldn't take back once I'd made it.

When we pulled in, and the headlights glinted off a piece of metal sticking out of a tree, I knew. It was a pretty obvious sign, after all.

I told Chase not to drive any closer, to park where we were. He gave me an annoyed look and rolled his eyes but turned the engine off. I twisted to face him, gave him one last chance, but he didn't want to take it.

"I've got to warn you, he's kind of crazy," I said.

I wasn't sure exactly how I was going to pull it off, I was

pretty much winging it, but the vague outline of a plan was taking form in my mind.

"How crazy?"

"Walls with ears and tinfoil hat crazy."

I could tell by his expression that Chase needed me to elaborate.

"He's paranoid. Convinced that the government or someone has his house bugged so they can listen to his conversations. Sometimes he gets the feeling that they're tapping directly into his thoughts, so he puts a tinfoil hat on."

I almost felt bad for what I was saying, since I'd never actually met Jack Murphy, but I'd heard Alma joking about her father-in-law before, and it seemed a good fit. It must have sounded good, too, because I had Chase's full attention.

"You go wait in the outhouse, I'll let him know you're here."

"What?"

"I told you. He thinks his cabin might be bugged. The only place he thinks is safe to talk is the outhouse."

"If he's that crazy then forget about it. I'll find another way."

"How long will that take? He might be a bit looney, but he's crazy smart and mean for the sake of it. He's got the proof you need, and he'll give it to you just to stick it to some rich outsider. All you've got to do is jump through a couple of silly hoops."

"I'm not stepping one foot inside someone's shit box."

I remember shrugging, turning around to head back to the car, but Chase grabbed my arm and stopped me. When he realized he was touching me, he let go like I was an infectious disease. I was real mad with myself for ever trusting a no good con-man. Self-loathing accomplishes nothing, though, so I directed my rage toward Chase instead.

"Okay, I'll do it. Go get him. Just try to make it fast, okay?"

I nodded and set off toward the front door of the cabin, the same route that would lead me straight to the machete protruding from the tree. His footsteps grew fainter as he went his direction, and I went mine. Approaching the weapon, I wrapped both hands around the handle and yanked. I was like some modern-day King Arthur. If it wasn't meant to happen, I wouldn't have been able to pull it free.

I took a couple of light whacks at the bark, just to make sure there was a decent edge on the thing, and then I stalked after Chase with the blade held down, along the length of my leg. It was so dark in the woods, away from the lights of town and with the thick tangle of trees blocking out the moon and stars overhead, that I couldn't see him. But I heard the creak of the outhouse door as it swung on its rusty hinges.

Then the shape of the building emerged against the gloom. Chase stood in the doorway, arms folded across his chest.

"What's the hold up?"

I closed the last few feet between us with quick steps and gave Chase a hard stab to the chest, causing him to stumble back into the outhouse and free himself from the blade. The door swung shut after him. I jerked it open and ran him through again like Joan of Arc wielding her mighty sword. It didn't take much. The first blow was dead solid over the heart. He never even put up a fight.

I took my jacket off and used it to cover his bloody shirt as I pulled him free of the outhouse, onto the ground. I dragged him to the back of Jack Murphy's beat-up old pickup truck. But it was getting him up onto the tailgate that was the real challenge.

I'm a pretty stubborn person when I get an idea in my mind, but I almost had to abandon this one. All the heaving and hefting and struggling left me in a full sweat, sharp pains lancing through my stomach.

Although almost crippling and certainly not enjoyable, the piercing agony in my uterus was welcomed. It sharpened my senses, made me think about what I was doing, the careful steps I'd need to take to cover up my crime. It made me think of the car keys in Chase's pants pocket. If not for the pain I probably would have forgotten to grab them, and I would have been stuck out at Jack Murphy's place in the woods with a dead man's useless car.

Climbing into the cab of the truck, my foot went through a rusted-out hole in the floorboard. I was worried that the old clunker wouldn't make the trip I had in mind, that I'd get stranded somewhere along a vacant dirt road with a dead body, but when I flipped the visor down and the keys fell into my hand, my concerns just melted away.

I'd never driven a car, but I'd watched enough times, and it was pretty much as simple as it looked. At least it is when you don't go over twenty miles an hour. And it helped that we were already so close to the old logging roads.

But not everything was in my favor that night. The cramping got worse, so bad that I was afraid I might pass out. The thought made me panic and dump the body too soon. I'd wanted to drive him deeper, maybe even to the pond, but I still had a lot to do before the night was over, and I couldn't think straight knowing there'd be no way to deny my guilt with a corpse in the back, the body thumping with every dip and bump of the road, so I went ahead and stopped the truck.

There was a whole collection of garbage in the cab, so I borrowed a couple of plastic bags and tied them over my shoes. Then I got out, lowered the tailgate, grabbed my jacket, and got back in. I had an idea that if I gained speed and veered suddenly that the body might fall out of the back by itself. It took a few tries until it worked. Then I left Chase Gibbons lying dead along the side of the road like the piece of trash he treated me as. I never looked back, not even once, on the return drive to Jack Murphy's.

I did my best to leave everything as I had found it—truck parked in the same spot, tailgate shut, keys folded up in the visor. I took the machete with me, though. Didn't think Jack would mind too much if I stole it, considering it was now a murder weapon. I bundled the blade in my bloody jacket and got into Chase's car. I made pretty much the same drive I had just done to dump the body, only this time I kept going until I reached the rough path through the trees that led to Craig's Pond.

Had it been summer there might've still been tourists hanging around on the shore, cooking on their expensive portable grills, or playing in the water. Luckily, it was already too chilly for that. I had the place all to myself, the gravel beach crunching loudly under the tires as I circled around to the far side.

I remember almost drowning there once. I was seven, maybe eight. I couldn't swim, but I could splash like a champion, and the pond wasn't too long of a walk from our house. It was a stifling hot day, and my brother and I hiked out to the pond to cool off.

But the spot where we usually played was overrun by vacationers, so we walked around to the far shore. I ran into the water full speed, only to find myself flailing, struggling to keep my head above the surface, not knowing the pond bed dropped off suddenly less than ten feet in. I fought to dog paddle my way back to where I could touch the bottom. I feel like I haven't stopped treading water since.

I lowered the driver's side window, tossed the jacket-wrapped machete onto the rocks, then pushed the gas pedal to the floor, and braced myself as the car surged forward.

Even after my bad experience, or maybe because of it, I never learned to swim. After the car launched out into the pond, it started filling with water a lot quicker than I had anticipated. I pulled myself out the window only seconds before the roof of the car submerged. I kicked against the metal hulk, trying to propel myself toward the beach, paddling for what seemed like hours before I felt the pebbled bottom shifting under my shoes.

I'm not sure how long I laid on the hard, uncomfortable rocks on that beach, curled on my side, hugging my bloody jacket as I breathed through the pain. By the time I managed to pull myself to my feet my clothes were halfway dry. I was also freezing cold, so I got my bearings and started hiking home to Momma's house.

I passed a gnarled old tree with a hole at its base that I remembered using as a cubbyhole when I was little. I stashed my jacket and the machete in there, knowing I'd have no problem finding it in the morning. I needed to free up my hands because I realized that whether I liked it or not, even though it was still too early, the baby was coming.

I did my best to get home, but it was so dark, and I was so tired, and every time the pain came I had to stop and hold on to a tree for support. Waves of dizziness left me disorientated. I couldn't keep my course straight. I knew I was lost, I just didn't want to admit it to myself.

I was cold, and alone, and terrified, but I didn't have a choice. I wanted to keep it in, but it was just like on TV when the doctors tell the women not to push but the women say they have to. I barely got my pants down before the baby came.

I sat there, panting, staring down at the silent infant with the blue tinged, translucent skin and the hollow, closed eyes, wondering what would happen next. Nothing did. My teeth started chattering, so I pulled my pants up. Still I sat there, watching the motionless baby. My motionless baby. But I don't recall ever having the thought, *my baby is dead*.

What I do remember is that I didn't want an animal to make a meal of it. Him. The son I'd made with Chase.

One of my shoes still had a plastic bag tied around it, soggy and worn, but it was better than nothing. I wrapped the baby in the bag and placed him in the bough of a tree. I thought about burying him, but something about the dark and the dirt and the worms just seemed wrong. I considered taking him with me, but

I had no idea how to get home from wherever I was or who I might run into on the way.

It was just too risky. And I doubted I'd be able to find my way back to where I was. So I knew it was goodbye when I took that first step, which led to the next step, and all the other steps as I walked away from my baby, the life I had carried with me, inside of me, leaving him behind.

I'm not sure how long I stumbled around the woods after that. I've never been one for wearing a watch. Something about keeping track of time makes me feel like I don't have enough of it, like I have to watch it because it's running out. On some level, I suppose that's true. Who wants to carry a constant reminder with them of how much of their life they're wasting?

I'm pretty sure I was suffering from shock, or maybe I was just kind of out of it from being so cold, but I wandered around until I came upon Chief Riley, who had found Chase's body. I know I was in shock then.

The deception that followed was necessary, I have no apologies for that. But now... now it's all done. I'm free of Coyote Cove, and all the unspeakable acts I've committed. No one knows that I'm the one who killed Chase Gibbons. And no one ever will.

75

MAGGIE

By the time I make my decision my fingers are stiff and burning from the cold. Dusk has fallen, shrouding the world around me in darkness. Somewhere near the lake a loon gives a mournful call, a lonely cry for companionship. It's answered by the howl of a pair of coyotes. This is a dangerous world we live in.

I stand and stretch, taking a deep breath of the crisp air. When I was growing up, my parents raised me to believe that there was right and wrong. But the truth is, reality consists of everything in between. Which is what's making this so difficult.

Heather killed Chase Gibbons.

It took me a good, long while of staring the obvious in the face before I could believe it. I'm still not entirely sure how she pulled it off. I have to give the girl credit. Most teenagers lack the focus to become a criminal mastermind. But not Heather. The whole mental impairment thing was obviously an act. She used me. Maybe I felt bitter for a brief second, but this isn't about me. It isn't really even about Heather.

It's about the lives of all the people she'll have the opportunity to come in contact with if I stay silent about what she's done. And the harm she could potentially cause them.

I don't believe Heather's a bad person. I'm working with only a fraction of the puzzle, but the pieces I do have—Chase Gibbons being over twice Heather's age, the man working on projects to blackmail both me and Steve, Heather somehow managing to get the murder weapon to a location that would clear any suspicion that Steve and I were under when she could have just left us behind to take the blame without ever looking back—those pieces reveal a picture of a girl who doesn't deserve to spend her life behind bars.

A picture of a hopeful, helpful girl who found a place in my heart. Maybe part of that girl was an act, but I truly believe that the core is the same. Knowing that Heather is a murderer doesn't make me stop wanting the best life the world has to offer for her. We all have a dark side. We all lose control. We just don't all use a machete when we do it.

But it doesn't matter what I think. Or even what I feel.

Because in this tiny corner of Maine, it's my job to withhold the law. To serve and protect. As much as I'd like to, I can't let this go. But I can't just turn my back, either.

So, although I text Detective Robbins and tell him my suspicions about Heather being the killer, I also request that they run a DNA test comparing the profile of Heather's baby to that of Chase Gibbons. And that he lets me know who the judge is when Heather's arraigned so that I can request leniency. I know that there will be no halfway house now, no freedom for the girl for a good, long while, but that doesn't mean all hope is lost.

Heather needs help. And I intend to make sure she gets it. Because one day, I could be the one who's gone too far. So, I plan to do everything I can to make sure a second chance is in her future.

I pull open the sliding glass door with clumsy hands. Steve looks up from the book he's reading on the couch, a dog curled under each arm. The flickering light from the fireplace dances across the scene. This is my heart personified. Before me is my hope, my dreams, my soul, my everything in life that I never thought I'd have. That I thought I didn't deserve.

In a way, Heather gave me this. Steve and I were drawn to each other because we were both damaged. We both have secrets we can't bear to share, dark spots that reside between us. If it hadn't been for Heather, we may never have taken the first step in confiding in each other, in moving toward the light that will hopefully, one day, chase away the dark.

A LETTER FROM SHANNON

Dear Reader

First, a most sincere thank you for choosing to read *The Girl Who Lied,* the first installment in the Chief Maggie Riley series. If you'd like to keep up to date with my latest releases, you can sign up at the following link. Your email address will never be shared, and you can unsubscribe at any time.

www.bookouture.com/shannon-hollinger

I had a great time writing this book, rediscovering the knowledge and skills from my past as Maggie rediscovered hers. I hope you had as much fun with it as I did, and I can't wait for you to discover what I have in store for Maggie and the rest of the residents of Coyote Cove!

If you enjoyed the story, I would be incredibly grateful if you'd leave a review and recommend the book to your friends and family. I love reading what you think, and it also helps other readers find my books for the first time.

And, finally, it gets lonely in the writing cave, so please feel free to get in touch with me directly and keep me company! You can find me on Facebook, Twitter, Instagram, Goodreads, TikTok, or my website.

Thank you so much for your support—it really is hugely appreciated!

Shannon Hollinger

shannonhollinger.com

facebook.com/thiswritersays

twitter.com/thiswritersays

instagram.com/thiswritersays

goodreads.com/shannonhollinger

tiktok.com/@shannonhollinger

ACKNOWLEDGMENTS

Once upon a time, there was a writer. One day, she got married, and she and her new husband spent their honeymoon in a cabin in a one-stoplight, blink-and-you'll-miss-it town in Northern Maine. I wrote the first draft of this novel when we returned home, and though it sat on a shelf gathering dust for years, this story has always had a special place in my heart. I was just waiting for the experience and skill I needed to do it justice.

So first, I have to thank my husband, Ben, for not minding that I was plotting murder on our honeymoon (at least it wasn't yours, right?), as well as for his continuing support over the years. He brings the light to my dark side. Whether we're hiking down the wrong side of a mountain or having to jump over a giant alligator blocking the path at the end of a five-mile trail, we'll do it together. Goonies never say die (although they might say other colorful words, and worry about death, when the local wildlife is too busy digesting the last hiker it ate to share the trail).

A huge thanks to my mom, Stacy, who isn't just my number one cheerleader and the person who instilled in me a lifelong passion for reading and writing, but is also my best friend, and to my grandmother, Marvis, who introduced me to Agatha Christie at an early age and changed the course of my history forever.

To my dad—thank you so much for always believing in me, and know that I still miss you every day.

Many sincere thank yous to my publishing team at Bookouture. I'm so very grateful to have found such an amazing tribe, one that feels more like a family than a publishing company. Special thanks to my editor, Susannah Hamilton, for her excellent guidance and input, and to everyone else whose hands, talent, and skill have touched this book and helped make it into what it is today! Also, to my fellow Bookouture authors, who are unbelievably friendly and supportive across both genres and oceans.

Finally, and most importantly, endless thanks to all the readers, reviewers, Booktokers, Bookstagrammers, book tweeters, bloggers, and librarians out there who spend so much of their valuable time sharing book love! Please don't underestimate how important you are! Knowing that there are people who enjoyed reading the book you've spent so much time, sweat, isolation, and occasionally tears on is a tremendous feeling, and your kind words mean the absolute world to me! The best part of this journey has been 'meeting' you. Thank you so much for brightening my days!

.

Printed in Great Britain
by Amazon